Happy Birthday Susan!

THE WIDOW OF WATERFORD

By: Jessica Kidd

Jessica Kidd

Dedicated to Shay Kidd, the love of my life. Thank you for all your unconditional love and support. You are my everything.

And to the many friends and fellow writers who bore with reading all my rough drafts. Thank you, friends.

Prologue

Across the lawn, the forest shadows stretched out as if reaching for the well-lit house. From a high vantage point in the trees, he was able to see the guests gathered in the dining room. Most of the staff were in the kitchen or serving among the guests. This left the servants quarters on the third floor vacant. A difficult entry point, but manageable.

Sliding down from the tree branch he had been resting in, he landed with a soft thud on the leaf strewn ground, the movement startling his horse. Using soothing words, he calmed the beast and checked again that the reins were secured to the tree. The last thing he needed was for the animal to become frightened in the darkness and run away.

Once certain the horse was calm, he moved with the agility of a fox across the lawn towards the stately house.

It was always easy to pay off one servant or another to do odd things. Most were desperate for the money, like the maid whom he had paid three shillings just so she would leave her window open. He climbed up the uneven brick wall until he reached the window and slipped into the empty room.

Without making a sound, he crossed the floor to the doorway. He listened for any signs of activity on the floor but only faint laughter from the party below could be heard. Cautiously, he inched the door opened, and peered out into the hall. No one was around. A sigh nearly escaped him, but he knew he still had a long way to go before he reached his goal.

Holding to the shadows, he crept through the house in silence. Once he came upon two servants, giggling girls more interested in their gossip than anything else. Silently, he ducked into the shadows, waiting for the maids to pass him by. He held his breath, not wanting to bring any undue attention to himself. The girls passed by him, their chatter fading down the hall. He praised luck for her goodness towards him.

Coming to the family quarters he slipped into the dressing room of the largest room. No one was about, not with the dinner party happening downstairs. Any servants that had once been in the room were now in the kitchens, resting from their daily tasks.

Vigilance, man, he thought to himself. Vigilance was always needed. The man who got cocky was the one who got caught. Keeping a clear head, he moved about the room, using the moonlight from the windows as his guide.

At last he found his prize. On the dressing table was an engraved wooden box, left out so the lady of the house could store her jewels later that night. While the box was locked, it did not make him hesitate for a moment. Using his well-honed talent, he picked the lock with a satisfying *click*.

Throwing the lid back, the contents of the box sparkled in the moonlight. Diamonds, pearls, ruby rings to fit any size of finger, all begged to go with him. Greed glinted in his eyes. He quickly pulled a velvet sack from his pocket and filled it with the contents of the box.

The thief closed the box and went to the window. When it was locked from the inside, the room was secure. He unlatched the window and swung himself out onto the narrow ledge. Facing back into the room he let his eyes linger on the nearly empty box before he scaled down the wall and disappeared in the shadows.

His mount was right where he had left it. The horse neighed, startled by his sudden appearance in the darkness. "Easy love," he crooned to the animal. "No need to fear, my darling." At the sound of his voice, gently in the air, the animal calmed and allowed him to come near.

As he rode away, he let out a quiet laugh at his own success. How arrogant some people were, thinking wealth was enough to prevent disaster from coming. Still, this house was rich enough that the loss of a few jewels would barely faze them. The thief spurred his horse into the woods and was swallowed by the night.

I.

Vivian Reed looked at the sky, distrust in her expression. The sky had been red in the morning. Not pink, or even the soft orange she enjoyed so much. That morning it had been as crimson as blood.

Red sky in morning, sailors take warning. Red sky at night, sailors delight.

Isn't that how the rhyme went? Vivian should have taken that for a sign, as she had every other day for the past decade.

She had stared at the sky for a long while, deciding what to do, when *his* voice entered her head.

"You know perfectly well what the correct decision is," came his condescending tone. It was that same tone he always used whenever she tried to have a discussion with him. "It is only that stubborn Irish pride of yours that would make you question the sage advice of your elders. If only you would listen to sense, Vivian."

So, Vivian Reed had done something she had always wished to do, the exact opposite of what the Admiral would have insisted upon. Without further deliberation, she boarded the Kensington.

She regretted her obstinate decision almost as soon as the ship made its way out of Plymouth harbor. The usually blue English Channel had become black and choppy. The rough waves rocked the ship back and forth in the most unfavorable manner. Her stomach protested even as she stood out on the open deck. She looked out at the horizon to settle her insides, but the solid line of the sea and sky was blurred by the distant sight of rain.

A stiff breeze blew her red curls about her face. She brushed them back yet again. Why hadn't she worn her bonnet when she went on deck? The cold sea air made her shiver despite her wool dress. She pulled at her shawl, trying to keep herself warm but was unable to fight off the chill.

"Mrs. Reed, won't you be more comfortable below deck?" The portly captain of the ship asked her for the third time.

She gave him a sweet smile, trying to hide her annoyance at his unwanted concern. "I'm perfectly content *on* deck Captain Seymour. Thank you for your inquiry."

He sighed, shaking his head as he walked away. She thought she heard him mutter something about women not having enough sense to be out at sea, but she couldn't be sure.

He meant well; she knew. If it had been any other woman on deck in such weather, she would have been worried herself. But she was more comfortable here in the open air, even if it was blowing profusely, than she was below trying to take no notice of the other passengers pitying stares.

Vivian had started the voyage off in the company of the other passengers on board the Kensington, a merchant vessel of some rapport. But that had been before Mrs. Seymour started to talk about her as if she weren't there.

"And poor Mrs. Reed, you know how badly she has been doing since the passing of her dear husband," she had said to another passenger, pretending not to notice Vivian sitting right next to her. "The little darling just can't manage without Admiral Reed there to guide her."

Vivian had forced herself to *not* roll her eyes at such a ludicrous comment. She had been doing just fine without her dearly departed husband if he could have ever been called that. The admiral hadn't been intentionally cruel, He had just been as cold and unpredictable as the sea he had loved so much.

Instinctively, her hand moved to a small pendant that hung about her neck. The silver around a small amber stone was carved into the Celtic rings of Ireland. It had been a gift from Vivian's mother on her wedding day. She never took it off, even when the Admiral demanded she did. Rubbing the smooth stone had become a habit whenever she felt the least bit uneasy.

Lightning flashed overhead, a crack of thunder on its heels. The sudden noise made her jump. Vivian clung to the railing to keep from slipping on the wet deck. The wind went from stiff to fierce, the waves rising under its force.

The sailors attempted to secure everything down that was on the deck. They shouted to one another as they worked with a frenzy. Vivian watched as they swayed and slipped on the ever-dampening deck.

The ship pitched in the growing waves. Vivian held onto the railing as the Kensington rose and fell in the churning sea. Her body protested the sudden movement. As her knees began to shake from cold and seasickness, she held tighter to the railing until her knuckles turned white.

The Kensington's bow rose at the crest of one wave, only to have nothing greet it on the other side. For a surreal moment, Vivian and the ship were weightless. She floated, noticing a water droplet that hung suspended in the air before her. Then the moment ended. Vivian slammed back onto the deck, forced to her knees with power only gravity could muster.

"Mrs. Reed!" Captain Seymour pleaded over the wind. "Please, it's time to go below deck."

She knew that he was right, she had stayed too long and should have been somewhere safer long ago. She nodded and released her grip on the ship's railing to head below.

She had only taken a few steps when the ship was struck on the port side by a wave nearly as large as the Kensington itself. The ship rocked so violently Vivian was certain they would capsize. She reached for the railing, needing something solid to hold on to. Her fingers brushed the slick wood as her feet slid out from under her.

The weight of her body crashed against the wet deck, knocking the air from her lungs. She hurtled across the vertical deck at an unbelievable speed. Vivian grabbed for something that could stop her. Again, and again she reached for a handhold but everything she touched slipped from her grasp.

"No. No! NO!" she screamed. In one last desperate attempt, she grabbed a handful of rope, but as her fingers closed around the coarse fibers her body sailed off the side of the ship, wrenching the rope from her grasp.

For an instant she was surrounded by nothing but air and mist. Her heart pounded in her ears, deafening her to the world. She didn't know if she was dreaming or awake until the icy water swallowed her whole.

The water pressed upon her, pushing her down. Thrashing her way to the surface, she gasped in a lungful of air. The waves loomed high around her, crashing down with a roar.

I am going to die! The disturbing thought rolled through her mind. Vivian fought off the paralyzing fear that threatened to pull her down, just as the currant was trying to do. Despair began to wash in when a hand grasped her arm and pulled her toward the surface. The movement was like a slap to her senses. Vivian burst above the surface, gasping in the air.

Turning her so Vivian faced the sky, her rescuer slid a strong arm under her own, keeping her head above water. Pressed together, he swam them toward safety. She clung to him, praying that she wouldn't slip from his embrace.

"I don't want to die," Vivian cried as she gasped for air.

"You won't. I got ye now," he reassured her in a tone that belied the strain he was under. "But you have to swim."

"I can't," Vivian gasped.

He cursed in Gaelic. It surprised Vivian so much that she started to correct him, but her mouth filled with salt water. All that she was able to do was to sputter and cough.

"You'll have to kick then," he said as he swam them toward the ship.

"What?" Vivian wasn't sure she was hearing him right.

"Kick, woman! No, not me. One leg at a time. Good lass. Now keep it up till I tell ye to stop."

Vivian kicked one leg, then the other, over and over again. She kicked with all that she had in her. It was exhausting work. Her boots were filled with water, making them heavy. They threatened to slow her down but still she kicked.

He held her close, the heat of his body dispelling some of the icy cold. Together they swam, he doing most of the swimming as she kicked. His movements were sure and even which made Vivian think he must be one of the sailors.

She felt so tired. Kicking seemed to take so much more effort now than it ever had as a small child. If only she could rest for just a moment. Surely just a little pause wouldn't slow them down too much.

"Wake up!"

Vivian's eyes shot open at the fierce sound of his voice.

"If you want to live, you need to work for it. Now swim!" He sounded so angry that she instantly obeyed. Despite cold and fear, she did her best to swim with him as they slowly made their way toward the ship.

Ropes came sailing out of the sky towards them. He looped one under their arms so the crew on deck could hoist them up. They were pulled out of the sea, one agonizing tug at a time until they sloshed onto the deck of the Kensington, a tangle of arms and legs. Extricating themselves from each other left both exhausted as they sprawled out onto the deck.

Vivian's hand flew to her throat. She let out a great sigh of relief when she found her mother's amulet still there.

They laid there for a moment, Vivian and the stranger who had risked his life for hers. Then he did the oddest thing. He laughed. A deep, resonating sound that dispelled all the fear that had consumed Vivian's heart only a moment before. And to Vivian's surprise, she found that she was laughing too.

II.

Vivian sat in the captain's cabin, her feet in a basin of hot water, a cup of tea in one hand. Her other hand rubbed at the stone in her pendant. Mrs. Seymour, the captain's wife, did her best to brush sea salt from Vivian's wet clothes. The pudgy older woman fussed about the cabin as if her very presence could bring relief.

For Vivian it did not. Mrs. Seymour made a disapproving sound every few seconds. It was enough to send the most patient individual into a fury.

"I just can't understand why you would put yourself in harm's way, Mrs. Reed," Mrs. Seymour said as she hung up the wet garments.

"I needed some fresh air." Vivian repeated. She wasn't sure how many times she had told the older woman her reasons for being on deck.

Mrs. Seymour continued as if she hadn't heard. "And then to not heed the call of the Captain. 'Tis a woman's duty to obey the men charged with her protection. Why, what would the Admiral have done if he knew you were parading about the deck during a storm?"

"Pray I'd drown," Vivian muttered under her breath.

Mrs. Seymour shook her cap covered head. "Now, Mrs. Reed, I know what you've been through. We all do. It has been a trying year for you, what with the Admiral dying so in the west Indies, and all. Now you've decided to move away from all your friends. It wouldn't be surprising for any woman in your situation to want to be with her beloved. Throwing yourself off the ship isn't the right way of doing it."

Vivian's jaw dropped. "You think I threw myself overboard?"

Mrs. Seymour looked at her with large, patronizing eyes. "There's no need to be ashamed, dear."

Vivian couldn't believe her ears. She stared at Mrs. Seymour for a long moment, doing her best to keep from screaming. The older woman meant to be kind, but all the pity and sympathy and good intentions was aggravating. It was beginning to drive Vivian insane.

Vivian forced a smile onto her face and calm into her voice. "Thank you for your concern, Mrs. Seymour. I appreciate all you have done for me."

The older woman made to speak but Vivian cut her off. "I should thank my rescuer."

An amused twinkle came to Mrs. Seymour's eyes. "I hoped you would say that. What a man Mr. Kade is, too! A look from those blue eyes sends me into the titters. Oh, but you mustn't be telling the Captain I said such a thing."

"I promise I won't," she reassured Mrs. Seymour. Though what a captain's wife was doing looking at a sailor was beyond Vivian. She had spent years on ships and had never gotten "titters" from looking at the crew.

"Now, you'll be needing some dry clothes, Mrs. Reed. I had your trunk sent up, so you get yourself into something warm," she said as she motioned to a trunk in the corner. "I was so glad to see you in the old style. What these girls are thinking nowadays is beyond me. A waist on a dress should be where the waist of the body is, says I. Not up in the armpits. And in my day, it was fitting to keep a bosom tucked away. Why, these girls today are positively sinful with how they show off their… er… assets."

Vivian sighed with relief when Mrs. Seymour shut the door behind her. The woman's endless chatter had given Vivian a headache. Now in the silence of the cabin Vivian felt at peace for the first time since she had boarded the ship.

Rifling through her trunk, Vivian found a midnight blue dress in the new style. The cut of this dress was so flattering it made her small bust appear almost ample. She might have worn something in the old style, but her wet dress was the last one she had.

Vivian agonized over how obstinate she would appear to Mrs. Seymour as she slipped into the dry clothes. It wasn't that she wanted to argue with every person that tried to help her. Vivian wished to be one of those demure women of society. She tried to be gentle and meek, to be like other wives who honored all their husbands wishes and never went against protocol. But that type of temperament went against her nature. She could never be demure when there were others who needed someone to fight for them. She refused to be meek in the face of those who would wrongly use her. As for being gentle? Well, her kind of gentility wasn't going to earn her an invitation to Almack's any time soon.

Once the dress was on, Vivian pulled out her brush and began to coax it through her tangle of red curls. Vivian brushed and brushed until her hair was nearly as smooth as the silk of her dress. Once she arranged it, she shook out a few of her shorter strands around her temples and the nape of her neck. Twisting the wet hair around her fingers she hoped they would dry into curls.

Vivian made certain that her pendant settled in its proper place around her neck. Looking in the age spotted mirror that hung in the cabin, she surveyed her appearance. For the hundredth time, she noticed how the amber stone was nearly the exact color of her eyes. It made her miss her mother all over again.

Movement outside the cabin door brought Vivian's attention away from her reflection. She closed her trunk and stood in the center of the room. Her stomach twisted into knots. What did one say to the person who saved their life?

Mrs. Seymour bustled into the room, and, with a motion to the man behind her, said, "Mrs. Reed, may I present Mr. Sean Kade."

Vivian stared at the man in surprise. She had been expecting a sailor, early aged and weather beaten as were most. The man who stood before her now was anything but weather beaten. Here was a man who could have taken the place of any Greek statue. By the way he dressed he was a gentleman of some means. The way his velvet coat fit on his athletic frame, was enough to make any woman's knees weaken. She remembered the strength of his arms about her as he held her afloat in the water. Vivian discreetly wiped the sweat forming on her palms onto her dress.

Mrs. Seymour cleared her throat, giving Vivian a disapproving look. The dress was obviously not to Mrs. Seymour's liking. Vivian blushed as she realized that she had been staring at Mr. Kade in what could only be an unladylike manner.

"I am pleased to be properly introduced to you, Mrs. Reed." His sapphire eyes shone, holding a hint of secret amusement. He bowed and a raven lock tumbled across his brow.

For a fleeting moment, Vivian wanted to cross the room and brush his stray lock away. Blessedly, she caught herself before she could do more than flinch in response to the impulse. Instead, she curtsied. "And I you, Mr. Kade."

Turning her attention to the plump figure at the door, Vivian firmly said, "Thank you, Mrs. Seymour. That will be all."

Mrs. Seymour protested but Vivian gave her a stern look, one the Admiral had so often used. It did the trick and the older woman scurried from the room.

Mr. Kade smiled at Vivian and whispered, "Poor thing. You couldn't let her listen in so she would have a bit of gossip to tell the rest of the ship?"

"She has received enough gossip at my expense to last a lifetime."

"Ah yes. The infamous Mrs. Reed," he said dramatically, the deep timber of his voice reverberating through Vivian's insides. "Throwing herself overboard from the despair of losing her late husband."

Defiance ignited within her. With hands on her hips she said, "I didn't throw myself in. I was weak from all the rocking and when the deck became wet, I lost my balance and slipped into the water."

Mr. Kade held up his hands, "I meant no offense."

Vivian sighed and rubbed her temple. "Neither did I. I've been with Mrs. Seymour and her views for far too long. It was starting to wear on my nerves."

Mr. Kade's face lit up again. "Well, I can say for a fact that you didn't jump. Not with how your feet flew over your head."

She looked into his lively eyes and the stress of the day melted away. She threw her head back and laughed.

"Thank you," she managed once the laughter had faded. "I needed that." She sat on one of the cabins practical chairs and offered the other to Mr. Kade.

"I am always at your service," Mr. Kade said. He flashed a charming smile. Vivian had a feeling that, as a boy, his smile kept him out of a great deal of trouble. Mr. Kade sat next to her, leaning forward so their knees almost touched.

Vivian tried to seem unaffected by his nearness. "I have to know; how did you get to me so quickly? I was barely in the water for a minute before you were there."

"A man must keep his secrets to seem irresistible," he winked.

"So, you fell in too." Vivian tried to give him a serious look, but it quickly dissolved into a grin.

He chuckled. "I saw you fall overboard and jumped in after you."

"What were you doing on deck in such a storm?"

"The same as you." Mr. Kade leaned forward in a conspiratorial manner. "Trying to get some peace from our devoted hostess."

"I am so grateful that you did," Vivian said with all sincerity. She reached out and took his hand in both of hers. "I hope you know that I'm eternally in your debt."

"It was nothing." His cheeks were turning a soft pink.

"It was something to me," Vivian said, her voice growing animated with each word. "I would be dead now if not for you. I owe you my life, sir, and I want you to know that I won't forget what you did." Vivian spoke passionately. Most people would have called it unladylike, but she wanted her sincerity to be known to this man. "Your quick thinking and your guidance in the water... well, I just can't thank you enough. To me you are the truest of heros, Mr. Kade. Thank you from the bottom of my heart."

With his free hand, Mr. Kade patted the back of her hands before he placed them on her lap. "It was no trouble. Truly. Although I do think I lost my quizzing glass in the process. No matter, you are safe and that is the important thing." He removed his hands from hers. He sat in the uncomfortable chair, looking nervous.

Vivian wanted to kick herself. Her fit of passion, heartfelt though it may be, was unwelcome by Mr. Kade as the sympathies of her Plymouth neighbors had been to her. In fact, he was more concerned about his lost quizzing glass than he was about her safety. She looked at the man across from her. His once god-like appearance faded into the image of a typical fop. Well, no matter. He had saved her, and she had expressed her gratitude. All that was left now was to gracefully end the conversation and part ways. If only she could think of something to say. The weather! When all else fails, the weather was a universally welcomed topic by all well-bred ladies.

"I do believe that the storm has passed," she said. "Many storms leave blissful sunsets in their wake. Would you care to view this one with me?"

Relief flashed over Mr. Kade's face and he readily agreed. Vivian was at the door before he had a chance to rise. She marched onto the deck, all the while wishing she was better at conversing with people, even if they were fops. Why did she always feel the need to speak her mind?

"I would like to apologize," she said as they walked about the deck together.

"For what?"

"For the whole day, I suppose. If I hadn't been on deck so long, then I wouldn't have fallen into the sea. Then you wouldn't have lost your quizzing glass and then I wouldn't have spoken like a brazen idiot a moment ago. The Admiral always told me I should guard my tongue, but I never do."

Mr. Kade stopped her and looked into her eyes. "Mrs. Reed, I don't think you need to apologize for the whole day. An accident happened and I was only too happy to help. Besides, it isn't every day that a man gets to be a fair lady's truest hero."

A blush pricked at her cheeks. "So, you don't think I spoke too passionately before?"

"Oh, I know you did," Mr. Kade said, and Vivian's blush deepened. "But I didn't mind. Please, say anything you want to me anytime you wish."

He placed one of her hands in the crook of his arm, keeping it there by placing his freehand over hers. The Admiral had always held her elbow when they walked, claiming it was easier to control her that way. With Mr. Kade there was no control, only two companions walking together amiably. Vivian felt completely at ease with the arrangement.

As promised, the storm left a brilliant sunset in its wake. The cool sea air pushed the ship along as it angled north. The Irish coastline came into view, and the Kensington began to leave the sea to make its way up the Barrow River.

The farther up the river they sailed; the more excited Vivian became about seeing her home. The smell of peat moss burning in the family hearths hung in the air. Vivian watched as children ran along the banks, trying to get passengers to wave at them.

One little boy with a tousle of sandy hair caught Vivian's attention. He waved his chubby arm in the air. Vivian waved back at him, a warm smile spreading across her face. The little boy whooped for joy and ran to his friends.

"You have a fondness for children," Mr. Kade said.

"Only the most rambunctious of them," Vivian replied. "I've always enjoyed the company of children. They're unafraid to have fun, even if it isn't fashionable."

Mr. Kade chuckled, "Spoken like a true Irishwoman."

Vivian turned to look fully at him. "How do you know I'm Irish?" She thought back on all that she had said to him that day, certain she had spoken only formal English. Even the Admiral would have been pleased.

"Your pendant," Mr. Kade motioned to her necklace. "Few members of English society would wear such a necklace. It's beautiful, mind you, but very Irish."

Vivian rubbed it between her fingers absently. "The Admiral hated it."

"Ah yes, your famous Admiral. Mrs. Seymour told me so much about him. He sounded like an interesting man." Mr. Kade released her hand so he could lean on the railing of the ship.

"He was a decent fellow," she said, staring at the river below her. "If you were a man...and of some profession...and, most importantly, not Irish. To him, we were all a bunch of layabouts."

"That's not how I would describe myself," Mr. Kade gave a broad smile.

"Are you a native of the island also?"

"Aye," he proudly said. "I hail from Dublin. And yourself?"

"Waterford. My father and brother live there still. I'm planning on staying with them for a time."

Mr. Kade nodded; a serious look furrowed his brow. "And then what?"

Vivian cocked her head to one side. "What do you mean?"

"You said that you'll be staying with your family for a time. But what happens after that time?"

"I have no idea." She tried to sound as if it didn't matter. She didn't want to admit to a person who was very nearly a stranger that she had no idea what she was going to do with her life. As outspoken as she was, even Vivian conformed to the belief that marriage was a female's highest priority. Honorable professions available to women were few. The thought of being anything other than a wife had never occurred to her. A woman was to marry, have children, and live her life for her family. But Vivian had no children and now her husband was gone. What was she to do now?

His deep voice rumbled, soft and low like thunder in the distance. "May it all go well for you, Mrs. Reed."

"Vivian," she whispered.

He looked momentarily confused which made her smile.

She shrugged. "I figure the man who saved my life should at least be able to call me by my Christian name. It's Vivian."

Mr. Kade straightened, taking Vivian's hands in his. "I am honored, Vivian." His blue eyes softened, sending a tingle down Vivian's spine.

A sharp *'Haloo'* disrupted their peaceful moment. Vivian glanced around Mr. Kade to see Mrs. Seymour coming their direction. The older woman waved her finger at the couple.

"Yoo-hoo! Mrs. Reed, I'm so glad I found you," she said in a sing-song voice. "We are going to be docking soon and you know what that means."

Mr. Kade smoothly moved Vivian's hand to the crook of his elbow as he turned to face Mrs. Seymour. He gave the woman a dazzling smile as she came closer.

"While I'm sure Mrs. Reed knows what that means I haven't the slightest idea. Would you do me the great honor of educating me, Mrs. Seymour?"

Mrs. Seymour giggled. "Oh, Mr. Kade! What a charmer you are!"

"Not nearly as charming as my fair hostess has been." He bowed to Mrs. Seymour and kissed her hand.

While Mrs. Seymour explained the process for disembarking, Vivian slipped away. Her trunk was easy to repack. As she shook the sea salt from her now dry clothes the image of Mr. Kade kissing the older woman's hand played in her mind. The thought of it made her stomach tighten, much as if a cobra had slithered around her middle and was slowly tightening its coils. Vivian shook the thought from her mind. If she didn't find the notion so preposterous, she would have thought herself jealous of Mrs. Seymour.

On deck once more, Vivian watched Waterford come into view. The city shimmered like a jewel as the sun sank behind one of its towers. The cathedral spire loomed above the city's stone walls. Lights shone from the windows of brightly colored buildings that lined the massive river. Vivian inhaled the fragrant air, heavy with spring blossoms and fertile earth.

"Happy to be home?" Mr. Kade joined her as the ship docked. Together they admired the view of the city before them.

Vivian smiled at him in the dimming light. "Overjoyed."

"How long has it been since you were last here?"

"Ten years," she said.

"That *is* a long time to be away from your family."

She nodded in agreement. A decade of separation was a long time for a family. She had received nothing but the occasional letter from her father and brother. Would she still know them after so long?

III.

It is a cruel trick of the sea to make a person long for land only to leave them unable to stand once they are finally on it. So, it was with Vivian. Her graceful steps faltered on the dock. Swaying, she grasped at Mr. Kade with two hands, doing her best to stay standing.

"Are you sure you've ever sailed before?" he asked with a laugh.

"I need a few minutes to get my land legs again."

Mr. Kade half-carried Vivian over to a nearby bale and helped her to sit on the dry hay. Then he left her there as she steadied herself. A triumphant expression illuminated his features when he returned to her.

"I have secured a carriage to take you home. Your luggage is being loaded as we speak," he declared, pride swelling his chest. "And don't worry about paying for the ride. I've already covered the cost."

Her eyes widened with surprise, then moistened with gratitude. In a voice thick with emotion she said, "Thank you, Mr. Kade. I don't know what I would have done without you today."

"It's what we hero's do." Mr. Kade effortlessly helped her to her feet. Slowly, he escorted her to the waiting carriage.

"If everyone I helped was as appreciative and pretty as you then I would go about assisting others all day."

Wiping her eyes, Vivian gave him a radiant smile. She didn't want a sad countenance to stain his generosity. Once settled in the carriage, she reached back to grasp Mr. Kade's hand. She looked earnestly into his eyes that still showed their blue in the dwindling light. "I cannot thank you enough for saving my life today, Mr. Kade. I am forever in your debt. If there is ever anything that I can do to repay you, please don't hesitate to ask it of me."

He leaned into the carriage just enough so she could hear him whisper, "Then I ask that you call me Sean."

"Sean," she whispered in return.

He bowed once more, kissing her hand in the process. When he released her hand, he shut the carriage door and sent them on their way.

While she enjoyed dreaming of Mr. Kade, or Sean as he wanted to be called, Vivian felt giddy with anticipation at seeing her family. When the carriage left the cobbled streets of Waterford to enter a country lane, excitement swirled inside of her. Her journey was near an end. Soon a manor house rose before her. It looked much as it had when she was younger. Tendrils of ivy climbing up the pale stone walls, curling around the shuttered windows. She breathed in the smell of spring blossoms and the moist earth, the smells of safety, of home.

Vivian leapt out of the carriage before it had stopped in the circular drive. She ran up the stairs to the front door and pushed on it. It didn't budge. Vivian pushed again. Still the door didn't move. She jiggled the handle to see if she was trying to open it wrong. When nothing happened, she hammered the knocker but there was no answer. Vivian went to the nearest window and peered inside. She had to wipe dust away from the glass to be able to see through.

"They're not there anymore," a voice with a thick Irish accent announced.

Vivian turned towards the sound. It was Mr. Kelly, the aged gardener of the manor. As glad as Vivian was to see him, she was surprised by his words.

"What do you mean?" she asked.

"They're all gone." He shook his grey head. "'Tis a shame too. They were nice people."

"Gone where?" Vivian felt panic rising. Where was her family?

"I don't know that I should be telling a stranger," Mr. Kelly said as he rubbed his stubble. He eyed her suspiciously, his face growing stern.

Vivian stared at him for a long moment. He had no idea who she was. To not be recognized by someone who had known her all her growing up years was something Vivian hadn't expected. She should tell him who she was, but would he remember that Dr. Warren had a daughter?

"Mr. Kelly, I'm Vivian Warren. I've come home to see my father, Dr. Warren," she said, tentative but hopeful.

Mr. Kelly, however, just stared at her. He looked so utterly confused by her words that she feared he had completely forgotten her. Then, as she was ready to turn away, his face lit up.

"Vi? Vi, me girl, is that really you?" The suspicion in his eyes vanished, his face lit with recognition.

"Yes," she said, relief seeping in.

Mr. Kelly tipped his hat back, scratched his head, and let out a low whistle. "My, how ye've grown. Ye're a regular lady now. Come now, let me have a look at ye."

Vivian stepped away from the house so Mr. Kelly could see her better. He reached his worn hands out for hers and shook them with a vigor that belied his aged frame.

"Well bless me stars. It be little Vi home at last. Not a bit of the scamp ye used to be. And what of that high and mighty English fellow of yours?" He leaned in as if he had some great secret to share with her. "Did ye run away from him?"

Vivian laughed despite herself. "No. He passed away."

"Oh. Now that is too bad." Mr. Kelly hung his head. He whispered a Gaelic prayer for the deceased.

"Mr. Kelly, where is my family?" she asked the moment the prayer was over. Vivian wrung her hands as her nerves began to well up inside her again.

The old man nodded his head. "Aye. They be down the field in the center of Waterford now. That wife of yer brother's had no love for the country. Pity he didn't take her farther away than that, if ye ask me."

"And my father? Is he still with them?" This was the real question that Vivian wanted answered but the one she feared most to ask. If her family had moved without telling her was there a chance that her father.... She didn't want to think about the words.

Mr. Kelly nodded. "He's alive if that's what yer worried about. Yer brother was good enough to take him in when his health failed. He's living in Waterford as well."

Relief swept over her, leaving her weak. She placed her hands on her knees for support. Mr. Kelly patted her back as she forced air into her lungs.

"There, there. It'll be alright," he crooned in a melodic way that only the Irish were capable of. Vivian had missed that sound.

Vivian nodded and straightened, allowing Mr. Kelly to walk her back to her carriage. She had more questions but was able to push them aside. At that moment all she wanted was to see her father.

Mr. Kelly gave the driver directions to the house in Waterford that her brother was living in and sent them off. Back down the winding lane. Back to the city of Waterford with its impressive walls standing guard around it.

It was dark when the carriage finally pulled up to the correct house. Nervously, Vivian climbed the stairs to the front door. While the house was large for living in the center of Waterford, it seemed stark and formidable, not at all like the home of her youth. Vivian rang the bell and waited. Then waited some more.

After what felt like an eternity in her exhausted state, the door was finally opened by a stiff butler. He looked down his beak of a nose at her.

"Yes?" his obvious disdain set Vivian on edge.

Vivian straightened up, matching the butlers cool distain. "Please inform Mr. Warren that his sister, Mrs. Reed, has arrived."

He surveyed her with a scrutinizing eye. "Hmm. Yes. You have been expected," and because he could, he added "for quite some time."

"It's important to build anticipation for my arrival." Vivian winked at him, making the butler bristle. He turned abruptly on his heel, hustling through a spacious foyer. Vivian entered the hall, her eyes widening with shock.

The polished white marble of every surface reflected light from the crystal chandelier that hung overhead. Oriental vases sat atop gold etched tables and beautiful paintings hung on the walls. Nathan Reed was a clergyman. Vivian wondered where did the money for such a house come from?

The butler opened a sliding door and announced her arrival to those in the room, Vivian close at his heels. If she had been expecting a warm welcome complete with embraces and kisses on her cheeks, she was left very disappointed. Despite the fire that was blazing in the large hearth Vivian could feel a solid chill in the environment.

The Warren family sat around the fire as if poising for a portrait. Her father, aged and stooped, sat in a wingback chair facing the door. He looked ashen, not at all the energetic man he had been the last time Vivian had seen him. It broke her heart to see him looking so forlorn.

Next to him stood Vivian's beloved brother Nathan, solemn in his black clothes of sobriety. On an elegant settee before Nathan sat his wife flanked by two children. Vivian curtsied to the occupants of the room as she entered. The feeling that decorum was demanded in the house felt overwhelming.

"Is someone there?" Dr. Warren asked.

"It's Vivian, Father," Nathan bellowed at the old ma. Turning his attention to Vivian he said, "You must forgive him. He can't hear well these days."

Vivian ran across a plush carpet to her father and dropped to the floor beside his chair. She kissed his hands and then his cheek, which was becoming wet with his warm tears. "My little girl. How I have missed you!" Dr. Warren held out his two shaking hands to his daughter.

"I'm here now, Father. I'm back," she said as she tenderly held his hands in hers.

Dr. Warren's dim eyes shone through his tears. He moved his hand to Vivian's cheek, and she leaned into his touch. It had been a long time since she had been with her father and she wanted to remember every second of this meeting. She closed her eyes as she committed it to memory.

Dr. Warren rubbed his thumb on his daughter's cheek. "My precious girl," he crooned. Then, remembering the others in the room he said, "Don't forget to greet your brother now."

Vivian jumped up and threw herself into the arms of her older brother. "Nathan!"

"Easy there, Vi," he said with a joyful laugh. "You'll have the staff questioning what type of lady you are."

"The type who could care less what the staff has to say," she said with a laugh. "I've missed you so much." Tears prickling at her eyes she hugged him fiercely. He hugged her back.

"You've grown so," Nathan said when he finally released her.

"That tends to happen over ten years." Vivian tried to laugh at her words but the truth of them stung.

After a moment Nathan remembered himself. Stepping away from his sister, he straightened his coat. Formally, he said, "Vivian, may I please introduce my wife, Claire. Mrs. Warren, I would like to introduce my sister, Mrs. Reed."

Vivian found the use of surnames formal and unnecessary. However, the grave look worn by Mrs. Warren, or Claire as Vivian was determined to call her, showed that this was a normal thing about this house.

Claire rose from her seat like a graceful swan taking flight. She offered Vivian a solemn curtsy which Vivian returned. Claire's eyes raked Vivian from head to toe and back again with a scrutiny most people reserved for livestock. Vivian wouldn't have been surprised if Claire asked to see her teeth.

"It is wonderful to finally make your acquaintance," Claire said. "Mr. Warren has told me so much about you that I feel I know you already." The words were kind, but the tone was condescending.

"And I you, Claire. I am so pleased to have a sister. After growing up with only brothers for company you can't imagine how happy I am to have another female in the family."

Claire didn't look at all pleased by the comment. In fact, she seemed more affronted than before. Vivian glanced over at Nathan, hoping that he would give her some idea as to what she had said wrong. She hoped it wasn't the use of her sister-in-law's Christian name. They were family after all.

Claire claimed the attention of the room by clearing her throat. With a polished air she said, "I would like to present my children to you Mrs. Reed." She motioned for the two children to come forward. Vivian looked down into the faces of two little boys who looked like mirror images of their mother. They had Claire's straw like hair, her round face, even her large brown eyes. The only thing they didn't have of their mother was her self-assurance. These two boys were as timid as any children could be.

"Bow to your aunt, children," Claire barked at the boys who stood staring at Vivian. They offered carefully practiced bows to her. She curtsied but watching their joyless faces made Vivian wonder if they ever had a day of fun in their whole young lives.

"I am pleased to meet you both." Vivian turned back to Nathan who hovered over her shoulder. "You never told me how grown up your boys were. They are true gentlemen."

The boys almost smiled at the praise. Almost.

Claire jumped in and motioned to the older of the two. "Master Warren is going to be a clergyman just like his father when he goes to Oxford, and young James here will become a clerk." Both boys nodded at what their mother said.

Vivian raised an eyebrow. "They are a little young to be deciding their future careers, don't you think?"

"Not at all." Claire said. "As you said yourself, they are more grown than most children. I have devoted all my time to my sons' studies so that they may enter the university early. It is my feeling that men of idleness, as most Irish are, have little to contribute to society. It is only the truly hard-working English that are of use to this island. But then I don't expect those who have spent their time climbing up the social rungs of society to understand."

Vivian's jaw dropped. If Claire had reached out and slapped her face, Vivian would have been less surprised.

Claire seemed to understand that she had gone too far. Quickly she changed the subject. "Speaking of studies, it is time for the children to retire to bed so they will be ready for their lessons in the morning. They spent too long waiting for our guest to arrive this afternoon."

Vivian was taken aback again. "The driver went to the manor instead of your home here," she said.

"Yes, well...come along boys." Claire sputtered. She swept out of the room with an air of indifference, her two children at her heels.

Once the door was shut behind them, Vivian felt the vice around her chest release. Breathing again, she turned back to her father and brother. Nathan was standing by the fireplace absently twirling his pocket watch around his finger. He hadn't seemed to notice the coldness that filled his wife's greeting to his sister. Or if he did, he refused to acknowledge it.

Dr. Warren looked exhausted. His eyelids drooped as he sagged back into his chair. Vivian noticed a wool shawl nearby. She tenderly tucked it around her father's lap as he had done to so many of his patients in his younger years. Vivian remembered attending to the elderly and the infirm with him as she grew up. She had always admired the great care he had given them.

Dr. Warren stirred as Vivian knelt before him. "You look tired, my dear. Why don't you rest your eyes a bit?"

Vivian smiled softly at him. She knew that he was really the one who was tired, but she had no desire to throw aside his fatherly concern for her. "I'll do that Father," she said. She kissed him on the top of his head, noting his thinning hair.

Vivian and Nathan slipped quietly from the room so that their father could rest. Nathan led her up the stairs to a small bedroom on the third floor. It was a simple room with nothing but the most immediate necessities. The small space was in complete contrast with the ornate decorations on the lower levels of the house. The sanded wood floor was bare of the lavish rugs that covered the parlor floor. The walls were stark with only a light layer of whitewash to hide the buildings bricks. The bed was narrow, with a patchwork quilt over it. There was no fireplace in the room and the singular, narrow window overlooked the stables. Vivian did her best to appear pleased with the room. At least she would have a space to herself while she was here.

Nathan was obviously happy with it and didn't try to hide the pride he felt in his home. "Here you are, Vivian. I know that you will be very comfortable. One thing that Claire excels at is making certain that all her guests are comfortable."

Hopefully more comfortable than she makes them feel welcomed, Vivian thought but she didn't dare say it. Nathan seemed very fond of his wife and Vivian didn't want to offend him.

As he turned to leave, Vivian stopped him. "Nathan, why are you living in town and not at the manor?"

"Claire wanted to live in town, and I needed to be near my parish. This is the best of both worlds. For now, why don't you rest and I'll have a tray sent up to your room. You must be hungry after your journey." He moved to embrace her but paused. Awkwardly, he patted her on the shoulder. "It's good to have you home."

IV.

The ship creaked around her as it rocked in the torrential sea. Vivian looked up to see the sails being snapped by the wind, bits of water spraying onto her. She shivered with cold as the air swirled around her. She hugged her arms about her body, trying to hold onto any warmth she had.

She knew this dream too well. It had haunted her sleep ever since her first voyage with the Admiral. He had called her a silly girl when she had told him about it, claiming she had read too many gothic novels. Vivian knew that wasn't the case. No book had ever filled her with the terror she felt now.

Her heart raced as she turned around to see *it*.

It was always there. Always watching.

Vivian backed up as the hood figure glided toward her over the damp deck, it's black cloak flapping in the wind. It made no sound as it reached toward her, its gloved fingers coming closer… closer…

Vivian snapped awake. She was breathing hard into the blanket that she was face down on. Pushing herself up to a sitting position, Vivian inhaled deeply and exhaled slowly.

She went to the washstand and splashed some cold water on her face. It helped to wake her up the rest of the way.

Vivian tried to survey the room about her. The eerie darkness was contrasted only the lucid shadows that swam on the walls. Vivian pushed the thin curtains aside, only to reveal a world darkened by a spring rain.

How she had missed the rain. There had been rain in England, of course. There was rain in every part of the world that she had ventured to but there was something about the rain in Ireland that was different. It was softer, calmer, as if it only rained this morning to welcome her home and for no other reason.

Vivian lit a candle that was sitting on the bedside table. The single flame illuminated the small space about her. At the foot of her bed was her traveling trunk. Someone must have brought it in before she had entered the room. At least that was what she hoped. She would have been so embarrassed if someone had come into her room while she was asleep.

With a creak the old trunk reluctantly opened. There were few possessions in there, which made traveling easy and settling into new places even easier. Under a pile of dresses was a battered wooden box, not much larger than her hand. Inside was a tarnished brass spyglass. Vivian sighed with relief. She didn't know why she felt so relieved to find the worthless thing still in its box, but she was.

With a lighter heart she placed the small box back into the bottom of her trunk. She wasn't sure what time it was, but she guessed it to be morning. She rang the bell in her room then began to unpack her trunk as she waited for a maid to come. Vivian was just laying out her attire for the day when a small knock came to the door.

A little maid entered when Vivian answered the door.

"I need a breakfast tray, if you please," Vivian said cheerfully to the girl.

The maids face took on a terrified expression. "Beggin' yer pardon, miss, but I can't be gettin you that."

"Why ever not?"

"The mistress o' the house don't like no eatin' cept in the dinnin' hall. No one get's a tray in their rooms. Ever!"

"But I had a dinner tray last night," Vivian said.

"That's cause- Mr. Warren said it was alright. But now the mistress is saying that there's to be no more of that." The girl fidgeted with her apron, refusing to look Vivian in the eye.

"Well how ridiculous!" Vivian couldn't help her outburst. "Then I will be down momentarily to eat."

"Sorry, miss. But it's all been cleared away. Breakfast happens at eight sharp rounds here. The mistress is most particular."

"Am I to go hungry then?" Vivian wasn't sure how much she believed Nathan's opinion that Claire made her guest feel welcomed.

"Sorry, miss," said the little maid as she shook in her boots. "It's what the mistress ordered."

Vivian could tell that the child was terrified. Calmly she said, "Very well. I will be at breakfast on time tomorrow."

The maid curtsied and hurried out of the room. Vivian rolled her eyes. She understood having an ordered house. After all, she lived on board a naval ship for years of her life. But when a maid was too terrified to even accommodate a guest in a house then the rigidity of a schedule had been taken too far.

Thinking of households and orders, Vivian attacked her tangle of curls. She would have to wash it soon, but she wasn't sure if the terrified maid would be allowed to haul water upstairs for her. Once her hair was set, Vivian dressed in a simple day dress of sky-blue muslin and wrapped a cream-colored cashmere shawl about her shoulders.

Venturing out, Vivian wandered about the house until she came to the drawing room she had been in earlier. Still sitting in his chair was Dr. Warren, looking as tired as he had the night before. Kneeling next to him was a man whom Vivian thought was Nathan from behind.

"Is all well, Father?" Vivian asked as she came into the room.

Her father looked up at her, his eyes brightening. "If it isn't my girl, returned at last." He tapped the man next to him on the shoulder. "Look and see Dr. Eldon. Tis me girl returned at last!"

Dr. Eldon turned around as he rose from his kneeling position next to Dr. Warren. "I am pleased to see you home at last, Mrs. Reed. Your father has talked of nothing else for some time now." He smiled kindly at her as he bowed.

In an instant of realization Vivian remembered who this man was. He was a former student of Dr. Warren's who had come into their home to be trained as a doctor. "Dr. Eldon! What a pleasant surprise. What brings you here?"

"I'm now a physician of Waterford!" He laughed as the words came from him, jiggling his portly frame. His friendly smile added a pleasant twinkle in his brown eyes.

Vivian couldn't help but smile back. Dr. Eldon had that effect on people. Even when he was just a student everyone had loved him because of his pleasant nature.

"I'm so pleased to see you again Dr. Eldon," Vivian said as she shook his hand.

Before another word could be spoken, the door burst open.

Nathan came in, absently reading a newspaper. He seemed to have no idea of the disturbance that he caused. Behind him came his boys, full of energy and mischief as little boys usually are. They raced around the room; eyes bright with life. Their entire countenance seemed so different from when they were with their mother the night before.

It filled Vivian with relief to see how lively these potential scholars could be. She had thought them overly controlled by their mother's aspirations for them that the boys never had a chance to be actual children. However, the noise did nothing but upset Dr. Warren. Every noise that was above a whisper caused him to jump in fright.

"Saints preserve me!" He gripped his heart and slumped back in his chair.

"Father?" Vivian rushed to his side.

Dr. Eldon was right beside her. He held his patient's wrist, feeling the pulse and timing it with a pocket watch he pulled from his stretched vest pocket.

Nathan barely looked over his paper. "He does this at least once a week. Sometimes more."

Vivian was shocked. Was her brother so unfeeling that he didn't care when his own father suffered? It was a thought that repulsed her. Instead of dwelling on it, she turned her attention to Dr. Eldon. "Is there something that can be done for him?"

He smiled at her, but the smile didn't extend to his eyes this time. "We shall talk of it presently. Right now, let's get your father to bed."

With Vivian on one side and Dr. Eldon on the other, old Dr. Warren was taken to his room. Dr. Eldon helped him get ready for bed while Vivian tried not to fret. She stoked the fire and drew the curtains all the while listening to everything that Dr. Eldon was saying.

"Try not to get overly tired, sir. You always suffer from an attack when you are most exhausted."

"I wouldn't be so tired if I could have some peace and quiet," Dr. Warren grumbled as he settled back onto his pillows. "And besides, I'm not sleepy."

Dr. Eldon nodded his understanding. "I know sir, but we must all do the best we can with what God has given us. Now, I want you to rest for a good long while today. I will have a servant bring some nourishing stew for you later. For now, enjoy the quiet while those boys are downstairs." He winked at his patient who huffed in return.

Dr. Eldon led Vivian out of the room and shut the door behind him. She was ready to ask her questions, but he held a finger to his lips. He motioned for her to follow him down the hall, away from the earshot of her father. Once safely away, he turned to her with a grim expression.

"I'm not going to mince words for you, Mrs. Reed, but your father is not well at all. He is greatly affected by loud noises, as you saw earlier. I'm afraid that his rheumatism has gotten so severe that he has difficulty moving about freely."

Vivian felt confused. "Surely having a desire for a quiet, comfortable place to be can't be causing my father such grief."

"You said the right word just then. Grief. Your father is suffering from a broken heart."

She gave him a quizzical look. "Are you serious? I didn't think that people actually suffered from such things as broken hearts."

Dr. Eldon smiled but no joy reached his eyes. "A typical, healthy individual may not. But you must remember that your father is an aged man. His career is over. Instead of being one of the most respected people in the whole community he is now reduced to being a guest in his son's house. Between you and me, he often feels like an unwanted guest. All those things weigh on a man's mind. And we must remember the loss of his beloved wife, your mother. I fear he truly has lost his will to live. You were the only reason he has been making any effort in his own health."

The understanding of her father's health left Vivian feeling cold. Tears pricked at her eyes. It took all her self-control to calmly say, "Is there anything to be done?"

"Spend time with him, as often as you are able. I think seeing your pretty face might do him some good." Dr. Eldon laughed at his words; his cheerfulness restored. "I also left some laudanum in his room. If he begins to become too difficult to manage, just have him drink a glass of it. You may need to mix it into some wine or brandy so he won't know he is taking it but the opium in the laudanum will quickly put him to sleep."

Vivian nodded her understanding. "Is it safe to leave in his room? I don't want him taking the laudanum without anyone knowing."

"It is perfectly safe for him to take," Dr. Eldon said. "Now let's go tell your brother."

Vivian followed him down the stairs and into the drawing room where they had left Nathan earlier. Sure enough, he was still there reading his newspaper. The little boys were nowhere in sight, and Vivian didn't know if that was a good thing or not. She watched Nathan as Dr. Eldon explained the situation about their father's health to him.

Nathan sat for a moment in silence. "So, what you're telling me is that my father is only going to need more and more quiet around the house but even that isn't going to make him well again."

"Essentially, yes. That is what I'm saying," Dr. Eldon said.

Nathan crossed his arms over his chest, his face in a clear pout. His reaction both confused and irritated Vivian. She had a higher expectation of his conduct than he was showing.

"I hate to be the bearer of such bad news," Dr. Eldon continued. "I think the best thing for Dr. Warren is to be comfortable in his old age. He hasn't much longer on this earth. It's best to make the most of it with him." He offered a sympathetic smile to the siblings, patting Vivian's arm as she stood by him.

She nodded her understanding and tried to smile at him, but it felt pathetic on her face.

"There you are," came the voice of Claire as she swept into the room, a flood of panicked energy in her wake. "I need to prepare this room for the dinner party tonight, and you still have to review my notes on your sermon for this Sunday."

"What dinner party?" Nathan asked in an agitated tone. Vivian took a step back and looked between the two of them. She wasn't sure if she should still be in the room, but Claire was standing just inside the doorway. It would be difficult to escape.

Claire gave Nathan an annoyed look. "The dinner party I've been planning for weeks. Sir Warren is coming, and I want to make a good impression. Now, I need this room."

If Vivian thought that Nathan sounded agitated before it was nothing compared to how he responded now. "Sir Warren? Why on earth did you invite Sir Warren to dinner?"

Claire put her hands on her hips, giving Nathan a vicious look. "He is the highest-ranking member of our community and a very near relation of your father's. Family lines are always worth preserving. Besides, he enjoys your father's company, though I have no idea why."

"Well too bad for that," Nathan scoffed at her. "My father is sentenced to bed for the rest of the evening because it's too loud around here. Isn't that right, Dr. Eldon?"

Dr. Eldon looked surprised to be pulled into the conversation. He had silently gathered up his medical bag and was in the process of slowly making his way around the edge of the room toward the door. Vivian pitied him for being dragged into Nathan and Claire's disagreement.

Regaining his composure, Dr. Eldon nodded. "Your father in law is doing very poorly, Mrs. Warren. I feel that the best thing for him will be quiet and plenty of rest."

"But what of my dinner party?"

"I'm afraid that he will not be going to any dinner parties for some time," Dr. Eldon said with a shake of his head.

Claire pursed her lips in frustration. "Well it simply won't do to only have four people at a dinner. I even ordered a good roast for this evening. What am I to do now?"

"Cancel?" came Dr. Eldon's suggestion.

"Impossible! I have never canceled for any reason before and I don't want to now." Claire stamped her foot. She gave Vivian the impression of a very spoiled child demanding her way.

"I've got it!" Nathan jumped in, sounding excited for the first time all day. "Dr. Eldon, why don't you come to dinner tonight. Bring your wife. I'm sure two more will be a welcome addition to Claire's party. Won't it darling?"

Claire beamed. "Yes, it would be my love. What a wonderful idea. Do come, Doctor, and bring Mrs. Eldon with you."

The immediate change in Claire was almost comical but Vivian managed to suppress a laugh.

"I would gladly accept Mrs. Warren, but I have a guest at my house. I wouldn't feel right about leaving him home with nothing to amuse him."

"Bring him with you," Nathan said as he went back to his newspaper.

Claire nodded. "Yes, bring him along." She sighed with relief. "I will still be able to have my dinner party for Sir Warren after all."

With that she swept back out of the room allowing everyone to breathe easily again.

The moment was short lived, however. The instant Dr. Eldon had shut the front door Claire returned.

"How could you have just invited the Eldon's over like that? I was so embarrassed. This evening will be a complete disaster, and it's all because of you," she ranted at Nathan.

"I was only trying to help," he said, instantly defensive.

Vivian tried to edge away from the tension that oozed between the two. It grew rapidly until it encompassed the entire room.

"You ruined tonight." Claire was screaming. "Completely ruined it."

Nathan slumped in his chair, his face becoming red with rage.

"And furthermore," Claire shrieked.

"I was only trying to help!" Nathan screamed. Throwing down his newspaper he jumped out of his chair and stormed from the room without a backward glance.

"You think only of yourself." Claire yelled after him. "You think nothing of my feelings. Only of yourself!" She began to cry bitterly. She, too, ran from the room. In the distance several doors slammed. Then all was silent once more.

V.

Absently, Vivian rubbed her pendant between her fingers. She had been sitting in her father's room ever since the screaming match to make certain that he was taken care of. Claire couldn't spare any of the staff, as they were all needed for the evening's dinner party.

"You look tired."

Vivian turned toward her father. He was awake, propped up on a mound of pillows that made his old frame look small.

"I'm perfectly fine," Vivian gently reassured him. She went over to him and began to fluff his pillows and tuck the blankets around his thin shoulders.

"Don't fuss, child," he said, waving her away. "I'm being treated like a child. I don't need you jostling me around with it all."

"Do you need anything Father?" Her tone was light and cheerful. It sounded unnatural to her, but he didn't notice.

"Not at the moment. What were ye reading?"

"Shakespeare's sonnets. Not that they're really holding my attention today."

Dr. Warren looked at her as she hovered over his bedside. Finally, he said, "Well don't just stand there, girl. I'm not dying this minute so why don't you read me something from that book."

Vivian laughed, releasing all the tension that had filled her. She went back to her chair where she had left the book and, sitting down again, she opened it to a random page.

My mistress' eyes are nothing like the sun;
Coral is far more red than her lips' red;
If snow be white, why then her breasts are dun;
If hairs be wires, black wires grow on her head.
I have seen roses damask'd, red and white,
But no such roses see I in her cheeks;
And in some perfumes is there more delight
Than in the breath that from my mistress reeks.

"I don't think he liked her too much," Dr. Warren said when Vivian had finished reading.

She giggled. "Me neither. But I suppose we will never know for sure."

"Well I know," Dr. Warren said with conviction. He sat upon his pile of pillows and looked at his daughter. "If a man loves a woman then she becomes the most beautiful of all things on earth. Like how I felt about your dear mother, may she rest in peace. She was an angel from heaven. I remember the first time I saw her. She was sitting down by the river Suir, and I remember thinking that never had God made anything so perfect as He had made her. So, if'n I tell ye that this Shakespeare fellow didn't care for that mistress of his, you best believe me."

A lump had formed in her throat at the sentiment he had just expressed about her mother. A part of Vivian wondered if there would ever be a time when a man would feel like that about her. She turned her head away so that her father wouldn't see the tears she wiped from her eyes.

"Child, I'm so sorry," Dr. Warren said when he saw Vivian's reaction. He too began to tear up, his chin, with its white stubble, trembling as regret surged through him.

Vivian leapt to her feet and ran to his side. She took his shaking hands in her own, holding them fast as she sat on the bed.

"Forgive an old man for asking so much from his child," Dr. Warren wept.

Vivian's heart went out to her father. "There is nothing to forgive, sir. You asked for my help and I willingly gave it."

He shook his head. "I never should have let you go through with it. I should have found another way. You were too young to be married, especially to someone who wasn't even your friend."

Vivian smiled at him through her own tears. She wanted to ease her father's suffering, but it was difficult to pretend that the last ten years of her life hadn't happened. She couldn't simply tell him that it had been fine, and she had been happy. That would have been a lie. So, she told him the truth.

"There was no other way. You know that. I did what I had to do to save my family and I don't regret that," she said.

"Such a burden should have never been put on your young shoulders-"

"-But it was. And it's over now, so please don't dwell on it for another minute. I'm home with you and that is all that matters." She gave him a genuine smile which seemed to reassure him. He settled back onto his pillows.

His burst of emotions had left him physically drained. Within minutes, Old Dr. Warren had fallen fast asleep. Vivian tucked him in and quietly slipped out of the room.

As she turned away from the door she came face to face with Claire.

"You startled me," Vivian said, placing a hand on her beating heart.

Claire's eyes narrowed momentarily but then she smiled a forced smile to cover her annoyance. "What should startle you is how little time you have to get ready for this dinner," came her honey-dipped words.

Claire herself was already dressed in an evening gown of bright pink silk with a matching turban wrapped around her pale hair. The color didn't look well on her at all. The pink in the fabric only heightened the pink of her cheeks and the paleness of her skin, giving her a sickly look.

Vivian smiled kindly, feeling that any other reaction might make Claire feel slighted. "I was just on my way to find something suitable."

Claire took Vivian's hand in her own as she eyed her from head to toe. "I know that things have been hard for you lately," she said with false sympathy. "If you are in need of any attire, I would be happy to loan you something. It is no bother for me. I only want to help you. It would be a shame if Sir Warren saw you in anything that wasn't… resplendent."

Vivian pulled her hand back from Claire. She could hear the undertone of derision in the words. Anyone could have heard them; they were so subtly veiled under the thinnest film of generosity.

Understanding dawned then. Vivian knew why Claire was willing to invite her to her home. For the appearance of generosity. What better thing for a minister's wife to do than to allow her husband's poor relation to live with her. It almost made Vivian feel sick inside.

Instead of giving into loathing for her sister-in-law or pity for herself, Vivian squared her shoulders and cheerfully responded, "Thank you so much for that gracious offer but I think I will try my luck with the few things I have in my trunk. I might just have something that isn't too ragged."

Before Claire could protest Vivian turned around and hurried into her own room. Of course, Vivian knew that Claire had wanted her to be resplendent. After Claire's accusations to her husband, Vivian had figured the better she looked the more pleased Claire would be. The first chance Vivian had had after she heard the words 'dinner party,' she had laid out her best evening gown. It was emerald green silk with an overlay of shimmering French lace.

The Admiral had hated it.

"It shows too great a preference toward Ireland."

"But I am Irish, my dear," Vivian said in a cheerful way that always annoyed him.

"You are a subject of the crown and His Majesty," he fumed.

"Not by choice," Vivian muttered under her breath.

The Admiral glowered at her. "Go change this instant! And be quick about it. I want to be punctual."

"If you want to be on time then insisting that I change is a silly idea. You know how long we ladies can take."

Admiral Reed grew red about his collar. His jowls shook, and spittle flew from his mouth as he screamed, "Go now and be quick about it!"

She knew she had pushed him too far. Even after changing, and in record time too, he still gave her the silent treatment. All through the evening he didn't look at nor speak to her. His intention was to make her feel his anger, and it had worked.

Even now, as Vivian dressed for dinner, thoughts of the Admiral floated through her mind. She did her best to push them aside, but the thoughts were persistent. Then she reminded herself of an obvious truth.

"He isn't here," she said to her reflection in the tiny washstand mirror. "He is dead and gone. I can wear whatever I like."

Vivian did her hair in a way that, while very becoming on her, the Admiral had always objected to. He never liked it when any woman allowed her curls to tumble down her back. She even refused to wear her pearls; the only jewelry Admiral Reed had ever deemed appropriate for the wife of a naval officer. So tonight, the only jewelry she wore was her amber pendant.

Vivian took a step away from the tiny mirror so that she could catch as much of herself in the reflection as possible. Vivian Reed looked resplendent.

She entered the parlor with every intention of making a fuss over Claire, complimenting her on her housekeeping, her generosity, her loveliness. Instead, the moment Vivian stepped into the room, her attention was immediately drawn to a pair of sapphire blue eyes.

"Mr. Kade!" She was so surprised that she forgot the rest of the room.

His smile could have illuminated the darkest trench in the sea. He was before her in an instant, bowing chivalrously.

"Mrs. Reed it is a pleasure to see you again. Especially in such dry circumstances," he said with a wink.

Vivian blushed at his teasing. "And here I thought you enjoyed a good swim."

"It depends on the company," he whispered.

Vivian felt her heartbeat faster as she looked at the charming man before her. She wished she could think of something witty to say in return, but flirting was hadn't ever been one of her strengths.

"You know each other already?" Claire asked, appearing at Vivian's side. Her annoyance was barely contained.

"Yes," Vivian said. She hadn't told her family what had happened to her on the ship and now seemed like the worst time. "Mr. Kade was with me on my voyage to Waterford and was kind enough to help me in a difficult situation."

"I see." Claire seemed pacified by the answer but no less perturbed at being upstaged at her own party. "Well, now that you have met Mr. Eldon's guest, I want you to meet one of mine." Claire pulled Vivian away without further explanation. Dragging Vivian over to the fireplace, they stood before a seated old man.

"Sir Warren, may I present my sister-in-law, Mrs. Reed."

The old man looked up at the two women with a glazed expression over his beady black eyes. "Eh? What was that?"

Claire repeated herself louder.

"You have a present of a reed?" Sir Warren asked in an equally loud volume.

Claire tightened her grip on Vivian's arm in her frustration. Vivian tired not to yelp in pain as nails dug into her flesh. "No, Sir Warren," Claire nearly yelled at the man. "This is Mrs. Reed. Nathan's sister."

A horse sounding guffaw came out of the old man's throat. He slapped his knee, and his black eyes began to sparkle. "I heard ye the first time. Must keep these silly young things on their toes. Can't let all the women folk become full of themselves," he said to no one in particular.

Claire shoved Vivian's arm away from her and stormed off in a huff. Vivian curtsied politely to Sir Warren before walking away herself. She had little interest in talking further with such a rude man.

She had no sooner turned around than Dr. Eldon was before her, his wife on his arm. "Mrs. Reed, I would be honored to introduce you to my wife."

The woman stepped forward and Vivian had the oddest feeling that they had met before. Then it struck her as suddenly as a Caribbean hurricane. "Kathleen Taylor? Is that you?"

Kathleen smiled broadly at being remembered. "It is as I live and breathe. Only I'm not a Taylor anymore. I am now Dr. Eldon's wife."

Vivian smiled in return. It had been so long since she had last seen her school friend. She and Kathleen had attended a girls' school in Waterford before Vivian had been sent to a finishing school in Dublin. The two had been close friends until Vivian's marriage to the Admiral. As time and distance separated the two girls their letters had become farther and farther apart until they stopped altogether. The loss of a friend had made Vivian sorrow, but she had not become bitter. Life has a way of giving you a second chance and she recognized hers now.

With all the joy she could feel for her friends' good fortune Vivian said, "So you are, and I must say congratulations to you both! How long have you been married?"

"Nearly eight years," Kathleen said with a giggle. She looked up at Dr. Eldon who smiled affectionately at her.

Turning his attention to Vivian, Dr. Eldon said, "She might have gone for a better-looking man than I, but I'm blessed to have her."

Kathleen laughed again. "There is no better man in the world than you, dear one."

The look that passed between the two was filled with such love and admiration. Vivian felt as if she were intruding on an intimate moment. She looked away from the Eldon's and saw Mr. Kade coming toward her.

"I see you have met my charming cousin," he said in his soothing voice.

Vivian's eyes widened. "Oh?"

"Mr. Kade and I are distantly related," Kathleen cheerfully supplied. "He came to visit me a few summers ago and we have made it a tradition ever since."

Mr. Kade smiled at his cousin. "And she spoils me to no end. Honestly, Kathleen is the kindest person in the world."

"Oh, Sean you are too sweet. Isn't he sweet Dr. Eldon?" Kathleen asked as she hopped around to face her husband.

Mr. Eldon rolled his eyes with an air of annoyance, but Vivian could tell that he was teasing. "If he was any sweeter then I would have a toothache."

Vivian looked between the two and could see some family resemblance. They both had the same blues eyes, though Sean's were deeper set than Kathleen's. Both were of the black Irish set, which she found charming. But where Sean was tall and lean Kathleen was not.

A gong sounded to announce dinner. Claire scurried around the room making sure that her guests were ready for dinner. *More like to put them in the proper order*, Vivian mused.

She was right. Claire had every person line up in couples before they could enter the dining room. Vivian was given the "most desirable pleasure," as Claire put it, of walking with Sir Warren. This also meant that Vivian would have to spend the greater part of the evening talking to him.

VI.

Vivian had no fond memories of Sir Warren. When she was five, she had snuck a cookie from his pantry and was severely scolded by both the cook and Sir Warren for being a little thief. When she grew older her father sent her off to finishing school. Vivian had returned most accomplished. Her mother, delighted with all that Vivian had learned, was eager to show off her daughter to the neighborhood. Mrs. Warren had hosted a lovely party in Vivian's honor, insisting that her daughter perform on the harp. Vivian had complied, wishing to make her mother proud. In the middle of a very difficult piece Sir Warren had belched. Actually belched! Then he said, "At least it sounded better than that infernal contraption she's on." The men in the room had burst into laughter at his untimely joke.

No, thought Vivian. *Not a single fond memory at all.* And now she would have to make pleasant conversation with the man all evening.

Vivian would have sulked during the first course of the meal if Claire's seating arrangement hadn't been so appealing. While Claire was at the head of the table and Sir Warren was given the seat of honor on her right hand, Vivian, who was sitting on Sir Warren's other side, had a perfect line of sight to Sean, who sat on the other side of the table. It was the only relief to the nearly suffocating formality of the room.

Claire listened intently to Sir Warren's dreary tale of his wealth. It held no interest for Vivian. She looked over at Sean to find his eyes locked on her. He gave her a devilish smile. Her heartbeat faster.

"Dr. Eldon tells me that you are quite the traveler, Mrs. Reed. How have you found the world outside of our humble island?" He asked, his blue eyes sparkling.

"Not as green and lovely as here," she said.

Vivian had the sense that he was ready to tease at a moment's notice. It was such a difference from what she had been used to. She wanted to be able to tease him back, but she had to admit to herself that she had no idea how. Growing up with two older brothers should have prepared her but after ten years with a husband who had more salt water in his veins than blood it was hard to remember that men could smile at times.

"You only say that because this is your favorite of all the locations you visited," Sean said kindly. "I want to know what you actually think about some of the places in the world you were able to visit."

Vivian thought for a moment. "I found the Bahama's enchanting, the Cayman Islands rockier than I would have imagined, and Jamaica didn't live up to my expectations."

"It didn't?" Kathleen chimed in from farther down the table. "How so?"

"After spending time in Nassau, Bahama, I came to love the white sandy beaches and clear water. On a fine day, I could see a fish swimming up to one hundred yards out at sea. And there was something so calming about the palm trees in the breeze. Where I lived there was always a cool ocean breeze to dispel the heat of the island. But it never felt so in Jamaica. The water around the island had a greenish hue to it so I wasn't able to see the ocean floor at all, and much of the earth was red there instead of white sand or black soil. I suppose it is all a personal preference, but I didn't enjoy Jamaica as much as I did Nassau."

"How long did you live there?" Dr. Eldon cut in.

"I was in Nassau for five years and Jamaica for one."

"And you were living on a ship the entire time?" Kathleen said. "I couldn't stand to be living on a ship in a harbor for five years!"

"I doubt you could stand to be on a ship for five minutes, my dear," Dr. Eldon teased.

Vivian smiled warmly at her friend. "I wasn't on a ship the whole time. Admiral Reed liked it when I would have a house on land for him to come to. I think he felt it was easier to deal with me on land than to always have me underfoot on his precious ship. Not that I minded really."

Sean's face gave a more serious expression. "I imagine that being in the navy is a full-time job. It must have been difficult to be separated from your husband so often."

"Not as difficult as one might think. I have no great love of sailing on the sea, as you found out on my last voyage. And there is greater security to living on land than a little ship that moves about with the ocean's whims."

"Was there a great deal of danger in the West Indies?" Kathleen asked.

Vivian nodded. "Considerably, yes."

"Like pirates?" Dr. Eldon said with the eagerness of a child.

"Yes," Vivian appeased him. "There was one time when a band of pirates tried to take control of the harbor at Nassau. All the civilians who lived in the town were taken to the fort for protection. The pirates fired a number of cannonballs at the fort with the hopes that the outer walls would break apart in the attack. However, the limestone that the fort is made out of is unusual stuff- when a cannonball would hit it, the stone would absorb the ball instead of crumble."

Dr. Eldon's eyes were wide with excitement. "Really?"

"Absolutely," Vivian said animatedly. "The next day there were soldiers trying to pry the cannonballs out of the fort walls. It was wonderful to watch."

Sir Warren scoffed. "A man's labor is always wonderful for a woman to watch. Too bad she can't do any of her own." He laughed at himself as if he had made the funniest joke in the world. Claire laughed along with him.

"Oh, Sir Warren, you are too much," she crooned as she placed her hand on his arm.

"I think that Mrs. Reed's story is very enlightening," Sean offered in support. "Tell me, how did the pirates get away?"

"They didn't," Vivian said seriously. "Admiral Reed came up behind them and between the twenty cannons on his ship and those from the fort the pirate ship sank just outside the harbor. Any of the pirates who didn't drown were hanged the next day."

"A fitting end for those who break the law," Nathan said, raising his glass.

Vivian was surprised by her brother's quick accusation but even more surprised by what came out of her mouth next. "I don't think that it was, Nathan. What of forgiveness? Some of those hanged were mere boys. I believe that, through proper guidance and education, those boys could have reformed and become useful members of society."

"Really?" Sean said with a quizzical look on his face.

I've come this far, might as well commit to the whole idea, Vivian thought. Taking a deep breath, she continued. "Absolutely. There are many experiences in life that can be overcome. I feel that if a person wants to become better and is willing to put in the effort to do so, then they can really achieve a great deal."

"So says a naive female mind," Sir Warren said with a laugh at his own wit.

Vivian could tell by the way he was tilting from side to side that he had had too much to drink already and he was going for another glass of wine. He had always drunk too freely. Yet another reason Vivian disliked him.

Claire patted Sir Warren's arm again. "Well put, Sir Warren. It may be difficult for some of the gentler sex to understand, but there are rules that must be abided by. What would our society be if not for our laws?"

"Well put, my dear," Nathan said.

Claire pursed her lips and pretended she couldn't hear him.

Vivian looked at her brother in disbelief. "Can you honestly say that it is right to hang every child who makes an unwise choice?"

"If that choice involves piracy, then yes," Nathan stated.

"And what would the good Lord say to those who are looking to turn away from sin." Sean asked Nathan. "Isn't his grace sufficient to save all men?"

Claire scoffed. "It's sufficient to save all honest men, not pirates, Mr. Kade." She turned on Vivian. "Really, I don't know where these ideas of yours are coming from, but if this is what a woman thinks after she traveled the world then I will happily remain in Waterford all the rest of my days."

"Well I find it all fascinating," Kathleen said coming to Vivian's defense. "New ideas, new places. I think that being able to see the world in a new light is worth a difference of opinions. If I ever become a pirate, Vivian, I want you to be the judge of my trial." She giggled at her words and Vivian felt her heart warm toward her friend more than ever before.

Mr. Kade raised his glass in his hand. "To Mrs. Reed. The most traveled, and kindest, of us all."

Everyone raised their glass, cheerfully repeating the toast.

Only Claire had looked less than pleased. Her eyes briefly turned cold as she looked between Vivian and Sean. No one else saw the look but if they had it would have made them uneasy.

Vivian beamed at Sean, her heart beating in her ears. He winked at her over his glass.

The conversation turned to other things. At times, Vivian joined in and at times she listened. Once dinner was over everyone retired into the parlor for some entertainment. As the whist table was set up, Claire came rushing over to Vivian.

"You must sit with Sir Warren," Claire said.

"I will be happy to be his whist partner if you like."

Claire shook her turbaned head vigorously. "No! He has no intention of playing whist. And there aren't enough people to make a second table so you will have to sit out anyway. I want you to go over to the sofa and engage him in conversation."

"What of Mr. Kade?"

"What of him? He didn't come with a partner so why should I worry about him?" Grabbing Vivian by the elbow Claire led her toward the sofa where Sir Warren was already seated. "Now I need you to entertain him with riveting conversation."

Vivian pulled her arm free and sat down on the sofa. Sir Warren was staring into the fireplace, nursing a brandy in his hand. Vivian had no desire to talk with him, but she had less of a desire to upset Claire. She sighed with frustration.

"Thinking of your perfect island again," Sir Warren asked. He didn't look at her, only stared into the flames as they danced in the hearth.

"Actually, I was wondering about you," Vivian said. Vivian did her best to act demurely. It took her a great deal of effort.

He scoffed. The sound set her teeth on edge. Vivian noticed that he did that often. How she detested such a sound.

"Business is well," he said. "I have been around to all of my tenants recently. I have to check on them often since you know how lazy the Irish can be. It takes a strong hand, an English hand," he emphasized, "to keep them on track."

Vivian forced a smile onto her face. She had never cared for Sir Warrens method for handling business. He acted as if he were superior to those who worked his land, no matter how dedicated they were. It frustrated her how he felt that the Irish were slothful. If she wasn't a Christian, she would have hated him.

Vivian wondered why she had to be related to such a man as Sir Warren. She blamed the monarchy. If King George I hadn't awarded her great-great-grandfather a title and lands, then she wouldn't be sitting here with Sir Warren now. Many of the Warren descendants had gone back to England to marry the aristocratic families there. Some would stay, some would bring their spouses back to Ireland. But there were a few Warren's, like her father, who had married into the native families of Ireland. Vivian had never thought about how her mother was treated by Dr. Warren's family. Now she wondered how her mother had endured them.

VII.

Vivian did her best to appear to be listening to what Sir Warren was prattling on about, but it was no use. Her mind drifted until she felt herself begin to nod off. She straightened up to keep awake. The fire they were sitting in front of did little to help, the warmth desperately tried to lull her to sleep. To fight off the drowsy feeling that kept creeping over her, Vivian focused on the old man's words.

"Then there was the siege of Fort Mifflin. Terribly long siege it was too. I remember my old friend Cromalin was getting letters from this Cornish lass through most of it. He kept on about her faithfulness, convinced she would wait for him till the end of time. All the rest of us had bets going on how long it would take for her to write him off. 'Course he died before she could turn him down. Fever it was, terribly bad one. It was a mercy when he finally died. A few weeks after that the letter we were all certain would come finally arrived. And wouldn't you know what it said?"

Vivian didn't bother answering. She had heard this story a million times and it always ended the same.

"It said she had taken up with a local farmer and was already big with his child. Ah, well. Women are never the most committed lot. Some new fancy takes their notion and they're off, aren't they little thief. No, first chance a woman has she will leave a man faster than rats of a sinking ship." Sir Warren chuckled to himself.

Vivian glanced at a small clock that sat on the mantel. Had she only been listening to him for a quarter of an hour? It felt like an eternity. She was growing weary of him.

"I bet I can guess what you are thinking," Sean whispered in her ear.

Vivian turned to the arm of the sofa to see him kneeling beside it.

"I doubt that," she whispered back. A glance back at Sir Warren showed he was talking on, oblivious to the side conversation that had begun. Another glance around the room showed that the whist party was completely absorbed in their game. Feeling relieved at being ignored, she turned her attention to Sean.

"I can indeed. You're wondering if Sir Warren's calves are his own or are padded to make them look so comely."

The thought had never crossed her mind, but now she had to look. Sure enough, Sir Warren's calves were as shapely as any footman's would have been. Vivian looked back at Sean.

"Are they real?"

He motioned with his head for her to look again. "You tell me."

Vivian turned back to Sir Warren just as he was scratching the back of one leg with the top of his opposite shoe. The padding of his calf shifted to the side of his leg and stayed there. Vivian had to stifle a laugh.

"You're such a tease." She looked into Sean's twinkling blue eyes.

"But you enjoyed it." He smiled broadly.

"How did you even know that about him?"

"Years of observation has taught me a great deal about humanity. And now it will pay off again. As you can see, your companion is so worn out from lecturing about salt that he has even bored himself."

Vivian looked back at Sir Warren to find his eyes closing even as his mouth still moved. The old man muttered as his head sagged, coming to rest on his chest. A snore escaped his still moving lips as sleep claimed him.

Clapping a hand over her mouth to keep from laughing, Vivian let Sean lead her away from the fireplace to the window. He leaned against the window frame as she giggled.

"That was wicked of you." Vivian tried to be serious but that only made her laugh more.

A mischievous grin flashed across his face.

"But you enjoyed it," he whispered to her. Looking into his eyes, she saw that they had darkened. If she fell into them, she knew she would be lost.

A cheer from the card table drew her back into the room. Someone had won the hand. Claire looked up at that moment, disapproval in her sour expression.

"Mrs. Reed, it's been ages since I last heard a song played on my piano forte. Play something for my amusement."

"I haven't played in a great while, Claire. I doubt my abilities will be to your liking."

"Nonsense," the other woman said dismissively. "Entertain the company."

Vivian reluctantly sat at the piano forte. She pulled a piece of music out of a stack on the piano forte and began to examine it. The piece looked simple enough, but Italian love arias could change at a note's notice. Vivian stretched her fingers over the keys but hesitated to play.

"Is all well?" Sean asked in her ear, his voice soft and low.

He was leaning over her shoulder, looking at the music. With him that close Vivian could catch the scent of him, fresh linen, earth, and something that was unmistakably male. It was enough to send any foolish girl into a frenzy. Vivian was no fool but even she had to admit his nearness made her heart pound. She felt certain that he could hear it beating in her chest.

She had to swallow hard before she could speak. "You're distracting me, Sean."

"Am I now?" A teasing grin tugged at his lips.

Glancing his way, she found him so close to her that their lips could have brushed. His serious gaze held her eyes for a long moment. Her heart pounded in her ears. Waves of heat and cold swept over her body as if they were sweeping over a virgin shore. The blue pools of his eyes held her captive. Knowing she needed to look away before anyone noticed them, she forced her eyes toward any other thing. They fell to his lips which looked soft and inviting.

Another cheer from the card table startled Vivian out of her own thoughts. Turning her attention to the piano forte she began to play the aria. The first few measures were halting but her fingers quickly remembered some of their training. If any of the company was proficient in music it would have been evident that Vivian hadn't played in a great while. Still, the sounds of the music were pleasing enough to the company and no one offered any objection.

Her fingers danced across the ivory keys. They were not a nibble as they once had been, the Admiral having not kept an instrument on his ship. Yet she enjoyed the feel of creating something where there had been nothing before; even music, that could only be listened to for a short while before the melody faded away.

The end of the page neared, and Sean reached out his hand to turn it.

"Signal when you are ready," he said.

Vivian gave a great nod as he quickly turned the page so that she could continue to play without interruption. He watched her with a devotion she had never had from the Admiral. The realization of that his eyes were on her filled her with delight and dread. Was he pleased with what he saw? What if she made a mistake and embarrassed herself?

The continuous questions that raced inside her head distracted her from the music. Her hands faltered and a mess of notes sounded throughout the room. Claire threw her a sharp look, her displeasure permeating the room. Removing her hands from the piano forte, Vivian found they were shaking.

"You are doing beautifully," Sean encouraged.

"Do you think so?" She asked, a slight quiver in her voice.

"I know so." His low voice rumbled through her, sending warmth with the sound.

As the evening ended, Sean pulled Vivian aside.

"Your views of the world were fascinating. I would love to hear more about what you think."

"I didn't terrify you with my idea of forgiving pirates?" Vivian asked, a tentative smile on her lips.

Sean beamed at her. "Not at all. In fact, I would love to know who else you think we should forgive. The colonies? Maybe even the French?"

"I am willing to forgive all except Marie Antoinette. I can never forgive her for being able to wear pink while I know I can't."

"I think you would look like an angel in anything you wore." Sean took Vivian's hand and kissed it. "Until tomorrow then."

VIII.

Morning sunlight struggled to filter through the narrow window of the attic room. It did little to dispel the chill that hung around Vivian. She had dreamed of the sea. She often did. Even when sequestered on land, the endless motion of the waves haunted her. She shivered as images of the Admirals ship floated behind her eyelids. There had been something wrong with the ship but as sleep slid away, she couldn't remember what. With a sigh, she got out of bed, hoping to be relieved of all things aquatic.

She dressed and set her hair in a hurry, wanting to do anything that would distract her mind. She was used to taking care of herself after years of sailing with the Admiral. He had always said that a lady's maid was for women who were too inebriated to take care of themselves. He insisted that Vivian manage her own life without the assistance of another woman. While Vivian felt no need to have a maid of her own, those years on the Admiral's ship without any female company had left her feeling isolated.

Vivian stretched out her shoulders after she finished her hair. One thing the Admiral had never understood was the strain caused to the arms when a woman had to do her own hair. It would have done him good to hold his arms above his heads for at least half an hour every day. Then he would appreciate a lady's maid.

Taking a step away from the mirror she examined her appearance and smiled with approval. The simple print dress gave her figure an appealing silhouette. She wondered if Mr. Kade would like her dress and then remember that he would call on her during the course of the morning. For an instant she felt excitement trying to bubble inside of her, but she pushed it down. It wouldn't do to expect anything different from him.

"All men are the same at heart, old girl," she told herself. It was better to be realistic. Heartbreak rarely came to the realistic.

At breakfast, she found her father and brother in the dining room, each immersed in their respective newspapers. She went to her father and placed a gentle kiss on his cheek. His color had improved from the previous day and he seemed to have some of his vigor back.

"You are looking much better today, Father. Do you feel well?"

"I feel years younger today. In fact, I was thinking of sitting in the parlor this morning. Would you care to join me?"

Vivian readily agreed. She had longed to spend some time alone with her father since she arrived home. There were things she wanted to discuss with him without being overheard.

"Anything of interest happening in the world?" She asked as she settled in a vacant chair near Nathan.

Nathan huffed. "There was another jewel robbery in Dublin. It's the fifth one this month."

"Good heavens," she exclaimed. "What is being done to stop it?" Vivian gripped her pendant. She would be heartbroken if anyone stole her mother's necklace from her.

"Not much to be done if no one can catch the thief," Nathan said behind his paper.

"*The* thief? As in a single person?" Vivian couldn't think why one person would want to risk their life for stealing. It was well known that the law frowned on thieves. Jail sentences were extreme, including deportation. If the judge felt the case was strong enough, a person could be hanged for stealing, even if it *were* to feed their family.

Nathan peered at her over his paper for just an instant. "The magistrates are claiming that it's a singular person. The real trouble is that there is no evidence of who it is. Could be a man. Could be a woman. Who knows?"

"A woman? No one would think a woman would do such a thing. They are fat too gentle for such a thing. They are too delicate to even contemplate such actions." Dr. Warren said.

"Odder things have been known to happen. Haven't you ever read the bible? There are some interesting women in those pages," Nathan said, his eyes never straying from his paper.

Vivian thought about the idea. Would she ever be in a position where she would be willing to steal from others? She felt certain that she would not but then she had never been desperate. Desperate people do dangerous things.

After breakfast, Dr. Warren let Vivian help him into the parlor. While he had been cheerful during the meal, he was starting to look tired.

"Start at the beginning, if you please," he said as he handed Vivian the newspaper.

"Father, you've already read some of this."

"It doesn't hurt to go over it again."

Vivian sighed. In a clear, strong voice she began at the first article. She read all about the recent robberies that had been happening in the north of Ireland. The thought of such an active thief on the loose made her nervous. Would this person come to Waterford?

By the time Vivian reached the third page of the paper, she was beginning to feel tired herself. The constant reading was giving her a headache. When she began reading about the prices of pigs in the nearby city of Kilkenny, her voice was hoarse.

"It's time for some tea," she announced.

"Keep reading," he said sleepily.

"No," Vivian said emphatically. "The price of pigs holds no interest for me today. Father, there is something I'd like to talk to you about."

Dr. Warren looked at her, his faded eyes slowly taking focus.

"I was left an inheritance by the admiral. I want to use it to set up a home of my own. Would you like to join me in it?"

"You wish me to live with you?" Dr. Warren sounded as eager as a child on Christmas Eve.

Vivian couldn't keep her own excitement from her voice. "Yes, father. I do."

"There's nothing I would like more," Dr. Warren said. "When? Where?"

"I have to talk to the bank first. Admiral Reed stored all his wealth there and they will have a copy of his will. Once I do that then we can start to look for a place to call our own. I was thinking of a cottage in the country."

"That sounds marvelous," Dr. Warren said. "But why did the Admiral keep his money in a bank? I thought he would never part with it."

"He wanted to see if he could increase it through investments," Vivian said. When her father made to ask further questions, she said, "It was just his way." Her husband had never allowed her to be involved with his income, despite her natural gift with numbers. It hurt that he had kept so much from her. If he had allowed her to help with their finances at any point, she would have some idea of what was due to her now.

"And you say his will was left with this bank? Did he never give you a copy?"

"I've never seen it," Vivian admitted. "I know I should have but the Admiral promised that I would be taken care of. I have always assumed that meant monetarily."

"Doesn't the Admiralty compensate you for his loss?"

"Oh, yes. They are very generous. I receive five hundred pounds a year from them but that would only go so far. It would be better if I had the money from my late husband as well. Then we can combine the incomes and still have a little to set aside."

The maid came in then and Vivian ordered tea.

"To live with my girl," Dr. Warren mused after the maid left. "Now that's a change worth making."

A noise came from outside the parlor. Thinking it was the tea, Vivian turned her attention to the newcomer.

Instead of a tea laden maid, Vivian watched as Claire came into the room and began pacing. Her round face was pinched with concern, making her small eyes appear even smaller than usual.

"This is too much. It can't be done," Claire muttered to herself as she wrung her hands. Vivian wondered how long Claire would keep up the dramatics. She watched as Claire paced the length of the room again and again.

Stifling a laugh Vivian asked, "Is all well, Claire?"

Claire threw herself onto the settee in the most dramatic fashion.

"It is unbearable. Too much for me today! I have children to educate, a household to run, I'm hosting tea this afternoon, and I also must deliver the baskets to the poor. Oh, what am I to do?"

"That does sound like a full day," Vivian said. Vivian stared at her, unsure what Claire wanted. Was the woman looking for sympathy or help? Or was she wanting to make herself appear more important by being overly busy? Whatever it was, Claire made a fuss as she continued to wail.

"How am I to manage it all? Oh, what is to be done?"

Vivian watched as Claire dissolved into a fit of tears.

"Best get on with it," Father Warren muttered. Annoyance was all over his face as he glowered at his daughter-in-law.

Claire's frigid glare turned on the old man. "If I wasn't so *burdened* in my own home, I could manage it all better. But I have to think about what is best for everyone else before I am able to think of myself!"

Vivian had to stop herself from rolling her eyes. In the short time she had been with her family she could tell that there was no love between her Claire and Old Dr. Warren. It was a miracle the two didn't announce their loathing for each other openly.

"Couldn't you send a maid or two to deliver the donations to the poor?" Vivian asked.

Claire jumped up and placed her hands on her hips in a pose of absolute offense. "Absolutely not! How would it appear to the parishioners if a servant delivered their donations to the poor? No, it must be a member of Nathan's family otherwise it would reflect badly on him."

"Then why doesn't Nathan deliver the donations?" Vivian asked.

Claire fumed. "You clearly have been without a husband so long that you forget how busy they are with their own pursuits."

Now Vivian *did* roll her eyes. Reluctantly she asked, "Claire, is there anything that I can do to be of service?"

Claire clapped her hands in delight. "Why, what a wonderful idea! You could assist me today. Since you have no house of your own to manage and no family to care for, you are naturally the person with the most disposable day. The donations are in the kitchen waiting to be sorted and there is a list with the housekeeper so you will know who to go visit."

With that Claire flounced out of the room.

Vivian felt her jaw go slack.

"Close your mouth before you catch flies," her father said.

"Did you... did you know she would do that?"

"She pulls that trick on anyone who'll listen to her. Always too busy for life. Always too proud to do the meaningful work herself."

"So now I have to make and deliver care packages?"

"It appears so," he said.

"But Sean- I mean, Mr. Kade is going to call today."

Her father gave her a sad smile. "Best get on with it then."

Vivian sighed and resisted the urge to tug at her hair. She handed the newspaper to him and left the room. As she went out into the hall she nearly collided with a wall of muscle.

"Easy there, my dear." Sean laughed as he steadied Vivian. His hands felt warm as they held her shoulders.

"I didn't know you were there."

"That makes me wonder if I'm as dashing as I think I am," he said with a dazzling smile. Vivian knew that he knew how dashing he was. The last thing Sean needed was his ego to become farther inflated.

She looked down the hall past him. "Where is the butler? He should be here to announce you."

"He seemed annoyed by my arrival, so I told him he didn't have to bother with me." Sean said.

Vivian raised an eyebrow. "And he listened to you?"

Sean ran a hand through his dark curls. "I may have also told him we were very well acquainted, and we had no need to stand on ceremony anymore."

"Lying to the butler? Mr. Kade, I am shocked." But the twinkle in her eye said otherwise.

"It's such a lovely day. I was hoping to take you for a drive. Maybe we could go all the way to the sea?"

A drive with Sean Kade? It sounded blissful. While the sea had no appeal for her, the drive would take several hours. Vivian felt elated at the idea until she remembered the job that Claire had pushed onto her.

"On any other day I would love to. Truly, I would. But today I'm not sure if it will be possible. Claire gave me the task of making and delivering bundles of food stuff to the needy. I need to get that done before teatime."

"Then it looks like we have our work cut out for us."

"We?" Vivian asked, hoping she had heard him correctly.

"Aye. We. You don't think I would leave a lady with such a project to do alone? You will let me help, won't you?"

"Yes, please," Vivian said before she could talk herself out of it. She didn't want to refuse him, even if it was considered polite to do so.

Smiling broadly, Sean followed Vivian into the kitchen where they found all the supplies for the care packages. Everything was piled into a heap in the larder.

"I can't have all that in here," the cook said, her hands on her ample hips. "Takes up too much room and I need all the space for the dainties I need to make for tea."

Vivian could tell that the cook was proud of the project but also overwhelmed. She felt for the woman. It certainly had to be difficult to live up to the expectations of Claire.

Trying to ease the cook's burden, Vivian and Sean took the supplies into the dining hall, vacant since breakfast. Without the presence of Claire, the formal room seemed almost cheerful.

"We should be fine in here." Vivian said as she started to lay out the items for the packages on the table. She glanced at Sean as he laid his tailcoat over the back of a chair. In his shirt and vest it was easy to see the outline of his muscular arms. His skin looked tanned against the bright white of his shirt and cravat. Vivian tried not to watch him as he rolled up his shirt sleeves, exposing his forearms.

The Admiral had always, *always*, been dressed in his uniform. He felt that anything less was disrespectful to the crown. Vivian had rarely seen anyone as casual with their attire as Sean was now. Even the sailors on the Admiral's ship were in their full uniforms at all times. To now see a man so relaxed in his dress was nearly scandalous. Vivian looked away as her face began to burn.

Trying to keep her composure, Vivian straightened her shoulders and faced the work that was before her. Together, she and Sean made as many care packages as they had supplies for. Every package was filled with bread, cheese, dried ham, and an array of dried fruit. By the time they were done, the table was covered with brown paper packages.

"Now what?" Sean energetically asked.

"The housekeeper has a list of people I need to take these to. I can get it from her but then I'm not sure of the best way to deliver them."

"Leave that to me," Sean winked. "You get the list and get ready to go out. I'll meet you out front in ten minutes."

Vivian nodded. She was so grateful for the help he offered. The Admiral had never been willing to assist in any of her humanitarian projects.

It was hard for Vivian to suppress a smile as she went in search of the housekeeper. The older woman handed over the list of names as if she were passing on a valuable heirloom. It took all of Vivian's concentration to keep from laughing. While helping the poor was most admirable, it certainly didn't need to be dramatic.

By the time Vivian was done assuring the housekeeper that she would see to all the needs of the poor in the parish and returned to the front door Mr. Kade was standing next to a small donkey cart. The care packages were already loaded into the back. Sean had a smug expression on his face, evidently pleased with what he had done. But when he looked up as she began to descend the steps, his expression changed. His eyes widened slightly, and his jaw slackened, making his lips part.

The change that came over his face both surprised and startled Vivian. She had received a million looks from men before, mostly the Admirals annoyed looks. Never had anyone looked at her in the way Sean was now.

Trying to sound unnerved, she asked, "Is there a bee on my bonnet?"

Sean shook his head slightly, then his cheerful smile returned. "Not at all. I was only thinking."

"Of what?" Vivian asked as they began to walk down the cobbled stone street.

Sean pulled at the donkey's lead, encouraging the animal to follow along. "I was actually thinking about heaven. Have you heard of it?"

Vivian threw her head back in a laugh. "Oh, I've heard of it. My brother talks of nothing but the next life in his sermons."

"I was wondering what he would say to angels walking among us."

"Nathan would say we are too fallen as human beings for heaven to want to have anything to do with us. According to him we are all destined to burn in a pit of fire and brimstone."

"Really?" Sean asked, sounding incredulous. "I know of some people who would never deserve such a fate."

Vivian gave him a side long glance. "Like whom? Nathan should meet them."

"My mother, you," he said, giving her a wink. "But most definitely my father. May he rest in peace."

Vivian slowed. "I'm so sorry. I didn't know you had lost your father."

Sean gave a shrug of his shoulders. "It happened years ago when I was but a lad. But I always thought him the best of men and if anyone was deserving of heaven it was him."

They walked on in silence for a few minutes before Sean said, "I have wondered if he would be proud of the man I have become."

"I'm certain he would be," Vivian said.

"And how would you know," Sean asked, a playful tone in his deep voice. "Has he come down from the clouds to tell you?"

"No," Vivian said timidly. She wasn't sure if the suggestion of angels coming to speak with her was blasphemous or not. "But I would think any father would be proud of a son who risked his life for another. I know I would be."

"That's because you have such a kind heart, Vivian. I'm not sure everyone would agree with you."

"What if they don't? Is their opinion more important?" As soon as the words were out of her mouth, Vivian heard how they could be misconstrued. "Not that my opinion of you needs to take precedence or anything. I'm sure there are more important people who have clearer ideas that you would rather hear from."

Sean caught her arm and gently slowed her, turning her to look at him. His blue eyes were soft as they looked into her own. "Of all the people I have known, your opinion is one that I value most."

Heat rose up her neck and over her cheeks. She looked down, hoping he hadn't noticed.

"Come," he said, taking her hand and placing it in the crook of his arm. "We have people to help."

IX.

The recipients of the care packages resided on one small street. The two-story houses were packed together, most being broken up into apartments. The smell of sickness filled the air. Piles of refuse littered the ground, making it difficult for Vivian to walk without the risk of stepping in something she would rather not name. Laundry hanging from lines crisscrossed above the street, sending everything below into shadows. It was a dismal, vile place to be and Vivian found herself pitying the residents.

Wishing to forget herself, Vivian and Sean quickly worked on passing out the packages to each family. The gratitude of the people was enough to make Vivian forget her surroundings. The children were especially excited about their newly obtained treasures. One grimy little urchin threw his arms around Vivian's knees, hugging her with all his might to show his appreciation. When he released her, he left a smear of soot across the lower part of Vivian's blue dress, but she didn't mind. The child's joy was enough to make Vivian forgive a dirty dress.

They came to the last of their packages as they reached the end of the road. Vivian checked and rechecked the list but found that they had visited everyone.

"I think we're done," Vivian said with a sigh. She was hot, tired, and thirsty, but very pleased with what they had accomplished. "I can't find anyone on the list that we missed. And there is only one package left. We should take that back to Claire. She might know of someone else who needs it."

"Or we could use it ourselves," Sean said, a mischievous glint in his blue eyes.

Vivian hesitated but then the bells in the nearby church rang, letting everyone know it was after two o'clock.

"It has been a while since both of us have eaten," she said, slowly warming up to the idea.

"Aye."

"And we both need a rest."

"Aye. I like where this is going."

"I know a meadow that isn't very far from here where we could have a picnic. If you want to, that is."

"I want to," he said quickly.

She smiled at him, timid in the knowledge he wanted to spend more time with her. She scolded herself for being foolish. Any man would agree to a free meal. She shouldn't be reading into things.

Sean took up the lead for the donkey. "Lead the way, love. I'll follow you anywhere." And Vivian wondered if he meant it.

She turned and led the way farther out of town. A short walk later, she came to a pasture surrounded by a low stone wall. Opening the gate, Sean led the donkey in.

They unhooked the donkey from the cart so the beast could have a chance to rest. Vivian laid out her shawl on the ground and sat on it, offering the seat next to her to Sean.

"I can't thank you enough for all your help today," she told him.

"Of course, you can." He winked at her which made her blush. She hoped he didn't think she always blushed like a child.

Sean opened the last package and spread the contents out before them. Vivian's stomach gave a loud grumble when she saw the food which made Sean chuckle. He broke off a large chunk of bread and handed it to her. They ate in companionable silence, each enjoying their well-earned meal after a long day.

"How did you find this spot?" Sean asked as he settled onto the grass.

"You see that house down the field," she pointed to the south of them, a thatched roof visible over the stone wall. "That's where I grew up. This pasture is part of the property. I figured since no one is in the house then no one would mind if we picnicked here."

Sean looked around at the pasture. There was a small stream running through one corner, and hedgerows growing along the road with the occasional lilac bush mixed in. It was a picturesque spot.

"I can see you here as a little girl having tea parties with your dolls."

Vivian laughed softly. "Can you also see me learning to fence and playing croquet?"

He sat up to look at her. "Really?"

Nodding, she said, "I was a wild child. I loved nothing better than to climb a tree or chase after my brothers. One winter it snowed, so George, my eldest brother, had the idea that we could go sledging. Only there are no good hills around here and we didn't have a sledge. We took buckets and gathered up all the snow we could find and piled it into a mound that was taller than any of us. We climbed to the top and used our mother's serving platters as sledges."

Vivian's sighed happily, remembering the wonderful time the Warren children had.

"That sounds like a perfect day."

"It was until our mother found us," Vivian said. She had to laugh as she remembered how angry her mother had been that day. Mrs. Warren's face had turned all shades of red. "She was so mad we had used her silver that she made us clean out the barn. We were working very hard until George started throwing muck balls at Nathan and myself. We spent all evening running around the barn, trying to make each other dirty. It sounds ridiculous now, but I can't remember a happier day."

"Where is George now?" Sean asked, evidently hoping to hear more about childhood mishaps.

Vivian looked down at the earth, hoping the anger she felt showed as grief. "He died when I was seventeen."

"I'm so sorry," Sean said.

Forcing a smile on her face, Vivian said, "Don't be. He's the reason I had to marry."

Sean's look was confused so she explained.

"Admiral Reed was willing to pay off a large gambling debt that George had accumulated in exchange for my hand in marriage. So, because of my brother I had to marry at fifteen."

"That sounds terrible," Sean offered.

Vivian nodded, turning her face away so he couldn't see the tears that welled in her eyes. The memory of why she had to give up her childhood to become a cold mans wife always filled her anger. She should forgive, but she was still angry with all she was forced to lose.

Sean slipped an arm around her shoulders, holding her close. Vivian let out a shuddering breath, the pain that often accompanied thoughts of George and her mother dissipating.

Vivian felt as if she were anchored in a safe harbor after being adrift on a torrent sea. The walls of ice that had protected her for so long melted as waves of warmth filled her. Here was the place she wanted to stay.

She lingered in Sean's embrace, listening to the beating of his heart. The scent of him wafted over her. She wanted to stay here in his arms, even to grow old there, but propriety looked down at a man and a woman even touching. What would someone think if they were seen embracing?

Regretfully, Vivian pushed away. "We should be getting back."

He nodded his agreement and began to get himself ready for the walk back into town. Vivian couldn't help but smile as she watched him try to catch the donkey. The little beast seemed to know what was coming and wanted nothing to do with it. Together they chased the donkey down and finally got it hooked up to the cart.

During the walk to town, Vivian and Sean talked about everything and nothing at the same time. She enjoyed that Sean listened to her opinions and seemed to respect them. He laughed with her and acted as if he enjoyed her company. It was such a difference from what Vivian had experienced with the Admiral. When they finally reached Nathan's street Vivian felt disappointed that they would have to part ways.

"Thank you again for all of your assistance, Sean."

"It was my pleasure. I hope you have an enjoyable afternoon."

They said their goodbyes and Vivian reluctantly started down the cobbled street. As Sean was beginning to turn away, he stopped and called out to her.

"I will be out of town tomorrow on business, but could I call on you the day after?"

"Yes." Vivian tried to hide her joy.

Sean smiled and warmth grew in her again. "Well aren't you difficult," he teased. "Until the day after tomorrow."

She could have jumped for joy, but that would have been unladylike. Instead, she smiled all the way to Nathan's home, her excitement knowing no bounds.

"What is so amusing?" A friendly voice asked.

Vivian looked up to see Kathleen smiling at her from the front step.

"What are you doing here?" Vivian asked, completely bewildered.

"Mrs. Warren hosts a tea once a week for the ladies of the parish," Kathleen said, as if that was obvious. "Now, what was so amusing that it had you smiling all the way down the lane?"

The door sprung open, and the butler led them through the hall to the parlor. Inside were an assortment of women, varying in age and status. Among them was Claire, who beamed at them as they entered the room.

"Mrs. Eldon, what a pleasure," Claire gushed. Coming forward she took Kathleen's hands in her own and drew her in to place a kiss in the air on either side of her cheeks.

"And my dear little sister," Claire said as she turned her attention to Vivian. She kissed the air by Vivian's cheeks as well before she ushered them into the room.

"Do make yourselves comfortable," she said as she motioned to the chairs that had been arranged into a circle. Then her attention was called to another lady entering the room.

"What was that about," Vivian asked as she settled onto the sofa with Kathleen.

"That is how she usually is with her guests," Kathleen responded. "She was very out of sorts last night. I wonder what happened?"

Vivian knew, but had no desire to tell Kathleen that she and Dr. Eldon had been unwelcomed at dinner. "Bless me if I knew," she lied.

"Well, whatever it was is over now. Mrs. Warren is usually the most attentive hostess. And her teas are divine. I can never get her recipes out of her cook though. Now, what was so amusing to you earlier?"

"You'll keep asking until you find out, won't you?"

"Most definitely. We may be older but I'm just as curious as ever," Kathleen said, a smile tugging at the corners of her mouth.

"I don't feel right talking about it here. There are too many ears."

"Tomorrow then," Kathleen said. "We can go for a walk together and you can tell me everything. Just like when we were girls."

"Exactly like girls," Vivian said, catching Kathleen's contagious smile.

Their attention was called to the center of room as Claire began to make introductions. The tea things arrived, and Vivian was amazed at the array of dainties the cook had prepared. Miniature tarts, petit fours, and macaroons were piled high on the tiered trays, along with a large selection of tiny sandwiches.

Throughout the afternoon Vivian watched Claire with an air of disbelief. This was not the same woman she had know the past few days. Somehow, her sister-in-law had transformed into a woman a grace and kindness. By the time the tea was removed and tables for cards were set up, Vivian wasn't even averse to the idea of pairing with Claire.

"Now, my dear sister," Claire said in her overly indulgent tone, "you have played whist before? I know the Admiral was opposed to cards, but he did allow you to play a harmless game with ladies, did he not?"

"He did not, no," Vivian said.

"What? Never?" a white-haired matron at their table asked.

"No. My late husband believed that cards in any form were an abomination. He never allowed them on his ship." Vivian felt foolish to admit such a thing but what was there to be done? She had never played a game of whist in her life. As a girl she was more concerned with other things and had never taken the time to learn.

Claire chimed in, as cheerful as she had been all afternoon. "Well, ladies, let us take this first round as a practice for Mrs. Warren."

All the ladies complied. They were most helpful in teaching Vivian the game, agreeing that she was a fast learner. No one was more fervent in their praise than Claire. By the end of the afternoon, Vivian was left to wonder which version of Claire was the real on. The stern mistress, or the devoted hostess?

X.

Darkness was his old friend. They had spent years together, getting to know and trust one another, just as he trusted the darkness now. With an overcast sky not even the light of the moon could be seen tonight.

He knew where he was going. He had walked that way several times, most of them this week. The house was vacant, except for a few servants who were in the kitchen below. The owners of the house were at the new opera that was premiering tonight. He had seen them there himself, just before the soprano began her first aria. As for the rest of the household staff, they were given the night off. No need to pay them when there was no one to be served.

He walked casually, not drawing any attention to himself. At the edge of the house was a small alley leading to the stables. He slipped down it, waiting in the darkness a moment to make certain he hadn't been seen.

Nothing stirred on the street he had just left except a stray cat. Confident that he was alone in the alley, he made his way to the water barrel that was stationed at the corner of the stable eaves. Since the barrel was completely full, the lid was closed. Standing on top of it, he easily reached the thatched roof above. Pulling himself onto the roof was simple. Now it was only a few yards to the attic window.

He was inside before the stray cat crossed the street. Then it was just down one flight of stairs to the mistresses dressing room. There were candles lit in the hall, set on golden candle stands, but there was nobody around to use them except him. He entered the dressing room and left the door opened behind him so the light from the hall would illuminate the small room.

The jewel box was sitting on the dressing table, completely open. Diamond necklaces lay strewn on the table as if they were cast aside at the last moment. He left those alone, as diamonds were not in demand now. Instead he focused on a large ruby brooch that lay on the bottom of the box. He pulled a velvet bag, no larger than his hand, out of his breast pocket. Into it went the brooch, a sapphire ring, and matching sapphire earrings. Before he turned away, he grabbed the diamond necklace and placed it into the velvet bag as well. Diamonds may not be in fashion at the moment, but fashion was known to change.

Placing the full bag into his breast pocket, he slowly made his way to the door. No need to rush now and make a mistake. He listened before he exited the room. Hearing nothing, he made his way back toward the attic window he had entered from.

The street was still deserted, just as it had been a few moments before. Luck was with him tonight, as she often was. He easily made his way out of the alley and back to the opera house. Smiling to himself, he settled back into his seat before the end of the first act.

XI.

True to her word, Kathleen arrived at the Warren's residence before the sun was high in the sky. When the butler announced her arrival, Vivian all but threw down the newspaper she had been reading aloud. The women set out, ready to traverse the whole of Waterford together.

"I haven't had a chance to look at the city since I returned," Vivian said.

"Anyplace in particular you would wish to see?"

Vivian thought for a moment. "The bank."

"What? We live in one of the most beautiful parts of the world and you want to go to the bank?"

Vivian laughed at Kathleen's outrage. "I have a small errand to run and then you can take me to any location you wish."

After Vivian delivered a note to Admiral Reeds banker requesting a meeting, the two women began to walk through the city streets.

"This is refreshing after being isolated at sea," Vivian commented.

Gently, Kathleen asked, "Was it terrible for you? To be always on a ship, I mean,"

"Not so terrible, no. It was really just the person I was with who was the problem."

"Vivian, my dearest friend. I understand."

"You do?" Vivian asked, almost afraid to hear the truth.

"Yes. You were unhappy in your marriage as many people are. It isn't until death separates a married couple that they get relief from each other. You are not the first to be glad to be widowed and I hardly think you will be the last."

"I certainly hope others are happier than I have been," Vivian said, looking at Kathleen.

Her friend smiled, reassuring her. "In that regard I am very happy. Dr. Eldon is the best man in the world for me. Now if only I could get my cousin to be as happy as myself." She gave Vivian a mischievous grin.

"Whatever do you mean?"

"Don't play coy with me, Vivian Warren. I know my cousin called on you and spent the better part of the day with you. And when you arrived at Claire's for tea it looked as if you had been rolling around in a field. Not to mention that my cousin couldn't wipe his grin off his face for the whole evening. I need full details before I start coming to conclusions on my own." Kathleen shot a wicked look at Vivian, daring her to contradict her conclusions.

In near panic, Vivian told Kathleen all about he the day before.

"So, you see, nothing untoward occurred," Vivian finished.

Kathleen sighed, looking dejected. "I had almost hoped."

"Hoped what?" Vivian asked, her voice rising in panic.

Kathleen spotted a bench and pulled them toward it. "Let me be frank, Vivian. Sean has never taken an interest in any woman as he has you. He would call on his dance partners the morning after a ball, yes, but he would only stay a few minutes. The other night, with you... Well, he couldn't keep his eyes off you. Then to learn that he was with you yesterday... I feel that he has taken a liking to you."

Vivian didn't know if she should be panicked or overjoyed. Sean Kade taking an interest in her. Such a thing had never happened to her before. "What should I do?"

"For now, nothing. Let his conduct guide your own. But you must decide how you feel and how you wish to proceed at some point. Do you want to marry him or not?"

Vivian's hands became damp in her gloves. Her heartbeat quickened with the onset of her anxiety. "Am I supposed to have an answer for that now?"

Kathleen took her hands. The steadiness of her friend's hands made Vivian realize that her own were shaking. "No, you don't need to have any answers yet. All that will come with time. For now, just enjoy the attention."

Vivian nodded. When Kathleen released her hands, Vivian's fingers instantly found her pendant. The smooth stone felt like a solid anchor in a sea of confusion. She had never learned the fine art of flirting. She had studied the language of fans but there had been no use for it in the navy. How was she to act with a man who may or may not wish to court her? And did she want him to?

As with all things, their walk came to an end. Kathleen left Vivian on the edge of town to begin her trek to her country estate and Vivian turned her feet towards Nathan's. She took her time, knowing there was nothing to do once she got there. Her father would be napping in his room by this time, and Claire would have the boys practicing their instruments which meant Vivian would have no access to the piano forte. All that would be available to her would be quiet needle work in her room. The thought did not appeal at all.

She paused and watched a Punch and Judy puppet show perform on the corner. The local children flocked to it. The joy on their small faces made the secret longing of her heart come to the surface again. If only she had such a little one to look at her with a face full of joy. The thought always brought a pinching sadness to her, twisting her disappointment into pain. The sight of the children no longer brought her peace, so she hurried away to find solace with the family she did have.

The second that Vivian opened the door; her ears were assaulted by the sound of someone wailing. The noise was deafening. It was a compliment to the construction of the house that the sound couldn't be heard outside. Rushing to the source of the commotion, Vivian found Claire prostrate on the ground in front of the stairs, sobbing uncontrollably.

"Claire, what happened?" Vivian asked as she knelt by her sister-in-law. The only answer was more sobbing.

"Please tell me what's the matter Claire," Vivian tried again. Claire let out a hysterical shriek. Vivian knew that she would receive no answers from the distressed woman. Her fears mounted the longer she heard Claire's sobs.

Vivian looked around for some evidence of Claire's hysteria. Sitting on the stairs were Claire's young boys, both distressed by their mother's weeping. Large tears rolled down their round cheeks. The smaller of the two tried to get close to his older brother, hoping for some comfort only to be shoved away. This only made the younger child cry harder.

Vivian called for her brother to come help. There was no reply from him, or from anyone. In fact, there seemed to be no one in the house at all.

Hoping to find some help from the servants, Vivian ran to the kitchen. She burst through the door to find the butler whispering with two of the maids around the kitchen table. At the sight of Vivian, the staff jumped. Looks of guilt covered their faces.

Seeing the servants gossiping made Vivian swell with anger. "Your mistress is in need of help."

The staff just looked at her dumbly. It was apparent to her that, while these people were capable of gossiping, they were not about to do something unless instructed to. Probably a result of Claire's fickle nature.

Without trying to suppress her anger, Vivian yelled, "Go and assist her!"

The butler and maids rushed past her out of the room.

Vivian followed along behind them giving instructions as they went. The butler and one maid picked up their mistress and carried her into her room. There the maid set about stoking the fire and soothing her mistress, searching for any illness that could have befallen her.

The younger of the maids helped Vivian take the boys into the nursery. The poor maid looked beside herself until she pulled out a story and began to read to the children. Slowly their tears stopped as the girl read to them.

Vivian stopped the butler in the hall. "Have the cook send up some tea for Mrs. Warren and some treats for the children. Perhaps something to eat will help calm them all."

The butler nodded and hurried downstairs, grateful to be free of the commotion.

It wasn't until the tea tray arrived with its crumpets and scones that the boys began to act like themselves again.

Pulling the maid aside, Vivian told her about the puppet show down the street. "Once the children are done with their tea, take them to watch the show. Be most mindful of them. We don't want them wandering off to add to the stress of this day." Vivian pulled out a few coins from her reticule. "To give to the performers when the basket is passed."

"Yes, miss." The maid curtsied and Vivian left her nephews in her care.

Leaving the nursery, she went to check on Claire. The wailing had reduced to muffled sobs under the maids comforting attention. Satisfied that things were as under control as possible with Claire and her children, Vivian went to find the rest of the family. She ran into the butler as she descended the stairs.

"What caused this commotion," she demanded.

He seemed taken aback by the sternness in her voice but bowed to her wishes. "I don't rightly know, madame. A gentleman came to visit the Reverend and his father earlier. A few minutes after he left Mrs. Warren came bursting out of the parlor in hysterics."

"And where is Mr. Warren? Was he here during all of this?"

"He shut himself up in his study the moment the gentleman left. He hasn't been out since then."

Vivian nodded and turned on her heel toward her brother's study. Without waiting to knock Vivian barged into the room on the back of the house. Oak shelves lined the walls, filled with books and knick-knacks Nathan had collected. Lit only by a small fire in the hearth, the room felt small and stuffy. Before it sat Nathan and their father in comfortable leather chairs, smoking their pipes. Smoke hung thick in the stagnant air. Going to the window, she flung it open and gratefully gulped in the fresh air.

Only then did the two men look at her. Vivian could see the grief lining her father's face. The sight of his downcast countenance pained her. She would do anything to make him happy.

"What happened here?" she asked as she knelt by her father.

Nathan made a disgusted scoff. "Mr. Fletcher was here."

"Who?" Vivian still felt confused.

"George has still found a way to torment us from his grave," her father said. "He has left debts that need to be paid. The money collector came to make certain that the debts are paid in full." A tear rolled down his wrinkled cheek, landing on a pile of letters in his lap. Vivian glanced at the letters. There was at least a dozen of them.

"Mr. Fletcher is the money agent from Dublin. He was a horrible little man." Nathan spoke as casually as if he were talking about the weather. "He left Claire in quite a state. She was in the parlor when Mr. Fletcher called. He said all kinds of things about how the responsibility of George's actions now rests on his family. If we can't do something, we will all suffer. Claire was in a fit by the time he left."

One would think a well-bred lady, particularly one who was so proud to be English, would be able to contain her emotions until she was behind a closed door.

"But George died nearly eight years ago. Why are we just now hearing about this?" Vivian's mind was reeling. Images of her long-dead brother floating through her thoughts. Had George really been so stupid as to get into more debt after the family had worked so hard to pay it off the first time?

"Mr. Fletcher claimed he had no knowledge of George's demise and was waiting for George to pay the debt himself. With no word from George, Mr. Fletcher took it upon himself to find George's family and bring the problem to their attention," Nathan said.

Dr. Warren held up a letter in his shaking hand. Vivian took it, curiosity mounting inside her. She read carefully, finally finding the amount of money owed hidden in a long passage of writing. It was the most confusing loan document she had ever seen.

"How much do we owe this man," Vivian asked her brother.

Nathan shrugged. "He didn't say an exact amount, and I can't make heads or tails of these documents. He was willing to give us a month to collect the money. If we fail, then he will have us all thrown into the poor house."

That information made Claire's hysterics make sense.

"Have Vivian look at the loans," Dr Warren said. "She's always had a head for figures."

Vivian went to Nathan's cluttered desk and cleared off a spot. Taking a clean sheet of paper and a quill she sat down with the letter, carefully writing down any amount of money mentioned. She motioned for Nathan to bring her the rest of the letters. There were fourteen in total, each as confusing as the first. Vivian wrote down the amounts of money mentioned in each one, some were amounts loaned, some were installments paid, and some interest that had accumulated on the loaned amount. She calculated and calculated again. When she was certain that all her math was correct Vivian sat back in the chair, resting her head in her hand.

As the weight of their situation rested on Vivian, she couldn't lift her eyes to face her father and brother. She double checked her calculations, praying that she had made a mistake that would lower the amount they had to pay but she hadn't. She sighed, trying not to cry.

"How terrible is it?" Nathan asked. Vivian could tell that he didn't want to hear the answer either.

"It's terrible," Vivian said as she rubbed her hands over her eyes.

"How much?" Father Warren's raspy voice sounded choked. "How much do we owe?"

Vivian buried her face in her hands. "Fifteen thousand."

"What?" Nathan yelled.

She removed her hands and stood to face her father and brother. "We owe this Mr. Fletcher fifteen thousand pounds. That includes the interest."

Father Warren slumped into his chair allowing the tears to flow freely down his cheeks. Nathan threw his pipe at the fireplace. Vivian watched as it shattered and sprayed bits of smoldering tobacco onto the floor. She made no effort to clean the mess up.

Looking back over the papers that lay in front of her made her feel queasy.

"Are these the only copies of George's loans?" A small idea began to form in her head. If there were only these copies of George's debt, if no one else knew, she could burn them and pretend that Mr. Fletcher never existed.

"No. George signed two copies. They were identical, at least that's what Mr. Fletcher told us." Nathan growled.

Vivian's hopes crashed to the floor. It would have been dishonest anyway, she told herself. She went to her father and knelt beside him. Doing her best to comfort him, she said, "We'll make it through father. I know we will."

"I wish I knew that" he sobbed. "All I can see right now is ruin."

An idea formed in Vivian's mind. A realistic one, much better than burning letters.

"Father, I can speak with Mr. Clay, the Admiral's banker. I've already requested an appointment with him. We can use my inheritance from Admiral Reed to pay off Mr. Fletcher."

Both men turned toward her, hope appearing in her father's eyes. Vivian looked over at Nathan and was almost frightened by the hard look that appeared on his face. Was he angry with her? It disappeared as quickly as it came.

"And if it isn't enough?" Nathan asked.

"We'll worry about that after I talk to Mr. Clay."

Nathan stared at the fireplace. "Let us be glad for the Admiral then. His widow can now save all our skins."

Vivian wasn't sure how to take his comment. It felt condescending. Still, she would go to Mr. Clay and see what could be done. With hope back in his life, Old Dr. Warren was easily able to go to bed. Vivian stood in the hall, watching her father settle onto his pillow.

"At least he'll sleep well," Nathan muttered.

"Won't you? I mean knowing that we can have this whole business behind us?"

Nathan sneered. "Yes, I can sleep well now knowing that the great hero, Vivian, has once again come to save the day."

He turned and stormed away, leaving Vivian feeling as if he had slapped her face.

XII.

Vivian was nervous as she left Nathan's house the next morning. She had awoken in a panic, fearing she had missed the appointment. After being assured that she still had plenty of time, Vivian felt restless. She paced around her room for an hour until the staff began to wake up. Then she had dressed and waited. And waited some more.

Not wanting to appear as a destitute widow, Vivian had dressed in some of her finest, a pure white muslin gown with a green velvet spencer. Her bonnet and reticule matched her spencer. For the finishing touch she placed her red fox fur over her shoulder. Vivian wasn't fond of furs, but this had been one of the few gifts from the Admiral. The only other gift he had given her was a string of pearls interlaid with gold beads. She had that on as well, hoping that they would bring her luck.

Nathan met her in the foyer as she descended for a bit of breakfast. His foul mood was evident in his scowl.

"What are you dressed up for?" His sullen expression seeped into his voice.

"I'm meeting the Admiral's banker this morning."

"Ah, yes," he said, his words dripping with sarcasm. "Off to save the family again."

Taken aback by his rude tone, she had no reply for him. Nathan had always been a sweet boy growing up, her favorite brother in fact. Why was he treating her with such negativity?

"Are you feeling well, Nathan?"

"Why would you ask that?" he said with a sneer.

"You don't seem like yourself at all this morning."

"And you would know what I'm like. You, who have been gone from this family for so long."

Vivian saw a dark shadow pass over his face as he looked at her. It frightened her to see someone she had always counted on to be supportive and loving turn into a different person. He began to walk away from her.

"Nathan?" Vivian timidly said.

He spun around, glowering at her with his dark eyes. "What?"

Vivian lost all courage when she saw his expression. Never had anyone looked at her with such hate. Not even the Admiral.

He stormed toward her, his hands clasped behind his back, giving him a hunched appearance. "What?" He demanded.

"I need the carriage today."

The words spewed out of her mouth before she could stop them. It wasn't what she had wanted to say but she had been so startled by him that she couldn't think straight. Vivian had never been one to handle confrontation well. She would have preferred to run away than face a problem with another person head on. Only there was no running away from Nathan. He was one of the few people she still had left in her life.

Nathan barked out a laugh. "You live under my roof for no cost; eat the food from my table for free. You can pay for your own carriage."

With that he stomped away leaving Vivian open mouthed.

It took several minutes to regain her composure. When she did, she sent one of the footmen to order her a carriage from the nearest livery while she tried to eat something. She could only sip at her tea, feeling her stomach churn inside of her. The whole conversation with

Nathan played again and again in her head. She couldn't think of anything she had done to offend him. When the footman returned, Vivian was almost calm.

As the carriage pulled up to the bank, Vivian felt more in control of herself. She pushed thoughts of Nathan out of her mind. All she needed to do now was to be charming. She was confident that the bank would give her whatever she needed.

Her father had no love of banks. He had once used a bank to hold his money only to have it stolen by a dishonest clerk. Vivian knew her father had had little success with money in his life. If he had then she wouldn't be here right now.

The bank's shining interior was as intimidating as its exterior. The polished marble floor and columns reflected the sun's light but none of its warmth. Vivian offered her card to the bank manager who ushered her into his office on the second floor. He introduced himself as Mr. Clay, the Admirals personal financial advisor. He was a portly man with a traditional white wig that hid his balding head. Every few minutes Mr. Clay would pull out his handkerchief to mop at his brow which pushed his wig back. It seemed the warming weather didn't agree with him.

After over an hour of consultation, Vivian felt as tired as Mr. Clay looked. They had been over every legal document that Admiral Reed had ever signed. She was tired of sitting in the uncomfortable wooden chair that Mr. Clay had offered to her. The back was too low to lean into and the arms were too wide to be of any use to her. She noted how these chairs were built for short, wide men, much like Mr. Clay himself.

Clearing his throat, Mr. Clay looked as uncomfortable as Vivian felt. The look in his eyes reminded Vivian of the look her father used to give to patients who were going through a dreadful illness. It was pity.

Mr. Clay laced his fingers together and placed them on the desk in front of him. "As you can see by all the papers, we have been through, and there is no easy way of saying this… but your husband has left no will."

"What?" Vivian wasn't sure she had heard him right.

"Admiral Reed left no will, madame."

"You jest." Vivian wasn't sure if she wanted to laugh or cry at the statement.

"I wish I was," he said with a defeated air. "The Admiral left no indication with me as to who should be his beneficiary in the event of his death."

Vivian felt his eyes on her as the weight of what he was saying settled in. He may have expected her to cry, or even become angry but Vivian kept her composure. Even if she hated to admit it, there was a tiny part of her that was English. She wouldn't give anyone the satisfaction of seeing her emotions. Especially not after this morning.

"But he does have funds in your bank?" she asked after a moment's reflections.

Mr. Clay brightened. "Most certainly, he does. He left a large sum of money, *all* his money I believe, in the bank's care, along with the title to the land he owns."

Vivian smiled. "Then as his wife, I should have access to these funds. How much did he leave in total?"

"I can't tell you that," Mr. Clay said.

Vivian's smile froze on her face. She gave him a hard stare. "Why ever not?"

Mr. Clay hunched down behind his desk, trying to appear smaller than he was. "You are not listed on Admiral Reed's account."

"But I am his spouse. We were married under the eyes of God. That must be enough to grant me access to my husbands' funds."

"In a perfect world it might." Mr. Clay looked at her, regret in every line of his face. "Admiral Reed's accounts were left in such a way that without his final will and testament I have no authorization to give away any of his funds, even to you. To be perfectly frank, Mrs. Reed, there is no money available to you."

Vivian felt her jaw drop. "No money? But surely something can be done."

Mr. Clay hesitated. "In terms of giving you access to the Admiral's funds or even his land I'm afraid not. Without any indication from the Admiral about his accounts the bank feels it is best to leave them undisturbed for the time being."

"Undisturbed? But I am his wife. Was his wife," she corrected. "How am I to live if I am denied access to the only income available to me?"

"You were left with an annuity form the Admiralty, weren't you? That should let you live comfortably." Mr. Clay looked so pleased with himself for thinking of the idea. Vivian wanted to slap the cheerful look right off his pudgy face.

"There isn't much left of the annuity I received. I had to spend most of it on my journey home. I can use what I have to establish myself somewhere but then what? There isn't enough to live from from one year to the next, at least not for long."

"The bank does offer its deepest sympathies-"

"Sympathies? How am I to live from sympathies?" Anger rose but she pushed it down. Calmly she stated, "I am left destitute by the actions of others. I am now forced to live by the hand of my brother."

"At least you have family who is willing to care for you. I have seen many who are in far worse situations than yourself, Mrs. Reed. You should consider yourself fortunate."

"Fortunate? Have you ever met my sister-in-law?"

Mr. Clay shook his head. Vivian narrowed her eyes and leaned toward him. Her words were heavy with derision. "Then until you do, *sir*, don't go about reminding people how fortunate they are. You may have no idea what you are talking about."

Mr. Clay apologized, then pretended to organize some of the papers that were piled on his desk. Vivian felt some remorse in making him uncomfortable. He was only trying to help after all. She knew that she should be kinder.

Trying again she asked, "Can anything be done at all?"

Mr. Clay looked at her seriously. "No. Not by me there can't. But perhaps you can do something to relieve your own situation."

"And what would that be?"

"Remarry," he said confidently. "You're young and pretty. Quite a catch for any man. I will tell no one of your financial situations and neither should you. That way some unsuspecting man may think you are the wealthy widow of a British Naval officer. It would be the perfect beginning to a new life for you."

Vivian twisted her reticule strings hard around her fingers, letting the pain distract her from the anger that was bubbling up inside of her. She was angry at Mr. Clay and his ridiculous ideas, angry at the Admiral for leaving her in such a situation, angry at George for his gambling. She was even angry at Nathan for being angry with her.

She opened her mouth to reply but no words came out. Vivian was certain that if she'd been hit in the stomach, it would have hurt less than realizing there was no help for her family now. With a sense of hopelessness, Vivian left Mr. Clay's office.

Wandering wherever her feet wished to carry her, Vivian eventually came to Reginald's Tower. She rested her back on the cold stone. Slowly, she forced air in and out of her lungs.

She wanted to scream with frustration. How could the Admiral leave her without a will? Vivian felt utterly abandoned by her late husband. They had never been in love, but she had thought that he was an honorable man. Thinking of Admiral Reed made Vivian's insides feel like ice. She had done her best to be a good wife. She had been dutiful, obedient, demure, but the closest thing to kindness that ever came across his face was a look of pity.

The urge to plunge her fist through the stone tower behind her was overwhelming. That wouldn't do any good, though. No amount of anger or tears was going to make this situation any better.

Resting her forehead on the cool stone soothed her heated face but it did little to dispel the self-pity. It tightened around her stomach, making her feel loathsome. She remained this way until a little tug on her dress drew her attention out of herself. Vivian turned to see a dirty child staring up at her.

"Spare a copper," the child asked as it held up a grubby hand.

Vivian stared down at the child, coming to her senses. Before her was a little being in obvious need, far greater than her own. Her heart ached for the child.

Without thinking, she pulled a coin out of her purse and handed it over. The grubby face before her lit up.

"Bless ye, miss," the child said. Then it turned and ran off.

It wasn't until the child had left that Vivian realized her situation could be much worse. She shook her head as Mr. Clay's words rang in her head. She was fortunate. Her situation could be worse. She would work on counting her blessings every day.

XIII.

One blessing she had to count on was Mr. Kade calling on her later. It was barely noon, which meant there was still plenty of time to walk home before he came. With a renewed spirit, Vivian started on her way, enjoying the sunshine as it warmed the city around her.

At the doorstep of the house she hesitated, unsure if she should knock or let herself in. Being an unwanted guest could be such a tedious situation. If this were truly her home she could go in, but if she was unwanted, she shouldn't make any presumptions. With a shrug, Vivian opened the door and let herself into her brother's home.

She was pleased to find there were no cards on the hall table. She hadn't missed Mr. Kade then. Clinging to that happy thought, she went into the parlor. As she had expected, Vivian found her father and brother sitting by the fire smoking their pipes. While Nathan had been too busy that morning to accompany Vivian to her banker's, he hadn't been too busy to purchase himself a new pipe.

Claire was pacing the floor, oblivious of anyone else in the room. She wrung her hands, occasionally letting out a small moan of distress. It took a great deal of restraint for Vivian to keep from rolling her eyes. At least someone was making a fine spectacle of their problems.

Vivian walked over the plush rugs to her father's side. Kneeling beside him she took his hands in her own. He looked at her expectantly, a glimmer of hope in his greying eyes. She wished she had some good news for him. It would have been so easy to tell him that all his troubles were over, and she would take care of the rest. But how would she be able to pay back fifteen thousand pounds? No, she had to be honest and upfront about the whole situation. Looking at him she shook her head.

Claire burst into sobs. "We are lost!" she wailed, throwing herself down on her velvet settee. She whipped out a silk handkerchief and proceeded to wail in the most dignified fashion.

Vivian turned her attention back to her father. "There is no money, Father."

Nathan stood. "How can that be?" He looked shaky on his feet.

Vivian stood to face him. "The Admiral left strict instructions with his bankers that he should only release money to the person who possessed his will-"

"-Then we'll find that person," Nathan jumped in.

"-Only he didn't leave a will with anyone." Vivian finished.

Nathan's face was a wash of confusion and anger, but whether at the Admiral or at herself, she couldn't say.

"My poor child," came Father Warren's weak voice. "To be wronged by the man who swore to protect you. It is abominable!" He slammed his withered fist on the arm of his chair.

Vivian's heart ached for her father. It wasn't that he felt sorry for her, but he had also been wronged by his trusted friend. Admiral Reed had promised Dr. Warren that his daughter would be well provided for throughout her life. It proved a cunning lie the entire Warren family had willingly believed.

"Fear not, Father. We will be fine. You'll see," she said to him.

He tried to smile at her, but the effort was weak.

A tapping at the front door made everyone in the room jump.

"Who in the world could that be?" Claire grumbled as she stomped to the window. "It's Dr. Eldon. Father Warren, did you send for him again?"

"No," he feebly said.

Nathan came up behind Claire. "His wife and cousin are with him. This must be a social call, my dear."

Claire fumed at the idea. "We don't have time for a social call. Send them away, Nathan."

"No!" Vivian yelled out.

Claire and Nathan turned toward her.

"Why ever not?" Claire asked, her tone cold with anger.

"They came to call on me. I told Mr. Kade that he could."

Claire's eyes narrowed. "When did you say that?"

Vivian tried to stop herself from wilting under Claire's burning gaze. "The other day after he helped me deliver the packages to the poor."

"He helped you?" Claire enunciated each word as if they were something vile. "You went about the parish with that… that man?"

"I did." She was not about to be made to feel guilty over accepting help with a difficult task. "He was kind enough to offer his assistance and asked if he could call today."

Claire glowered. "And you said yes?"

"Obviously."

"Well you can just tell him he can leave." Claire said.

"My dear," Nathan interrupted. "If we send *him* away, we will have to send the Eldon's away. It will reflect poorly on us. Besides they are already in the house. They can stay for a few minutes and then we will get back to the matter at hand."

Claire didn't look happy, but she consented to her husband's plan. When the butler opened the door to announce the arrival of Dr. and Mrs. Eldon, the room was a scene of tranquility. Apart from old Dr. Warren, everyone was standing as the visitors entered the room.

Moving as gracefully as an angel, Claire welcomed the visitors. She acted the part of the perfect hostess, doing all that was considered gracious.

Vivian realized that this must have been how Claire was when Nathan first met her. It was hard for a young man to resist the smiles of a pretty girl, and if she was capable of turning those smiles on and off as Claire was, then the young man stood no chance.

Chairs were given to the ladies first, leaving a few gentlemen standing. Sean leaned against the mantle opposite Vivian. She could feel his eyes on her, following her every movement. She risked a glance at him. The moment their eyes met he winked at her which only made Vivian smile. She ducked her head to keep her expression hidden from Claire.

Vivian was so wrapped up in her thoughts of Sean that she didn't follow the conversation until Claire was mentioning her.

"She was disinherited by Admiral Reed, you know. Poor Vivian is now completely destitute."

"Claire!" Vivian felt mortified. Heat began to burn in her cheeks as the shame of her situation became public.

"Well it's true," Claire said with a contemptuous smile. She leaned toward Kathleen Eldon in a conspiratorial manner. "I can't help but think that he left her penniless because she refused to give him any children."

"That's not it at all!" Vivian was beside herself with disbelief. How could Claire openly share Vivian's financial situation with anyone? In that instant, Vivian hated her sister-in-law.

"Men can be strange creatures, can't we Sean?" Dr. Eldon joked.

Sean smiled at Vivian. "Aye, we can be."

Vivian gave Dr. Eldon an appreciative smile. It was kind of him to try to relieve the tension of the situation.

Kathleen joined the conversation. "If I had a penny for every odd notion Dr. Eldon took into his mind then I would be the wealthiest woman on the island."

"Tis too true," Dr. Eldon laughed.

Kathleen patted her husband on the arm. "Now, the real reason we have come to call is because we are having a ball in a few days' time and I wanted to make certain that you have received your invitation. You didn't mention it at your lovely dinner the other night, so I wasn't sure." She pulled a sealed envelope out of her reticule and handed it to Claire. "You can never be too sure if those messenger boys get things where they need to be. Why, just yesterday I found one playing near the river when he should have been working."

"That's how children are," Dr. Eldon chuckled.

"Irish children, perhaps. English children would never do such a thing." Claire turned her nose up.

"I've often found the behaviors of children to be the same no matter where they are from. The children in the Caribbean act the same as the children in England," Vivian said.

Claire gave a scandalized gasp. "The street urchins perhaps, but never a child of breeding!"

"We must be off," Kathleen interrupted, a cheerful smile on her face. "We don't want to take up too much of your time today. I know how busy you can become with your charitable services, Mrs. Warren. Please, do come to our ball. Your entire family is invited."

Kathleen stood and the rest of the room followed her lead. She curtsied to Claire, thanking her for her gracious hospitality. As she turned to leave the room, she linked her arm with Vivian's, dragging her friend out with her.

Vivian walked down the hall with Kathleen, expecting to be released when they reached the front door, but Kathleen walked out into the street without letting go.

"Where are we going?" Vivian asked once they were away from Nathan's house.

"Away from that woman." Kathleen's bright face darkened. "I have never liked her. To think that she was openly trying to humiliate you. I am so mad I could shake her!"

"Then why did you invite her to your ball?"

"It was the only way I could think to get you there."

Kathleen kept a brisk pace until Dr. Eldon called out for her to wait. Turning around gave the women the perfect view of stout Dr. Eldon running to catch up to his wife.

"You are a fast walker when you want to be," he puffed as he stopped before them.

Sean came jogging up behind him. "Are you alright?" He looked at Vivian, his face full of concern.

"I will be. Especially with friends such as you all." Vivian felt blessed to have Kathleen, who willingly stepped into the confrontation with Claire.

"And being disinherited by your husband? That doesn't bother you?" Sean seemed angry, almost angrier than Vivian felt about it.

She smiled weakly. "I wasn't disinherited. There is just no will saying who his beneficiary should be. I thought he would have left it with his banker, but he didn't. The bank was given instructions from the Admiral that they can't release any of his money without his will. Until it's found all of his assets are being held."

"You could make a fake will," Dr. Eldon offered. When all eyes turned to him a deep blush ran up his next into his cheeks. "Or not."

Kathleen gave a cry of disbelief. "Don't you dare say such an unlawful thing. Vivian would never do anything like that."

The idea swirled around in her head for a moment, but Kathleen was right. She could never do something so dishonest. If it were ever discovered, she would be labeled as a thief and could be punished to the full extent of the law. Vivian had no desire to be hanged to death.

"I'll be fine," Vivian assured her friends. "I know things look difficult now, but I will think of something."

Sean placed his hand on Vivian's arm. "Until you think of something you should stay with us. It would be better than being with Mrs. Warren."

Kathleen clapped her hands for joy. "Oh, why didn't I think of it? Yes, Vivian, you must come stay with us. What a wonderful thing it would be. The four of us could have a house party. You must come right away."

"That's so kind of you but I wouldn't want to put you to any trouble." Vivian did want to go but what would her family say?

"It's no trouble at all," Dr. Eldon said when he saw her hesitation. "You could come on the night of the ball. It's only a few days from now. Then you wouldn't feel like you're running out on your father."

"If you're sure it's no trouble-"

"It's not!" Came the collective reply.

"Alright then. I'll come." Vivian had to smile. So, this is what it felt like to be wanted somewhere.

∙∙

"What of Mr. Harrison?"

"The lawyer? No, he would never agree to something like this."

Vivian could hear Nathan and Claire discussing as she came closer to the parlor door. Silently, she edged the door open. The two were sitting with their back toward her, their heads close together as they plotted. Dr. Warren was still in his chair, his eyes closed in sleep.

"What of Mr. Ketene?" Claire asked.

"Already engaged." Nathan said. He had a piece of parchment in his hands, a pencil poised to write.

"Sir Walsh?"

"Didn't he die last spring?"

"Right you are, dear. Oh, if only there was someone we could think of?" Claire said as she leaned back.

"What are the two of you doing?" Vivian asked.

The pair started at the sound of her voice. Turing, their faces held guilty expressions, as if she caught them with their hands in a stolen dish of sweets.

"Nothing," Claire said. Vivian could tell it was a lie.

Nathan sighed, a dejected sound. "We are trying to think of possible husbands for you."

"What?" Vivian wasn't sure but it felt as if the room started to spin.

Claire was at her side, helping her into a seat by Nathan. "Vivian dear," she began in a patronizing tone. "I know this must come as a bit of a shock, but your brother and I feel that the best way, the only way, to get us out of the financial bind is to try another marriage for you."

"You're joking," Vivian said. She tried to laugh but no one joined her. "You do know it was a miracle that worked the first time."

"We know," Nathan said without feeling. "We are asking God for another miracle."

Vivian glowered at him. "Can't we think of some other way to pay off this Mr. Fletcher? I'm sure if we got creative, we could gather the money to pay of George's debt."

"And what would that look like?" Nathan asked, his voice stern. "Claire and I would have to sell everything we owned, and we still wouldn't have enough money. I know this sounds unfair Vivian, but there aren't too many choices for us. Our brother took no thought of us when he borrowed money and now, we have to clean up his mess. Everyone has to help."

"I'm selling the piano forte," Claire said, as if the loss of the instrument was a great sacrifice.

"I don't want this," Vivian said.

"And I don't want to see my wife and children in a poor house," Nathan spat. "Or we could place the whole responsibility on the shoulders of our father. Let him take the fall for George. Such an aged man as father wouldn't last six months in debtors' prison." Nathan stopped and took several visible breaths. In a gentler voice he said, "I know it seems unfair, but if you don't help us with this mess that George left, we will all suffer."

Vivian nodded. She knew too well what it took to fix one of Georges mistakes. She'd paid the price for him before. Her fingers found her pendant. She held on to it as if it could save her, as if her mother could save her. But she couldn't. She hadn't then and wouldn't now. She needed to find a way to save herself and her family.

"What of Mr. Kade?" Vivian asked.

"You've taken a great liking to this gentleman," Nathan said.

"Is he even a gentleman?" Claire asked. "We know so little of him. What is his background? And if he has money, which I doubt, how much?"

"We could always aske and find out," Vivian said.

"We could, but we don't have forever. We need to find a potential candidate and begin working on them no later than the Eldon's ball."

"That's only a few days away," Vivian said, disbelief washing over her.

"Then we have to hurry," Nathan said.

XIV.

The days leading up to the ball were filled with discussions of possible spouses for Vivian. There was an intense search made of the area for the man with the most money. Vivian could barely control her outrage at the idea. Still, she went with Nathan to call on every gentleman he could think of. She smiled at Claire's impromptu teas.

"I can't take much more of this," Vivian said after one afternoon with Nathan and Claire. "I feel like I've been shown at a meat market."

"If that were so you'd have been sold already." Nathan laughed at his own ill timed joke.

Refusing to let him know how much his comment had stung, Vivian went into her attic room to pack her things. She hadn't told her family that she was going to be staying with the Eldon's and she didn't want to now. Let them find out later when she refused to leave the ball with them. It's not as if they would care anyway. They would plot and plan her life whether she was there or not. She felt irrelevant to them, merely a pawn to be played. She was beginning to loathe them all, especially George for getting them all into this situation. Again.

Anger and misery swirled around inside of her creating a whirlpool of anguish. Frustrated, she wadded up the shawl that was in her hands and threw it into her open trunk. She felt as if she were drowning and no one even cared. Hot tears burned their way down her cheeks. Vivian slumped on the floor, giving in completely to her despair.

She had come home to find comfort and support in her widowhood. Now all she found was a vindictive conspiracy. She wished she had never come back. She wept bitterly, then she wept some more. Isolation washed over her, leaving her beached on the shores of exhaustion.

***

Vivian knew the ship as it creaked beneath her feet. She hated every splinter of it. All around, the black sea stretched toward the ends of the earth. Occasionally its waves turned to an eerie green, lit by the distant streaks of lightning. There was no escape.

She stood there in the center of the deck. She turned every way to find someone, anyone, but she was utterly alone. Calling for help did no good. Her voice came out as a whisper that the wind swept away.

The spray of the sea chilled her. Vivian held up a hand to protect her face from the droplets that bombarded her and found that she was holding a small brass cylinder. She turned it over, studying the tarnished metal. As her hand slipped along its length, she found that it extended into a spyglass. She knew that spyglass. It was the same one the Admiral had used every day on his voyages. The one he had given her.

Vivian held it up to her eye, trying to find some help on the horizon. All she saw was a hazy line that blocked most of the sea beyond. She lowered the glass, hugging it close to her as if it were her only friend.

Black gloved fingers came toward her. Closing around the spyglass in its vice like grip, the fingers tore it from her grasp. Her eyes followed the fingers to find a hooded figure standing before her. Vivian tried to get the glass back. She reached for it, but the figure was beyond her grasp. She attempted to run after it, but her feet refused to respond. As desperation began to sink in Vivian lept for the spyglass, trying to wrench it free of the hooded figure's grasp.

Her fingers brushed brass, and for an instant she was certain that she had it in her hands. Then she was sliding across the deck, watching the hooded figure holding the spyglass recede as she fell overboard and was swallowed by the watery depths below.

Vivian sat up with a jerk. Her heartbeat wildly in her chest. Taking in gulps of air did little to settle the feelings that washed over her. Vivian leaned her head back against the wall, giving herself something solid to hold onto. Her whole body trembled with fear.

The darkness of the room confused Vivian. Had she really slept so long that the sun had set? Then she heard the noise on the slate roof. The rhythmic tat-tat-tat of rain drops as they fell.

It took several minutes before she was able to breathe easily. By then she felt spent and weak. She looked around the small room wondering what to do. She didn't want to be alone, but the company downstairs was less than desirable. Making a rash decision, Vivian got up and threw the last of her possessions into her trunk. She wrapped an old flannel shawl around her shoulders. The thing had been washed so many times it was nearly grey. She locked her trunk and left the small attic room her sister-in-law had so *graciously* let her stay in. Vivian ran down the stairs and out of the front door without a word to anyone.

In the street, the rain came down in drops as heavy as led. She was soaked in seconds, but she didn't care. Headlong she ran down the street, doing her best to dodge the puddles that filled in every space between the cobbles. Vivian didn't look back as she ran.

As country lanes opened before her, she jumped over one low stone wall to race through a pasture. Sheep bleated their protest at her intrusion, but she paid them no mind. She felt better than she had in ages. Why hadn't she done this before?

After several minutes of walking through fields and pastures, Vivian saw her destination. The rain was letting up, replaced by rays of sunlight through the grey clouds. With a spring in her step, Vivian approached a stately manor with a long gravel drive before it. She knew the place well, having spent a large part of her childhood there.

She smiled to herself as she knocked on the large front doors. The thought of how bedraggled she must look made her cheeks heat up. As if to confirm her thoughts the butler that answered the door nearly gasped at the sight of her.

"If you are here for assistance you must go to the kitchen door," he said.

Vivian gave him her most regal look, one she had mastered after spending more time than she cared to recall with the English ton. What she had learned from the ton was that appearances were deceiving but attitude was everything. "You may tell Mrs. Eldon that her friend, Mrs. Reed, has come to call with regards to our mutual business."

"I don't think that Mrs. Eldon has any manner of business to discuss with the likes of you."

"And I think that my presence will be most welcomed by Mrs. Eldon."

He looked her up and down, obviously less than impressed by what he saw. "Really?"

Vivian arched one eyebrow. "I could always go through the kitchen and find my own way to Mrs. Eldon's private parlor."

The butler looked flustered. Vivian could tell he didn't know what to make of her. Keeping her head high she turned away from him and took a few steps away from the door.

"One moment," he called out. Vivian turned to him, still giving him her regal stare. "I will let Mrs. Eldon know that you have come to call on her. If you will wait right there I will be with you in a moment."

"Yes. See that you hurry." Even though she was left standing on the doorstep Vivian couldn't help but laugh. The poor butler had looked so flustered.

A moment later the door flew open to reveal Kathleen.

"Angus! How could you leave Mrs. Reed on the doorstep?" Kathleen fumed at the butler. Vivian resisted the urge to say she told him so.

Kathleen led her into the main hall of the house. "Vivian, what in the world happened?"

"I walked here."

"In the rain?"

"Naturally," Vivian said with a cheerful smile.

Kathleen narrowed her eyes as she studied Vivian. "Why?" The word was drawn out as if she already knew but wanted to hear Vivian admit to it.

"I couldn't stand to be in that house another minute, so I ran all the way here."

Kathleen pulled her friend into a warm embrace. "I am so glad that you did. Now come, let's get you out of those wet things. We have a ball to get ready for!"

Kathleen led Vivian through the magnificent house of her ancestors. It had been built in the 1600's by some great-great-grandfather or another. It still held much of its ancient charm. When Kathleen's father became older, he had arranged his affairs, so his home was left to his only surviving child, Kathleen. It was a beautiful gift from him. Kathleen's home and land provided a comfortable life for her and her husband.

"Where is Dr. Eldon?" Vivian asked.

"He is checking on some of his patient's."

"Why does he continue to work as a doctor when he can just stay at home as a gentleman?"

Kathleen smiled. "He says the home and land were left to me, not him, so they are for me to do with as I see fit. He has his own profession he cares about."

Kathleen led Vivian into a lovely bedroom on the second floor. The walls were painted in a pastel blue with curtains on the four-poster bed and windows that matched. It was luxurious, especially compared to the bare room Vivian had just fled.

Kathleen ordered a bath for Vivian and sent someone to fetch her trunk. A maid stoked the fire in the marble hearth, filling the room with flickering light.

"I am so sorry to be such an imposition," Vivian said. She hadn't really thought about how busy Kathleen would be when she made the decision to come.

But Kathleen waved her concern's away. "Don't apologize. You saved me from having to review the menu for the fourth time. I feel as if everyone in this house needs to be spoon fed instructions. It will be good for them all to think on their own for once." Taking Vivian's hands in her own Kathleen said, "Now, why don't you tell me what is going on."

Vivian hugged her friend. It felt so good to be together, just the two of them. That old connection of girls who shared their hearts with one another was still there.

Sinking into a soggy pile in front of the fireplace, Vivian opened up to Kathleen about all that had happened since they saw each other last. She told Kathleen about the debt that George had incurred before his death, and about Nathan's plan for getting the money to pay it off.

"So, he wants to marry you to a wealthy old man? Didn't you already do that for your family?"

"Yes, and it needs to be done again," Vivian said defeatedly. She was so tired.

The water for the bath arrived, filling the room with its steamy heat. A Chinese screen was placed around the bath so Vivian would have privacy while Kathleen talked to her. "We have to come up with a plan." was Kathleen's reasoning. Vivian could only shake her head.

Once Vivian was settled in the hot water, she did begin to feel better. The problems that had filled her with so much dread seemed to float away.

"It won't be so bad," she told her friend. "Maybe this time I can find a gentleman who lives nearby. Then at least we could still see each other."

"I think it's abominable. You're being forced to give up any chance of happiness because of someone else's selfish actions."

"It's what you do for family," Vivian said. Having told Kathleen everything had helped Vivian work through her emotions already. Despite the burden that she still felt resting on her shoulders, Vivian was feeling cheerful again. She didn't want Kathleen worrying for her.

"It's not what I would do. I wouldn't have my own children marry for money either," Kathleen said.

"Yes, but you have money whereas my father doesn't anymore."

"That's his own fault. He never should have invested in that Argentina scheme. Diamonds come from Africa, spices come from India, not much comes from Argentina. What was he hoping to get from there anyway?"

"There was supposed to be a gold mine in Argentina. He felt very confident about it when he invested in it," Vivian said.

"And look where it got him."

"I think you're more upset about all of this than I am," Vivian said.

"You *should* be upset!"

"I was earlier but am now coming to terms with the idea. I'll admit, it's not what I want to do, but if it means that I can save my family from destitution then I am willing to try."

Kathleen snorted. "How in the world is your family expecting you to pay off this debt. It was a miracle that Admiral Reed was willing to loan your father money the first time your brother ended up in debt. He only did that because he was such a close friend of your father's. Now they're expecting someone else to do that again. What will happen if the man you marry won't pay off George's debt? Most men hold onto their money fiercely and will only give their wife a small allowance."

"I'll think of something, I suppose."

Vivian was starting to feel dizzy from all of Kathleen's questions. The truth was she hadn't thought about what would happen if someone else wouldn't pay off George's gambling debt. Her entire focus up until that moment had been on her own misery.

She splashed the warm water on her face, trying to wash some sense into herself. She had a duty to her family, and she would perform it. Frustrated with herself Vivian got out of the tub and toweled off. She wrapped a flannel housedress around herself that Kathleen had lent her until her own clothes arrived. It was too short for her, but it was better than nothing. Vivian shook her head, reminding herself that she couldn't be particular when she was begging her friends for help.

Taking the last of the hot water from a kettle hanging in the hearth, Vivian went to the washstand and began to wash her hair. Most women wouldn't have dreamed of washing their hair on the night of a ball. Too much washing and bathing was unhealthy for the body, but Vivian liked the way her hair looked right after it was washed. Her curls were most cooperative then and held the best shine. It was an added bonus that she would smell wonderful tonight.

Vivian looked over at Kathleen who was curled up on the foot of the bed, lost in thought. Finally, Kathleen said, "What about Sean?"

"What *about* him?" Vivian asked.

"You could marry him. He's kind and is very fond of you."

"Would he be willing to give me fifteen thousand pounds?" Vivian tried to sound sarcastic, but she felt a momentary flare of hope inside of her.

"Maybe," Kathleen said softly.

"What?" Vivian wasn't sure she had heard right. In fact, she was certain that she hadn't. "It isn't possible that Sean has an extra fifteen thousand pounds just laying around somewhere."

Kathleen laughed nervously. "You're right. What a silly notion."

"Kathleen? Is there something you're not telling me?"

"No." Kathleen answered too quickly. "No. Everything has been said."

"Kathleen, I am very fond of your cousin. You must see that. I know this situation isn't fair, but the thought of keeping my father out of debtors prison is my motivation for going through with all of this."

"Are you sure?" Kathleen looked close to tears. "Are you sure you are willing to marry without love again?"

"I'm more willing to do that than go to the poor house. That would be the only option for me if George's debts aren't paid off soon."

Vivian forced a brush through her tangled hair. It caught in her hair and refused to go farther. She yanked and pulled but to no avail.

A gentle hand took the brush from her fingers. "You were always too rough with yourself." Kathleen eased the brush through the wet curls a little bit at a time. Droplets of water fell out as Kathleen continued to brush. Vivian felt her shoulders relax even more during the attention.

Kathleen had just finished toweling out Vivian's hair when the door burst open. Two small children came running in. With a whoop of joy, they climbed upon the bed and began jumping.

"Get down this instant," Kathleen yelled.

Vivian could only laugh. The children looked exactly like Kathleen, dark hair and bright eyes, with dimples in their round cheeks. The oldest of the children was a little girl who was obviously leading her younger brother around. Neither of the children seemed inclined to listen to their mother.

"What do we have here?" Vivian asked cheerfully.

Kathleen looked distraught. "My very naughty youngsters have gotten away from the nursery again. It's their favorite game, but it has to stop now!"

She tried to get the little girl off the bed but was unsuccessful.

Vivian managed to catch the little boy in her arms. His chubby arms flailed about.

"Down! Down!" he shouted.

"Do you want to fly?" She asked him quickly.

This made him stop flailing and look at her. After thinking a moment, he gave a vigorous nod. Vivian laid him across her forearms and began to spin in a slow circle, lifting him up and down.

"Faster!" he cried.

Vivian laughed as she turned faster and faster with him until they were both dizzy. Together they fell on the bed.

"Again!"

"Me too!" called out his sister.

"I'm so sorry, Kathleen," came Sean's voice as he raced into the room. "They got away from me and-"

"Sean." Kathleen sounded impatient as she said his name.

"What?"

"Why are the children with you and not their nursery maid?"

"Oh. I took them riding when the rain stopped. We only just got back and haven't made it back to the nursery…"

"Well take them back," Kathleen said.

Vivian had to laugh to herself once Kathleen had ushered Sean and the children out. They were such a lively, loving family. The contrast between her own was like night and day. The love that flowed out of the Eldon household warmed her heart.

When her trunk arrived, Vivian hurried to prepare herself for the ball. The idea of Claire's criticism made her want to look her best tonight.

It wasn't that she wanted to make things easier for Nathan and Claire's scheme. There were some men who were intimidated by a lovely, confident woman. Those were the ones who were easy to control. Exactly what was needed for the plot to work. She could see Nathan and Claire having plenty of those men all lined up.

Setting her hair proved much easier after Kathleen had brushed it out. With the help of a curling iron she made ringlets that framed her face. It looked lovely but needed just one more thing. She pulled her pearl and gold necklace out of her trunk as well. With a few twists she was able to wrap the pearls around her head, creating a striking hair ornament.

Once satisfied with her hair, Vivian stepped into her silk ball gown. It had a gauze overlay that swirled around Vivian as if she was a fairy princess. Vivian looked at herself in the full-length mirror that rested in the corner of her room. Smiling ruefully at herself, she pitied any of the weak men she would meet tonight.

As she gathered up her fan there was a tentative knock on the door.

"Come in," she said, expecting Kathleen.

Sean stood in the doorway, looking dashing in his evening wear. Vivian felt her heartbeat quicken. She twisted the fan in her hands, trying to think of something to say to his sudden appearance. She was grateful she wasn't still in the old house dress. She hadn't been able to look at him knowing she was completely disheveled earlier.

"I-um… that is…," his faulty words stumbled out of his mouth.

"You look very elegant tonight, Sean." She offered him a warm smile.

"As do you," his voice cracked as he spoke. He cleared his throat. "I'm glad I found you. I was hoping to ask for the privilege of escorting you into the ballroom."

"I would be delighted." Vivian said, trying not to appear too over eager. "Should we go now?"

"Oh…um yes. Let's go." Sean turned to walk down the hall.

"Sean?"

He turned at the sound of his name.

"Aren't you forgetting something?" An amused smile tugged at the edges of her mouth as she stood in her doorway.

He laughed at himself. Returning, Sean offered her his arm. "Forgive me. I'm not my usual self at the moment."

"No need to apologize," Vivian said. When she placed her hand through his arm, he pulled her close, his free hand covering his own. Vivian regretted he couldn't keep her this close all night.

Reaching into his breast pocket he pulled out a narrow box tied with a silk ribbon. With a grand bow, he offered it to her. "I almost forgot that I got something for you."

"A present?" she said excitedly. "I've rarely been given presents before."

"I intend to change that."

"You don't need to do that," she said, suddenly shy from his attentions. She enjoyed them but wasn't used to them.

"But I want to, Vivian." His hands slipped around her own, even as she clutched the box. Vivian couldn't take her eyes off his. Their blue depths lulled her into tranquility. Sean's head bowed down closer to her own, a stray curl falling across his brow. Vivian reached up, brushing the dark lock out of his face. Sean clasped her hand, holding the palm to his cheek.

A burst of laughter from the party downstairs made him stop. He took a step back, releasing Vivian's hands.

"We'd better get downstairs before Kathleen sends a search party for us," he said sheepishly.

Nodding, Vivian pulled her door closed as they went out into the hallway.

"Open your present first," he instructed her. He acted as excited to see what was in the box as she felt.

Gently she pulled at the silk ribbon, setting it on a table in the hallway. She gave a gasp as she opened the lid of the box. Inside was a silver bracelet with polished amber stones set in it.

"Oh, Sean. It's lovely!"

"I saw it and new it was meant for you. The stones match the amber of your eyes."

He took the box out of her hands and put it on the table. Removing the bracelet, he laid it on her slim wrist, clasping it closed. He slipped his hand under her fingers and brought them to his lips, kissing her knuckles.

She was at a loss for words. A simple thank you seemed insufficient. To have been thought of, noticed. It was more than she was used to. It was all she had ever yearned for.

XV.

The bracelet Sean had given her matched her mother's amulet perfectly. They couldn't have looked better together if they had been a matching pair. She wondered how he was able to do that. Never, in all her searching, had she found a set of stones that matched so well.

She adjusted to the weight of the bracelet on her wrist as they made their way into the ballroom. It slid up and down her arm as they greeted acquaintances. As her eyes found her brother and his wife through the crowd, the bracelet felt like a painful reminder of what she had promised to give up. But not tonight. Tonight, she wanted to feel young and free, just once.

Before Vivian could turn about Claire was by her side.

"Vivian, darling! We were so worried when you left this afternoon. You didn't say a word to anyone. How happy I am to know that you are safe and sound."

She could only smile politely at Claire's faked declaration of concern.

"Now don't forget that Sir Warren is hoping to dance with you tonight, as is Lord McClalen." Claire laughed as if she were presenting the best news in the world.

Sean cleared his throat. "I'm afraid that they will have to wait for their chance to dance with Mrs. Reed." He gave Claire his dashing smile.

"Why?" She demanded without any attempt at civility.

"Because Mrs. Reed has promised the first two dances to me."

Vivian hadn't and Sean's lie annoyed her. When was someone going to ask her how she wanted to spend her time? Still, Vivian tried to suppress a laugh as she watched her sister-in-law open and close her mouth several times in consternation.

"I'll dance with them the next set," she assured Claire as Sean led her to a different part of the crowded room.

The musicians were beginning to warm up, signaling the beginning of the ball. Throughout the entire room, couples began to line up in neat rows. Sean led Vivian to the middle of the floor, taking his place across from her.

"You shouldn't bait her so," Vivian scolded him. "She gets very upset when things don't go as planned."

"Claire Warren isn't the only person who has plans for this evening. Take mine for example. I plan on spending as much time with you as possible. I *don't* plan on sharing your attention with two old members of the ton."

Vivian let out a bitter laugh.

"What's so funny?" Sean eyed her.

"You and Claire. You both have these plans that include me but have either of you asked me what I want?"

The music began, a waltz, and Sean held out his hands for Vivian to take. His fingers were warm as they circled hers. Grateful that she hadn't worn gloves, Vivian relished the sensation of his skin on hers. When his hand moved to her waist, she sucked in a breath as the heat of his palm penetrated deep within her.

He pulled her close to him, their bodies pressed together. She could feel the faint beating of his heart against her own.

Sean leaned close, his lips brushing Vivian's cheek. "What is it you want Vivian? Name it and it is yours."

She threw a glance toward Nathan and Claire who were standing at the edge of the dance floor. Even from across the room Vivian could feel the ice in their gazes.

"Tell me." His voice was low, earnest, rumbling through her as thunder rumbled over the sea.

"I want to choose for myself."

"And you can't do that with me?"

"I think the only person who lets me choose for myself is Mr. Eldon and that's only because we spend so little time together," she said. "Even Kathleen has plans for me. You didn't ask me to dance, you assumed I would. Is it so hard to ask for my opinion in something?"

"I'm sorry I offended you, madame," Sean said stiffly.

"Don't do that," she shot at him.

"Do what?"

"Become defensive. You asked me a question and I gave you an honest answer."

"And for you to accuse me of plotting against you is forgivable?"

"I never said you were plotting. And yes, you should forgive me. You have no idea the amount of pressure my family has placed on me for this night."

Sean's blue eyes were stormy as he stared at her. He slowly inched away, and Vivian felt herself becoming cold without him. She knew she needed to make amends with him.

"I didn't mean to snap at you Sean. It's not you. It's Claire and Nathan. I can't keep up with their unrealistic demands. I'm afraid any amount of time around them sets my nerves on edge. Please forgive me."

Hesitating only an instant, Sean pulled her close against him again. The warmth returned to her body and Vivian felt she could relax. He smiled his charming smile. "Only if you'll forgive my excitement to dance with you."

Vivian caught his infectious cheerfulness. "Absolutely." She was relieved he wasn't distant anymore.

"What is something you would like to choose," Sean asked as they danced.

"It could be anything. Where to live, who to employ. I don't care as long as I'm in control of it."

"With me, you could choose everything. You would be my equal."

"So, I'm not your equal now?" She smirked as she baited him.

"No." His casual answer made her eyes grow wide. He smiled, obviously proud of himself. "Right now, you're my superior. I only hope to be on your level someday."

She didn't know what to say. A part of her wanted to throw herself into his arms, to beg him to carry her away from this place with all its people and noise. But another part of her, the stronger part of her, reminded herself of her family's needs. They depended on her to save them from destitution. Yet even as she looked at him, this man who risked his life for her and was generous to her, she felt the resolve to heed her family's wishes fracture. The conflicting thoughts whirled around inside of her until she felt sick to her stomach.

"Sean, how much money do you have?"

"Enough," he said hesitantly.

"Enough to share?"

"It depends on who is asking."

She smiled at him, doing her best to keep eye contact during the dance. "*I'm* asking."

"I have enough to live like a true gentleman while supporting a wife and children," he said with one of his dazzling smiles.

"Do you have enough to share?"

"To share with whom?" he asked, his suspicion written all over his face. "I won't share with your family if that's what you're asking. Let them support themselves."

She forced a smile across her lips but inside her heart was screaming. If he wouldn't help her family then a relationship with him couldn't be.

The instant the set ended Vivian felt a cold hand grip her elbow and she allowed herself to be drug away to some unknown fate, all the while smiling at everyone she saw.

Vivian danced with the partners Nathan and Claire had arranged for her. There was Mr. Corey, the barrister, Mr. Evan's, who was a gentleman of some means, and a Lord McClalen, whom Claire fawned over. Yet through all the dancing and talk Vivian never let her eyes wander far from Sean.

The sight of him across the room nearly made her dizzy. She wanted to run to him and beg him to save her again. He had risked his life for her once, would it be so unthinkable for him to risk his money? But he had said he wouldn't share. He wasn't as generous as she had thought. She forced her eyes away from him to focus on others who would be more willing to assist her.

Finally, it was time to dance with Sir Warren. Vivian would have rather been in one of her nightmares. She glanced around, not knowing what she expected to find.

"Looking for something to steal, little thief?" Sir Warren said, pleased with his own cleverness.

"I don't think the Eldon's have enough cookies to tempt me," she said in a sarcastic tone. Sir Warren laughed, as if he enjoyed the humiliating banter. The music began, allowing Vivian to remain silent. She had no kind words for Sir Warren.

Within the first few steps of the dance, Vivian's toes were smashed by the sturdy heel of Sir Warren's riding boots. If not for the extensive training in keeping her composure, Vivian would have screamed a string of words that shouldn't be used outside a stable. As it was, his clumsy excuse for dancing left her certain that at least one toe was broken, and the rest were bruised.

The second dance of the set was much better for her. As Sir Warren's energy depleted, it was easier to keep her feet away from him. By the end of the set, the old oaf was huffing and wheezing for breath. Vivian almost felt sorry for him. Almost.

"Are you alright?" she asked as the set finished.

He gasped for air. "Just need a breather."

"Tea is being served. Do you want me to help you toward a table?"

"Aye, aye," he wheezed. Sir Warren grabbed Vivian's arm for support as they walked. The weight of him nearly toppled her over. Once he was settled into a chair, he turned his attention away from Vivian. She watched him a moment, almost wondering if he knew she was still there. She shook her head at the thought. Of course, he didn't.

"Why is Sir Warren sitting down?" Claire's impatient whisper rubbed Vivian's nerves raw.

"He's tired, Claire. Let the poor man rest."

She met the sharp eyes of her sister-in-law. The two women stared at one another, each trying to sense whose will was stronger. If God had made two beings out of separate materials, they would not have been more different than Vivian and Claire.

"You know your duty to this family, Vivian," Claire said icily.

"As do you," Vivian retorted.

Claire bristled at the words. Her lips pursed and her eyes bulged. Vivian could tell that if she didn't leave that instant Claire would certainly explode.

"Oh look! My friends!" Vivian lied and dashed away into the throng of party goers.

She left the ballroom behind, venturing down a less crowded hallway until she came to a large wooden door at the end. Slipping through it she leaned against it as it softly shut behind her. Relief washed over her as she looked at the familiar surroundings of the library. She had spent so many days with Kathleen among these books. These pages had been a witness to their lives. If she ran her fingers over the leather spines maybe she could rub some of those happy memories from them.

The sound of laughter from the other side of the door made Vivian remember why she had come into this room in the first place. She went to the opposite wall and threw open the French doors Kathleen's mother had insisted on installing years ago. The cool night air rolled into the room.

She should go back to the ball and dance with the long list of potential marriage partners Claire and Nathan had arranged for her. But the throbbing from her bruised feet kept her away.

Instead, Vivian ventured to the manicured gardens just outside the door. In the center was a small fountain, its water cheerfully bubbling in the night air. Gingerly, removing her shoes and stockings, she placed her bruised feet into the fountain, letting the cold water glide over them.

Leaning her head back, she caught sight of the night sky. The stars overhead look like diamonds spread across black velvet. As the tranquility of the night surrounded her, she let out a loud sigh of relief.

"Thinking of me?" A male voice asked from the shadows.

"Hardly," Vivian replied. She didn't want her thoughts going towards him, even if he always brought a smile to her face.

Sean sat on the edge of the fountain, facing her. "I'd like to say the same is true for me, but that would be a lie. I often think of you."

"Sean," Vivian began, looking away.

His fingers touched her chin, guiding her to face him. His touch made her breath catch in her chest.

"Tell me you think of me, the way I think of you," he said, his voice husky in the dark.

"I... I'm not sure," she started. His eyes were searching hers, pleading in their blue depths. "My family expects me..."

He huffed. "Don't tell me what your family expects. Tell me what you want, my darling. What you need." His fingers trailed along her jaw.

"I want... I need..." she couldn't say the words. Once said things could never be taken back. If she were to admit what she wanted in that moment would she ever be able to recover from it?

"I will give you anything, Vivian," he whispered. He leaned closer to her, his lips inviting her to do the same.

"Anything?"

"Name it and I shall give it to you."

She leaned closer, losing herself in the moment, refusing to think about tomorrow. "Kiss me."

He obliged. His lips were warm as they met hers. Tender, gentle. Moving against hers with a desire that stole her breath away.

She inhaled the scent of him, let the warmth of his lips, his hands fill her as she had never been filled before. Sliding her arms around him, she felt again how broad his shoulders were. On impulse, she let her hand tangle in his hair. The strands were silk against her fingers.

His kiss turned fervent, as his lips stole hers. Heat burned through her, igniting a fire so long dead she thought it extinguished. His arms wrapped around her, pulling her against him. As her body pressed against his Vivian knew she was losing herself to this man.

XVI.

"What happened to you last night?" Kathleen asked the instant that Vivian appeared in the breakfast room.

Vivian smiled at her concerned friend. "Nothing at all."

"That's not true. I know when you're lying."

"I most certainly am not."

"Are too. It's written all over your face. You have never been able to tell a lie in the whole of your life. You're too sweet for that." Coming around the table, Kathleen faced Vivian with her hands on her hips. "Tell me what happened. You disappeared before tea and then I didn't see hide nor hair of you all night. And Sean disappeared too."

Vivian glanced around, making certain they were alone. Pulling Kathleen toward the far corner of the room Vivian revealed what had happened, a part of it at least. She didn't want to tell her friend every detail of the night before. It had all seemed like a strange dream to her until she saw Kathleen's excited reaction.

"Sean spent the whole evening with you? That's perfect!"

Before Vivian could ask what Kathleen meant, the door opened, and Sean walked in with Dr. Eldon. Kathleen gave Vivian a smile that said 'I know what you're thinking' before she headed toward the buffet on the other side of the room. Vivian followed her lead and served herself breakfast.

The two men were deep in conversation about what was happening in the world. They talked while they filled their plates. It wasn't until they were seated that Dr. Eldon finally spoke to his wife. As they talked about their children, Sean leaned closer to Vivian.

"You look lovely this morning, my love." Sean whispered to her.

"You shouldn't call me that."

"Not call you what?"

"My love. I'm not, you know." She couldn't let him believe there was something between them when she needed to find someone else, someone with money, to marry. It was cruel, and that was the last thing Vivian wanted to be.

"Oh, aren't you now?" That teasing glint was in Sean's eyes as he looked at Vivian. It made her feel elated and angry at the same time.

She focused on the tea that was in her cup to keep from making eye contact with anyone. She feared if she did her emotions would erupt.

"I'm going to visit my father this morning," she blurted out.

Dr. Eldon and Kathleen stopped mid-sentence to stare at her.

"Then I'll join you," Dr. Eldon said after a moment's pause. "I've been wanting to check on him for a few days."

"I need to go to the milliners today. Why don't I come along?" Kathleen chimed in. "What about you, Sean? Care to go into town this morning?"

"Yes. I have some business to attend to."

"Then it's settled," Dr. Eldon said cheerfully. "We will all go to town this morning."

Vivian was glad to be in her father's presence again. After the horrific conversation a few days ago, old Dr. Warren had been nothing but sympathetic to his daughter's situation. It burdened his heart to ask so much of her. She paid attention as Dr. Eldon examined his patient, fearful things had changed since she saw him last.

"You need to stop worrying so much," Dr. Eldon told him as he sat on the edge of the old man's bed.

"It's difficult when you have to put so much on your wee ones," old Dr. Warren said.

Dr. Eldon nodded. "Just remember that they are grown now and can take care of you for a change."

"Aye, aye," old Dr. Warren said.

When his appointment was over, Vivian read the paper to her father until he dozed off. Smiling to herself, she tucked his blankets around his thin frame.

"I love you, father," she whispered to him. Then she slipped from the room.

She was nearly to the front door of the house when Claire grabbed her arm. With a mighty pull, Vivian flew into the parlor. The door slammed behind her, locking her in,

"Good morning, Claire," Vivian said as pleasantly as she could.

Claire flew across the room toward Vivian. Her eyes burned with anger. The sight of Claire rushing toward her made Vivian think of the ancient paintings of dragons, their wings unfurled and smoke rising from their nostrils.

"How could you disregard my wishes last night? You neglected all of my guests."

"The last I checked they were Kathleen's guests, since the ball was in her home."

Claire looked ready to scream. "Don't get smart with me. You know what is expected of you and yet you were negligent enough to leave the only opportunity you will ever have of rectifying the situation you caused."

"I caused? How on earth did I cause anything?"

"We all know that you lost the Admiral's favor, so he cut you out of his will."

"For the thousandth time Claire, there is no will. He never wrote one!" Vivian rubbed the bridge of her nose as she suppressed a scream. "What is it you would like to talk about."

Claire looked her up and down before turning her attention to the room about them. Wandering the room as she spoke, she said, "Sir Warren is thinking of taking a wife. He is getting older and would like to have an heir to pass his legacy on to. His only concern," Claire turned to face Vivian as she punctuated the words, "Is whether or not you are willing to produce that heir."

The air left her lungs, making Vivian feel like someone had struck her in the stomach.

"I will have you know that I am beginning to make arrangements for you to marry Sir Warren. It shouldn't take more than a month to get everything in order. The bands will be read in the next few days, and then the wedding will be fairly simple. Still, Sir Warren is willing to pay off your family's debts in exchange for an heir of his own. So, my only question is will you be able to provide him one?" Claire looked at her with such disdain that Vivian felt ashamed, but of herself or Claire she wasn't sure.

"You have no idea what you're talking about, Claire."

"It's a simple yes or no, Vivian." Claire's yelling made Vivian's ears ring.

"Why not let me choose whom I marry? I will make certain that the man has plenty of money to pay off George's debts."

Claire scoffed. "If I let you choose you would pick a common merchant or farmer. No, I will have you marry Sir Warren." Changing tactics, Claire's voice took on a pleasant tone. "It is the express wish of your father. And just think, you would have a title to go along with the marriage. Lady Vivian has a lovely sound to it."

It was then that the bud of understanding blossomed. Vivian realized what Claire truly was. A social climber.

Desperate for attention and the praise of others, Claire had married young herself. While being the first to marry gained her temporary superiority with her friends, that had soon come to an end as others made better matches. Claire had then insisted upon moving to town where her dowry money quickly furnished a lavish lifestyle. She did everything in her power to impress others, whether through her own accomplishments or those of others, such as her two boys. For Claire, appearances were everything. How much better would it appear to marry her sister-in-law to a Lord than to a simple gentleman. She cared nothing for the feelings of those closest to her, only the accolade of others.

"I refuse." Vivian folded her arms in front of her.

Claire's jaw dropped. It was clear she hadn't been told no very often. Recovering herself, Claire forced a smile onto her thin lips. "I understand your hesitation, dear Vivian. But you must think of your poor father. Why, even now he is lying upstairs in his sick bed. Death is so close by. You would ease his conscience. You could provide him with the peace he needs to enjoy his last days on earth."

The words pierced Vivian to her core. Her defiance crumpled. She knew, and Claire knew, she would do anything for her father.

"This isn't fair," Vivian objected.

"George leaving us to clean up his mess wasn't fair," Claire shot back. "But we are all doing the best we can. Mr. Warren and I have gathered two thousand pounds to help pay off the loan. We only need Sir Warren to agree to pay off the other thirteen and we should be safe from destitution."

"Where did you get two thousand from?"

"Never you mind," Claire said, pursing her lips and adjusting her shoulders.

"Suit yourself," Vivian said. She feigned indifference, examining the nails of her right hand.

"Oh, all right," Claire admitted. Vivian smiled to herself. She had known Claire wouldn't keep a secret for long. "We sold the piano forte, the harp, and many of Mr. Warrens books. I also sold a few of my jewels."

Vivian nodded. The loss of the instruments must have been hard. People would notice such fine things missing from this house. "Very well. Claire. You may arrange a marriage between Sir Warren and myself so long as I get to reside with Kathleen until the wedding day."

Claire thought this over for a moment. "You will need to come for certain social gatherings."

"Inform me when they are, and I will be there."

Claire beamed. "You see how easy things can be when you are willing to cooperate, don't you Vivian?"

Leaving Vivian alone at last, Claire went off to begin her scheming. Vivian smirked to herself. She knew that her sister-in-law had forgotten one crucial aspect of her plans. It would be Vivian who would climb higher on the social rungs, not Claire.

Instead of returning directly to Kathleen's, Vivian went for a walk in the country. She knew that Kathleen, while meaning well, would interrogate her about her visit. She wasn't in the mood to answer questions. She wasn't even sure she was in the mood to be around people after her conversation with Claire.

Feeling raw inside, Vivian wandered wherever her feet felt like taking her. She came to a small stream lined by bushes on both sides. Finding herself alone she removed her slippers. Her feet were still sore from the night before, so she set them into the cool water. It sent a pleasant chill up her spine.

Sitting on the bank made her remember other times she splashed barefoot in the ocean. In the Bahamas she had often walked barefoot on the white sand beaches, watching the fish swim in the clear bay. Then she would lay out in the shade of the palm trees for a brief rest before she had to return to her structured life.

Now, Vivian stretched out in the shade of the flowering bushes that lined the stream. Absently, she pulled the petals off a flower. When she was small, she would have asked the petals if he loved her or not. She didn't want to know the answer now. Knowing would only make future decisions harder. A tear escaped, sliding into her hair.

For the briefest moment she thought of running away. What was the point of money and titles when it only brought misery? And surely Nathan could manage the payments of the debt on his own.

Even as the hope of escape swelled inside of her an image of her father's face came to her mind. He looked so hopeful as he gazed at her. She knew that she could never abandon him, no matter what it would cost her.

Lost in her own thoughts, Vivian didn't pay attention to the passage of time until the murmur of voices called her back to her surroundings.

"This would be the biggest score by far." The voice was male and held a hard note in the tone.

"I've already done enough," came a second man. This voice Vivian knew.

Cautiously she pushed aside a thorny branch that hid the two men from her view. Sean looked agitated as he faced a man. The second man was as tall as Sean but had a hungry look in his hard face. Something about that man terrified Vivian.

"You think you can get out of this?" The man asked Sean.

Sean squared off with him, anger on his face. He clenched his fists until his knuckles turned white. "I've done everything you've ever asked, Miles. What more do you want?"

Miles's hard gaze turned cold as he looked Sean in the eye. "I own you. Don't forget that."

"All I have to do is walk away."

"And all I have to do is call the magistrate. Who do you think they'd believe first? Remember, one of us was born a gentleman and the other crawled out of the gutter." Miles didn't yell. He was quiet as he breathed out his threat. That frightened Vivian even more.

She trembled slightly with fear, making the branch she held aside rustle. She pulled her arm out of the bush to silence the sound but scratched herself on a thorn. Sucking in a breath to stop a gasp, Vivian cradled her arm as the scratch started to bleed.

"What was that?" Miles asked.

"I'll do the job," Sean jumped in, pulling Miles's attention back to himself. "I'll do it tonight just like you want."

"Good man. Let me know when it's done." He slapped Sean on the shoulder and sauntered off down the road.

Kicking a rock with his toe, Sean waited for Miles to be out of ear shot before he spoke. "Are you alright, Vivian?"

"How did you know I was here?" She tried not to sound surprised but failed.

Sean chuckled as he came around the bush. He sat himself on the bank next to Vivian, so close their knees were touching. Pulling his handkerchief out of his pocket he motioned to her arm.

"May I?"

Vivian nodded, holding out her arm to him so that he could press the handkerchief on the scratch until the bleeding stopped.

"I'm so embarrassed. You shouldn't have to take care of me this much."

"I like taking care of you."

After a pause she asked, "How did you know I was here?"

"I have my ways," he winked at her. Vivian had to stop herself from rolling her eyes at him, but he caught enough of the action to know how she felt. Good naturedly he laughed. "I saw you from across the field and decided to walk around to surprise you."

"Only your friend seems to have surprised *you*." Vivian didn't look at him as she said the words, but she could still tell that the smile left his face. He didn't sound cheerful when he spoke next.

"I wouldn't call him a friend even on our best days."

"He's wrong, you know. He doesn't own you. You can do anything you want with your life."

Sean gave her a grateful smile. He reached out, tracing his fingers over the edge of her cheek. "If only that were true."

Vivian couldn't hold his intense gaze and looked away.

"Did you enjoy your swim?"

Vivian looked back at him confused. Sean motioned with his eyes and Vivian followed his gaze. Her dress was bunched up around her knees exposing her bare legs. Vivian pulled her legs underneath her, covering them with her dress.

"I do apologize for my appearance," she said. Embarrassment made heat burn her cheeks.

Sean chuckled. "Don't fret about it. Tis a lovely day for a swim. I'd join you if I could."

"Propriety would never allow that." Although Vivian wasn't as shocked with the idea as she should have been.

"And it would allow you? What you're doing here would shock many a lady that I know." He cocked an eyebrow at her

"That's why I was hiding," Vivian said, unable to meet his eyes.

"Come now, Vivian. There's no need to be embarrassed when you're with me. Both of us just crave the freedom to do as we wish."

"Exactly!"

"We both just want the independence to make our own choices without all of society feeling the need to interfere," he said. His face darkened as he looked across the stream. Vivian felt forgotten for a moment.

"Shilling for your thoughts?" she asked him gently.

"That's generous. I only offer a farthing to most people."

"But you're not most people, are you Sean."

He smiled at her again, but it didn't reach his eyes. Those remained clouded. "I was just wondering if it were possible for a man to make something more of himself than he was born to. I feel it must be possible. What do you think?"

"Yes, I think it is very possible." Vivian wasn't used to a man asking for her opinion, but she liked it. "That is how the great kings of the past became so powerful. They didn't settle for what they were given but they worked to become something greater."

"Or they took it," he said flatly.

"True. Royalty of old were master thieves."

"And is that a crime?" He looked across the stream as he spoke. "Say a person took something that is not being used by anybody else but by taking it they helped improve the lives of themselves and others."

"I think many people would call that stealing," she teased.

"But would you?" He looked so intensely into her eyes that her heart nearly skipped a beat.

If it wasn't being used, did it really matter? It did, she decided. Theft would never solve any problem.

XVII.

Evening brought no respite from her troubles. Alone in her room Vivian thought more and more about what she could possibly do to free herself from an impending marriage to a man she couldn't stand, and simultaneously freeing her family from the severe debt that loomed over them. It was overwhelming and every solution she *did* fin was sure to be rebuffed by Nathan and Claire.

The thought of running away crossed her mind again. She knew she could walk away from it all and be free. Well, only as free as her conscious would allow. She had been raised to be obedient and compliant, even if it wasn't what she wanted.

Vivian rubbed her amethyst between her fingers absently as she thought about what to do.

Her eyes closed as she thought some more. Then sleep, with its soft intrusion, enveloped her.

Nausea threatened to overtake her as she felt the ship sway beneath her feet. The Gibraltar moved with every wave that came near it.

She was in Admiral Reed's cabin again, a familiar and unpleasant sight. It was as stark, and unwelcoming has the Admiral himself had been.

Vivian felt suffocated in a blanket of heat as she stared down at the Admiral. Lying there on his sick bed he looked so frail and small. She watched as he struggled to breathe between fits of coughing. Each cough racked his old body, sending a small stream of red spit down his chin.

Consumption.

There was no hope for him. Vivian could have walked out of the room; she knew he would have if she had been ill. She could have left him to die alone but she was too kindhearted for that. Despite his coldness to her over the years Vivian knew she had to do everything in her power to make him comfortable. It was the only way she knew how to be.

As she wiped his face Admiral Reed's eyes opened. With a great deal of effort, he focused on her.

"Wife?" It was his name for her. Never Mrs. Reed, my dear, not even her Christian name. He always called her by her rank, and wife was the best she could ever hope for. "Wife?" His voice was weak and horse.

"I'm here, Admiral," Vivian said. She didn't sound as frightened as she felt which pleased her a little.

"Forgive me, child," Admiral Reed whispered. He reached out for her. Taking his hand in her own, Vivian could feel how weak he had become.

"Rest now, Admiral. You must save your strength." Vivian tried to smile but she felt it must look pathetic.

Admiral Reed only held her hand all the tighter. "There isn't time. I must tell you how sorry I am. So sorry," his voice faded, and his eyes closed. Vivian almost thought he fell asleep.

"There is nothing to apologize for," Vivian whispered. She wasn't sure if he heard her or not.

Admiral Reed's eyes snapped open. "But there is!" He tried to sit up, but Vivian leaned over him, pushing him back down.

"I have been cruel to you, child," the old man wheezed. "I have criticized and belittled when I should have been loving. Forgive an old man his foolish mistakes. I never meant any harm. What do salty seamen know about wives. I'm so sorry."

Coughing began to overtake him again. Vivian held a glass of water to his lips, but he only pushed her hand away.

"Forgive me. Please say that you'll forgive me, I beg of you!" He searched her eyes, pleading.

She could only nod, finding it difficult to say the words. He needed to hear her say them, that was evident by the desperate look on his sickly face. Mustering all the courage she could Vivian pushed the words out.

"I forgive you, Admiral." Her voice shook but the relief that radiated from the sick man let her know she had done the right thing.

Relaxing into his bed, Admiral Reed repeated his thanks to her. He reached a shaking hand to the small table that was nailed to the floor beside his bed. From it he retrieved a tarnished spyglass, one that Vivian had seen him use for years. His fingers trembled as he struggled to grasp the object. Vivian helped him hold the spyglass.

Putting his withered hand over hers he pushed the object to her with the last of his strength.

"My gift to you," he wheezed.

"Thank you, Admiral," she said.

"You don't understand! I leave you all. I give you everything I have. You'll be provided for. I promise," He gasped out as another coughing fit began to overtake him.

Tears formed in Vivian's eyes. "Thank you for your kindness, Admiral." She held the spyglass to her heart.

"If only it were enough." Then the fit of coughing racked his body. Vivian tried to help him but there was nothing to be done. He only coughed and gasped for air until, at last, he lay still.

She called his name. She tried to rouse him. But Admiral Reed was dead. And Vivian was left completely alone. She didn't know she was crying until the tears dropped onto the cold brass of the spyglass with a plink.

She pulled it close to her. This little instrument felt like her only anchor. Vivian clung to it as tears flowed.

The cabin filled with darkness, so thick Vivian could feel it pressing on her. She rushed out onto the deck to call for help but there was no one there. As she turned about searching for anyone at all a faceless figure appeared before her. It started to move toward her as the blackness poured over the sides of the ship. The figure reached for her.

She ran as fast as she could, but her feet wouldn't move. It was as if she were running through quicksand. The blackness followed her, consuming all in its path. With all her strength, Vivian pulled herself to the bow of the ship. She clawed her way onto the beam that extended over the rough sea below.

Blackness pooled onto the deck until the only light was around Vivian. She could see nothing, hear nothing. Only feel the continuous movement of the waves as they threatened to send her plunging into their depths. The figure effortlessly pressed through the darkness. Its arms extended forwards as it searched for her.

She climbed farther out onto the bow, desperate to escape. Still the figure came towards her. It didn't stop, wouldn't stop until it had her.

Then, Vivian was falling.

Falling.

Falling.

Bang!

Vivian woke with a start. She rubbed the back of her head where it had hit something hard. Vivian sat up and stretched out her sore limbs. She had fallen asleep in the chair instead of going to bed.

"It was only a dream," she said to the moonlit room around her. Her hands still shook from the fear that had consumed her only moments ago.

She hated that dream. She hated how helpless and alone she always felt in it. It was happening more often now. Almost every night. Vivian stood up and started to ready herself for sleep in an actual bed when-

Bang!

"What in the world?" She pressed her ear against the wall to hear better. There was plenty of movement coming from the room. Then a man started to groan.

"For pity's sake!"

Vivian threw her dressing gown over herself and went out into the hall. Whoever was doing whatever in the room next door could have the courtesy of keeping the noise level down. She marched up to the door and knocked loudly. After the nightmare she had had, she didn't care what she interrupted. Real life was much less frightening than any dream.

The door slowly opened to reveal Sean, dressed in a black shirt and breeches. Vivian noted his odd attire but was too upset to comment on it.

"Will you kindly keep the racket down. Some of us are trying to sleep!" Vivian wasn't a pleasant person when her sleep was disturbed.

"My apologies," he whispered with a bow of his head. Then Sean slumped onto the door, sliding down it.

Instinctively, Vivian jumped forward and caught him under his arms. Bracing against his weight she kept him from falling onto the floor. It took all her strength to keep them both upright.

"Are you well?" Surprise surged through Vivian, along with a little panic.

"I can't rightly say," Sean replied in a groggy tone.

"Let's get you to a chair," Vivian said in a commanding way. If it wasn't so difficult to move Sean, she would have laughed at how much she sounded like the Admiral. Once he was sitting, Vivian stepped back to look Sean full in the face. It was then that the shimmering moonlight cast a glow across a deep red stain that covered the front of her white dressing gown.

Vivian looked back at Sean to find that the right side of his shirt was saturated with the sticky red liquid. Blood! She hadn't noticed it before because of his black clothes.

"What happened?" She tried to keep the fear out of her voice.

"Would you believe me if I said I fell out of bed?" Sean smirked at his joke, but Vivian was starting to see how pale he was.

"I need to get Dr. Eldon," Vivian started to turn away, but Sean grabbed her hand with a strength that belied his injured state.

"Don't," he begged. His blue eyes looked at her with such pleading that Vivian couldn't refuse him.

"Something has to be done. You're bleeding all over."

"Your father was a doctor. You can help me." Hope filled his ashen face.

"You need a real doctor Sean. It's been so long since I-"

"Please, Vivian. I can't get Eldon involved in this. Not after everything he's done for me. You have to help me."

She let out a long breath. She looked him over again. Her father had taught her basic medicine when she was younger, and the ship's doctor had relied on her as a nurse. She would need to see him in more light to determine how badly he was hurt.

"Fine. But if for any reason I need Dr. Eldon's help you have to let me get him."

Sean nodded slightly in reply.

Vivian raced back to her own room. She dug around at the bottom of her trunk trying to make as little noise as possible. Finally, she found her box of surgical instruments, a wedding gift from her father that had been invaluable to her over the years. Vivian held it close and said a little prayer to God, pleading for his assistance. Then she slipped back into Sean's room.

Once the door was firmly shut Vivian began to light every candle she could find. The room slowly became illuminated as the candlelight bounced off the highly polished wood paneling on the walls.

While trying not to disturb his injuries, Vivian cut away Sean's shirt.

"I don't think I know you well enough for such a relationship," he teased. There was a mischievous glint in his eyes that made the corners of Vivian's mouth want to smile.

Brushing all teasing aside she matter-of-factly said, "Sean, you are in need of medical attention. I am only trying to assist you with that." Vivian knew that she would need to work quickly, or he would lose too much blood and grow weak.

Carefully she washed his arm and chest. There was a bullet wound in his upper shoulder. Vivian let out a sigh of relief. The wound wouldn't cause any permanent damage. He also had a deep gash running across his arm where a bullet had grazed him.

"You're lucky that whoever shot you had such bad aim," Vivian told him.

"Bad aim? I have a bullet in me, woman! How do you call that bad aim?"

"Because a few inches lower and they could have hit a major artery," Vivian said. She laid out her instruments and bandages. She said another prayer, pleading for help from heaven. Then she took a deep breath and began.

Despite the unpleasantness of having a bullet removed from his shoulder and being stitched up afterwards, Sean did surprisingly well. He only pounded the chair with his good arm twice, groaned in pain thrice, and cursed all womankind in Gaelic once. All in all, he wasn't Vivian's worst patient.

When Sean was bandaged Vivian helped him into bed. As he lay there, he looked at the front of her dressing gown, touching the dried blood.

"I am so sorry to have put you through all this, Vivian. You've been an angel of mercy in my time of need."

"I was glad to be of service, Sean."

Vivian brushed a few black curls from his brow. Her fingers trailed down his jaw line. Sean pulled her hand to his lips, kissing her palm.

"Will you stay?" he whispered.

"I'll watch over you till morning." It was all that she could promise. She couldn't be caught in a man's bedroom, even if she was only acting as his nurse. If news of this was ever discovered her reputation would be tarnished.

The promise settled Sean though, and he laid back in bed, closing his eyes. Vivian pulled the blankets up around him, making sure that he was comfortable.

As he slept, Vivian went about the room cleaning up. She blew out all but one of the candles. She looked at Sean's blood-soaked shirt. She didn't feel right about bringing it to the washing girl. There would be too many questions. Vivian stirred up the fire in the hearth and threw the black shirt onto the flames. Then, not wanting to explain what happened to her own dressing gown, she tossed it into the fire as well.

Vivian stood before the flames in her shift as she watched the cloth burn until she was certain that every fiber of fabric was gone. With one last check on the sleeping Sean, Vivian slipped back into her own room.

Morning light was beginning to turn the grey sky a lovely gold when Vivian climbed back into bed. She rolled away from the window and fell into a deep sleep.

The easiest thing to do was to tell everyone that Sean wasn't feeling well. The most difficult was to check on him without anyone seeing her go in or out of the room. Reputations took years to build and seconds to destroy. Vivian had no desire for hers to be tainted even if it was to help an injured friend.

Thankfully, Dr. Eldon had her come into Sean's room with him to act as a nurse. To Dr. Eldon's reasoning, his beloved wife was far too delicate to be much use in a sick room. Once he had made that announcement to a few of the maids no one batted an eye at Vivian. The relief that filled her was immeasurable. She was able to check on Sean at any moment of the day or night without anyone thinking anything of it. If only things with Sean were as easy to manage as a few silly maids.

His body burned with an intense fever. His sweat dripped from his brow and soaked the sheets beneath him. Vivian sat on the side of his bed washing his face with cold water. She had seen fevers like this one before. If it broke soon then he would be able to heal. She didn't want to think about what would happen if the fever raged too long.

"If only I knew what was making him so ill," Dr. Eldon blurted in the late afternoon. "He was the image of health yesterday." The poor man paced around the room. "If I bleed him then I can drain the infection from his body," he muttered to himself.

"Don't bleed him!" The words sprang out of Vivian before she could stop them.

"Why?" Dr. Eldon gave a long look. "What are you *not* telling me, Mrs. Reed?"

Vivian looked down at Sean. Beneath the flush of his fever his skin looked almost grey. She worried about him. Even though Sean had wanted the truth kept secret, Vivian knew Dr. Eldon needed to know. He would be able to help best if he had the right knowledge.

Within minutes the whole story of the night before was out. Dr. Eldon's face flashed between shock and outrage. Finally, he settled with exhaustion.

"So, he's at it again," he sighed as he slumped into a chair.

"At what again? Is this not the first time he's been shot?" Vivian shouted.

"Not the first time at all." Dr. Eldon came over and examined Sean's wounds. "You did a fine job mending him though. We will sooth his fever the best that we can but in the end, we will have to wait and see."

Working together, Dr. Eldon and Vivian were able to change out all the linens on Sean's bed. They washed his body in cold water and cleaned his bandages. Sean seemed to be semiconscious throughout the process. He even was willing to drink some water. Then, exhausted, he rested again.

"I will stay and watch over him," Vivian told Dr. Eldon. "That is, if you don't object."

"It would be best," Dr. Eldon said with a slight smile. "I have a feeling seeing your pretty face would do him better than any remedies I can think of."

Vivian spent the long evening watching over Sean. At some points she spoke to him even if she wasn't sure he could hear her. At others she prayed for him. She sat on a chair next to his bed. Holding the hand of his uninjured arm, she drifted off to sleep.

XVIII.

The ship creaked and groaned around her. She felt certain that it would split apart at any moment. The darkness poured over the sides of the rail, the chill creeping into her bones. Through the mist came the hooded figure. His lurking mass filled Vivian with dread. He meant something sinister. Vivian scrambled backwards until her back pressed against the railing. As the arms of the figure reached out for her, Vivian thought she heard him whisper her name.

"Vivian?"

She sat up, confused by her surroundings.

"Vivian. You fell asleep, my angel." Sean was sitting up in bed, his hand on hers.

Then she remembered everything that had happened the previous night. "Your fever!"

Jumping up, Vivian felt Sean's forehead and cheeks with the back of her hand. His skin felt cool to the touch.

"Your fever broke. That's good news." Vivian let her fingers linger on him, then remembering herself she clasped her hands in front of her.

Sean's strong hand slipped into her own. He pulled her hands to his lips and kissed the back of her knuckles again and again.

"I owe you my life, Vivian. I can never thank you enough." His blue eyes were filled with sincerity.

"It was nothing," she shyly whispered.

"You and I both know that's not true, angel."

"What if I said I was happy to help. Would you believe that?" Vivian said with a smirk.

Sean gave her a lopsided grin. "Aye. Now that I'll believe."

Vivian set about redressing his injuries and making sure that he was comfortable.

"I'll need to get Dr. Eldon," she said when she was done. "He'll want to take a look at you."

"I'm feeling fine," he said stubbornly.

"Says the man who spent the past day fighting off a burning fever," Vivian stood with her hands on her hips. "I'm getting Dr. Eldon and there is nothing you can do about it."

"Fine," Sean pouted. "Can I at least get tucked in before you go?"

Vivian eyed him. While his face wore the most innocent expression Vivian could see the glint of mischief in his eyes. Wearily, she fluffed his pillows and arranged his blankets so that he would be comfortable. Once he was comfortably settled Sean again turned his innocent face toward her.

"What about a good night kiss?"

Vivian's brows shot up. "You must be joking!"

"Why? Can a man not get a kiss from his angel of mercy? Besides, I thought you wanted me to get better and a kiss from you would do the trick"

Vivian hesitated. Finally, she agreed. As she leaned forward, she saw Sean's eyes closing in anticipation. His fingers began to reach for her. His breath warmed her face. Then she planted a kiss on the top of his head and rushed away.

"I'll have Dr. Eldon check on you in a moment," she said from the door.

"That was a cruel trick, my angel. Cruel indeed." Sean put a hand over his heart and acted wounded.

Vivian smiled at him from across the room. "I did what you asked me to. Next time, be more specific." And with a wink she left to find Dr. Eldon.

Dr. Eldon thought it best if Vivian got a full night's sleep. She readily agreed. After a mercifully dreamless sleep, Vivian nearly skipped down to breakfast. She hadn't felt so good in ages.

"Well, don't you look lovely," Kathleen said with a smile. "I always did like you in lavender. It brings out the gold in your hair."

Vivian thanked her for the compliment and turned her attention to breakfast. She hadn't realized how little she had eaten until the smell of breakfast filled her nose. Everything tasted so good that Vivian had nearly stuffed herself silly by the time Dr. Eldon entered the room.

"Our patient is doing much better today. I have you to thank for that, Mrs. Reed. I don't believe I have ever seen a more attentive nurse in my life." Dr. Eldon smiled at Vivian good-naturedly.

Vivian waved the praise away. "I'm happy to help in any way I can."

Conversation fell away as they all began to eat. Dr. Eldon rifled through the morning newspaper. The article on the first page caught Vivian's attention. It spoke about a string of burglaries that had taken place in the grander homes along the east coast. Vivian read the portion of the article she could see as Dr. Eldon held it. There was something about the article that held her captive. The dates of the robberies, the locations, all sounded familiar to her.

"Well, I must be off," Dr. Eldon said as he rose from the table. He folded the newspaper and tucked it under his arm. Just as he was about to leave the room Vivian stopped him.

"Could I borrow that newspaper?" Her hasty words seemed to have startled Dr. Eldon, at least that was the impression his raised eyebrows gave her. Trying to sound casual she said, "I think that reading it might do Mr. Kade some good. Take his mind off his present situation, you know."

Dr. Eldon looked to Kathleen who nodded. He smiled at her as if they were sharing some private secret. "Of course, you can," he said handing the paper over to Vivian. "Just try not to tire Mr. Kade with too much company today."

Vivian promised she would keep her visit brief and snatched the paper away from him. Turning to the article she had started she continued.

> *While there is no firm information as to the identity of the thief, members of the gentry should be on their guard. There has been no indication as to how the items were removed from various houses.*
>
> *On the most recent attempt by the notorious burglar, Lord Ashby of Wexford attempted to stop him. Retrieving his pistol and with great aim, Lord Ashby was certain that he shot the menace no less than two times.*
>
> *"I heard the vagrant cry out after I fired my gun. That is always a clear sign to any marksman that the prey had been injured."*
>
> *While no one was found injured on the Ashby property the local magistrate is hunting for the burglar even as we speak.*
>
> *It is the duty of every citizen of the crown to offer up any information that they know of to the local holders of the peace that order may reign over us once more.*

She looked at the dates, she looked at the facts, and she had a sinking feeling in the pit of her stomach.

"Are you well, Vivian?" Kathleen's gentle concern broke into her thoughts.

"Absolutely," Vivian lied. "I am going to walk in the garden before I see Sean." Before Kathleen could say another word, Vivian sprang from her chair and left the room with the newspaper in her hands.

She walked the garden, looking and relooking at the words on the pages in her hands. It was wrong. It had to be wrong! Finally, after she could take the suspense no longer, Vivian marched inside and straight into Sean's room.

When he saw her enter, Sean's face broke into a smile. His blue eyes twinkled. He looked so much better than he had the night before. Vivian almost wanted to forget what she was planning on asking him. There was no possible way that this sweet, charming man could be a thief, a common criminal. But he had been shot. He had been laying on this floor, bleeding from two bullet wounds.

"Explain this to me," Vivian thrust the newspaper into his face.

Sean took the paper and began to read. His face fell with every word he saw. Finally, he threw the newspaper away from him.

"I didn't do those things because I wanted to," he said.

"You have to be joking! You don't have to do anything you don't want to do."

He snorted. "Says the woman who was married at fifteen."

"That was different-"

"How so?" he broke in.

"You're a man." she yelled

"So, men never have to do things they don't want to?" He crossed his arms over his chest.

"You shouldn't have to. That's the blessing of being a gentleman. But this," she picked up the newspaper and shook it at him. "This is unacceptable."

"Not all of us were fortunate enough to have a father who provided for us."

"Then get a job." she shot at him.

"I did." he said emphatically.

"Stealing isn't a job." she yelled.

"No, but it kept us from starving." he yelled back.

They were both seething with anger. After a long moment of glaring at each other, Vivian finally asked "Why?"

Sean took several deep breaths to calm himself. "For the usual reasons, I guess. At least that's how it started." He sighed and looked at the fireplace across the room. "I was very small when my father died. He left my mother with no way of supporting us. We were completely destitute. Then the creditors started to appear wanting to be paid. It turned out that my Father owed many people enormous sums of money, more than we could ever hope to repay. I took to the streets doing odd jobs for anyone who would hire me, hoping I could save my mother from the poorhouse. It was almost to no avail until one day a man approached me, wanting to hire me for a job. He said that he had left his watch at his friend's house. I was to go into the house and retrieve it. That was it. If I returned in half an hour the man said he would pay me a half-crown."

"Quite a sum," Vivian noted.

"Aye, for one as young as I, it was. And the money made my mother happy, so I continued to do small jobs for this man. I eventually realized that I was robbing houses for him, but it was paying off my father's debt faster than my mother could have imagined. Then one day I started thinking that if this man who hired me was able to pay me so well, how much more would I make if I took a few of those lovely things and sold them myself." He paused, looking down at his hands.

"How old were you?" Vivian asked

"Nine. I was nine the first time I stole for myself," he said without looking at her. He sounded so sad.

"And were you caught?" Vivian was riveted by his story and could hardly wait to hear how it ended.

"No, I was able to sell the jewel to a pawn shop with no trouble at all. The money from it paid off all the debt my father left on us. So, I stole another jewel and sold it to a different pawn shop. This jewel paid for the small flat my mother had plus enough for all our other expenses. The next jewel payed for my schooling. You see, I had no wish to become a thief or at least to remain one my whole life. I had my heart set on being a clerk."

"A clerk?" Vivian interrupted. "Truly?"

"Yes, truly," he said defensively. "A clerk is a very respectable profession. Besides, if I started as a clerk, I could eventually run my own business."

"I could see you having a business."

"So, could I. I wanted to be a merchant who bought exotic things from all over the world. I would travel to the ends of the earth for the finest silks and carpets. It would be called Kade and Son's Shipping." He moved his hands through the air as if creating the sign before him. He smiled a little at the idea but then his face darkened.

"Why didn't you go through with your plan," Vivian asked, curiosity burning.

"Because that man came back. I was in my apprenticeship. I was doing well for myself with a bright future and my mother was remarried to a kindly man. All seemed well in our lives until that man walked into my office one day. He said he knew I had been holding back on my takings from the jobs he assigned me. He said he had allowed me alone because I might be useful to him someday. He said if I didn't help him now, he would tell everyone what I had done. So, I gave in and did the job for him. Then the next one and the next. And before I knew it that old temptation of keeping a little for myself had come creeping back into my life." He sighed and rubbed his face with his hands. "I am ashamed of the life I have lived. So little has been right before God. I wish to be free of it, Vivian. I truly do. I want to go to a place where I might have a fresh start. The only way of doing that though is to bring about the fall of the man who got me into this whole mess and I am not certain how to do that. You understand, don't you?"

Vivian thought of Mr. Fletcher, and the mountain of debt her family seemed to never be able to be free of. She understood doing something that was against her conscience for the betterment of others. Yes, she understood better than most.

"Who is the man that you work for?" She asked.

"His name is Miles Fletcher."

XIX.

Vivian felt the pit of her stomach sicken. "Miles Fletcher? As in Mr. Fletcher, the creditor from Dublin?"

"Yes," Sean slowly answered. He stared at her confused.

Vivian jumped up and began to pace the room. "He's the man who loaned my brother George all that money. He's the one I'm trying to pay back."

Sean looked dumbfounded.

"The entire reason my family is in the situation they are, is because of this man. This Fletcher."

"Vivian, if your family owes him money then he will not rest until he has bled every last cent from you all." Sean looked concerned as he watched her pace.

"Really?" Sarcasm dripped from her voice. Noticing the hurt on Sean's face softened Vivian. She sat back down on the bed, facing him as she spoke. "It's not the amount of money that George borrowed that is the problem. It's the interest that is being charged. My family doesn't have any way of paying this man off."

"You'll think of something," Sean said halfheartedly.

Vivian scoffed. "I doubt it. Nothing seems to be enough. I'm out of ideas, Sean. I wish I could run away from it all."

Now it was Sean who sounded bitter. "That won't work. Trust me, I've tried and no matter how far I run he always finds me."

Vivian watched the frustration flash across Sean's face. It made her heart swell with pity for him. Reaching out, she gripped his arm to comfort him. He gave her a weak smile in return. Helplessness washed over the two of them as they sat there. Their own problems rolled over them like waves rolling over a stone, slowly reducing it to sand.

She insisted that he rest. Taking the newspaper with her, she slipped out of the room. Exhaustion threatened to overtake her body, but her mind would not rest. She paced the house, and then the gardens, all the while thoughts swirled in her head of what could be done. Eventually, there was only one place left she hoped to find solace.

The sun shone brightly as Vivian entered the gardens she had played in as a child. Mr. Kelly whistled as he trimmed the rose bushes. It seemed strange that she had been in Ireland for so long and had been to her home only once.

Vivian sat in her mother's favorite spot; a stone bench nestled among the flowers. She let the warmth of the sun pour onto her. It felt like a warm embrace. Almost as if her mother were there, holding her close.

"For a moment I thought it was yer ma sittin' there," Mr. Kelly said.

Vivian smiled at him. Then an idea struck her. "Mr. Kelly, if my family moved to town, why are they still having the gardens maintained?"

"They're not."

"Then who is paying your wages?"

"The bank be doin' that."

"The bank?" Vivian asked.

"Aye. Since ye married that Englishman, the bank has been payin' me. Promised to pay me if I work here and take care of the grounds. Not a bad offer, if I do say so."

Vivian thought on this a moment. "Do you know who holds the account your wages are taken from?"

Mr. Kelly shook his head. "Can't say that I do, Miss Vi."

She thanked him and he went off to tend to another part of the grounds. It was strange that someone had arranged for paying Mr. Kelly but had never taken the time to sell the house or lease the land. She knew it wasn't Nathan. Even if living in town, Nathan was smart enough to use the land for an increased income. So, who owned the property?

She closed her eyes and tilted her head towards the sun. She tried not to overthink what Mr. Kelly had told her. What did it concern her if someone else paid the man? Her family would have had to sell the house and the property anyway if it were still in their possession. These were the thoughts that were rolling around in Vivian's head when a shadow passed above her, blocking out the light. With how quickly the shadow arrived it should have left as fast. When it remained, Vivian opened her eyes. A man was standing before her, his black eyes appraised her. She jumped in surprise.

His smile was anything but cheerful. Vivian had to force herself to remain still and not shrink away from him. The last thing she wanted was Miles Fletcher to know how scared she was of him.

With as dignified an air as she could muster, Vivian addressed the man before her. "Mr. Fletcher, what a surprise to see you here."

"I see my reputation has preceded me," he said.

Vivian gave no reply. Without an invitation, Mr. Fletcher sat next to her on the bench. She slid to the edge, hoping she didn't appear rude. This man had her future in his hands, there was no need to make him aware that he was her enemy.

"What can I do for you today, Mr. Fletcher?" Sean's words kept ringing in her head. This was a dangerous man. What was more, Vivian felt he enjoyed being so.

He gave her a smile that didn't reach his black eyes. "Unfortunately, this isn't a social call, Mrs. Reed. I visited your brother, the Reverend Warren, earlier today. He gave me the impression that you were the one who is responsible for your family's finances."

"Did he now? That was very thoughtful of him." She fought the urge to scream at Nathan. How could he push all responsibility off on her? Then she remembered how derogatory he had been when they first found out about George's debt. Of course, he had named her the responsible party. He would push his responsibilities off on a child if he thought he could. "And what does that have to do with you?"

Mr. Fletcher gave a soft chuckle. "I am so glad that you asked, Mrs. Reed. As you know, your brother George took out several loans which he failed to repay in a timely manner. As I am unable to locate him, I am forced to turn to his nearest relations with hopes that they will be willing to assist him in his time of need." His voice sounded sincere, but Vivian could tell he was playing a part.

"I'm afraid that my brother George is dead."

"Oh," Mr. Fletcher crooned out in mock disappointment. It was obvious he already knew. "Well, that is so sad, Mrs. Reed. I do hope you will accept my deepest condolences for your loss."

Anger at this fake man swelled in Vivian. She wanted him to go away. Trying to get to the point she addressed him sharply. "Now that you know George is dead, I would ask you again what I can do for you?"

Sensing her anger only annoyed Mr. Fletcher. "Have I done something to offend you, Mrs. Reed?"

"Not at all," Vivian answered cheerfully. She needed to remember to tread carefully with a man like this. "I simply have places to be soon. We need to hurry things along if we are to discuss anything today."

Mr. Fletcher rose from his seat and offered her his arm. "Why don't I walk you to wherever it is you need to be then. We can discuss matters at hand as we go."

Vivian wanted to kick herself. There was no way to deny being in his company now and she would even have to hold his arm. Something about this oily snake made her insides want to cringe. Reluctantly she took his offered appendage. She led the way into Waterford.

She walked as briskly as Mr. Fletcher would allow, which wasn't very quick at all. He had a slow gate to his step, pulling her back to his side any time she tried to move faster. He appeared to enjoy this little battle of wills, and it made Vivian hate him all the more.

After what felt like an age, Vivian could finally make out Nathan's house at the end of the street.

"We are almost to my home, Mr. Fletcher. I thank you for walking me," she said with as much composure as possible. She wanted to run away from his leering gaze screaming but she knew that he would catch her.

"I will see you safely to the door," he answered. She felt he wanted to keep control over her as long as possible. If she hadn't been brought up to be a lady, she would have been willing to do anything to resist his power over her.

"Mrs. Reed, we spoke earlier about your late brother's debts," he said, every word drawn out. His attitude was full of mock sorrow, so much so that it reflected in his words. "I do hate to be the one to bother you in your time of mourning, but it is necessary that these debts be paid in full." He was full of fake concern. His insincerity rubbed Vivian's nerves raw.

"My family is working on gathering the funds you require. We will have the money for you shortly."

Mr. Fletcher smiled at her with his lips, but his eyes remained cold. "While promises of payment are most gratifying, Mrs. Reed, I need more than your assurances."

"And what sort of assurances would you require?" Vivian's words were clipped, her fear becoming evident in her voice.

Mr. Fletcher gave a sniff. "Nothing of great consequence, I assure you. I understand that your late husband was a member of the Royal Navy. Such a fine profession. One that serves our country well, don't you think so Mrs. Reed?"

His inability to remain on any one subject was an attempt to confuse her. His oily compliments were a way of drawing her in, making her trust him. Vivian wouldn't give him the satisfaction of an answer. Remaining silent, she watched him.

"Mrs. Reed, in lieu of your family's attempts to pay off the debt, I would need a sign of good faith. Some type of trinket that would show me that your family's intentions were sincere. I know," he said as if the idea had struck him out of the blue instead of being planned. "An item that belonged to your late husband would do. I am sure you have something that once belonged to him."

Vivian slowly nodded. Was that what he really wanted? Her old junk?

"Why don't you get me one of his possessions. Surely you could part with some small thing to let me know that I can trust your family in their desire to pay off this debt your brother incurred." His voice was pleasant, almost charming. But Vivian didn't trust him. Still, what would the loss of one small trinket hurt?

"If you would give me a moment and I will fetch something for you." She curtsied and hurried into the house without bothering to knock.

No one seemed to be about as Vivian rushed to the guest bedroom she had slept in before. Her original plan had been to stay at the Eldon's home for only a few days. A large portion of her belongings were still in this room. Sitting on the dressing table, where she had left it, was the box that contained Admiral Reeds spyglass. Opening the box, she let her fingers slide over the tarnished brass once more.

"I leave you everything," he had said as he placed the spyglass into her hands. Vivian shook her head. She had believed the dying man and he had let her down. Slamming the lid closed, Vivian carried it out of the house to Mr. Fletcher.

"A trinket of Admiral Reed's," thrusting the box at him. "I hope this shows enough of our intentions that you will give us some more time to gather the money you are asking for."

Mr. Fletcher opened the box to examine the contents. The faint sunlight reflected off the brass, giving the item a shine.

"This will do perfectly," a greedy expression played out over Mr. Fletcher's features. Closing the lid of the box, he bowed to Vivian. "It was a pleasure to meet you today, Mrs. Reed."

He strode away faster than Vivian would have thought possible, and with him the last of Admiral Reed's earthly possessions.

XXI.

Vivian turned back to Nathan's house. The imposing exterior didn't hide the truth from her this time. Inside was a family who didn't know themselves. Their desperation for the praise of their uncaring neighbors was ruining them. Vivian almost pitied her brother and his wife for a moment. They were doing everything they could to impress people whose good opinion didn't need to be gained in the first place.

Shaking her head, she walked into the house again. What was the point of chasing after the ton, as the English aristocracy were called, when they wouldn't have even cared to know the Warren family? If only Nathan and Claire would recognize that.

As Vivian went in again, she spotted one of the maids. Calling to the girl she inquired as to the whereabouts of the family.

"They all went out for the day, ma 'me. Says it was for the old Doctors' health." The girl bobbed in a curtsy and rushed off again, eager to get back to her work.

There was no point in remaining. She turned on her heal, making her way out of town and toward the only place she felt welcomed.

The Eldon house was empty of its usual bustle. Vivian went into the parlor, glad to be alone. She sat in front of the pianoforte and began to play. The music swirled around her as her fingers danced across the keys. High, cheerful notes helped her spirits soar. Low, haunting notes beat out the pain of her heart. She played for herself, lost in the place that only a few find, a place where there are only the performers and their music. She let the notes take her on a transcendent journey.

In the height of her reverie, she smelled him enter before she heard him. The smell of mold and mothballs and age. Lifting her eyes from the music she had been playing, Vivian saw Sir Warren shuffling into the room at the heels of a footman. Immediately, Vivian's elated spirit plummeted back to earth.

"So, I find you alone today little cousin." His voice held an exciting edge that didn't make Vivian feel anything more that agitated.

"So, it would seem, Sir Warren." Folding up her music, Vivian eyed her father's relation. There was nothing about the man that appealed to her. He had ridiculed and humiliated her far too long to have any place of affection in her heart. She didn't want his title or his money, no matter how badly her family might need them. Still, society demanded she behaved politely, even if all she wanted was to tell him to leave her in peace.

Leaving the piano forte, she offered him a seat on the settee and rang for tea, cursing protocol all the while. Why was it never considered good breeding to tell someone to get out?

Sir Warren prattled on about the price of sheep on the local market, declaring that he had never had a better year.

"I'm making more money that I know what to do with; all thanks to those Irish who haven't had a day of learning in their lives. I tell you what, a man can make a living by claiming to be the best at something even if he ain't. And no one here's the wiser for it. That's the difference between us English and those Irish. We set our sights on learning while they set theirs on the liquor. The devil's brew if you ask me."

Vivian hadn't. She wanted to remind Sir Warren that she was half Irish and loved her country. If she were braver, she would even tell him that she supported the rumors of an Irish rebellion with all her heart. But she wasn't brave, so she didn't. Instead, she offered him a plate of cakes, insisting that he try one. If his mouth was full then he would be less able to speak. Sadly, he refused the cakes.

"I have come here to speak to you on a most pressing matter, little cousin. It has come to my attention that you've gotten yourself into a rather difficult financial situation."

"I have?" Vivian tried to hide her indignation. Setting the plate down, she poured herself a cup of tea, hoping to gain patience from the warm liquid.

"Yes. Your sister, Mrs. Warren that is, was telling me of your debts. She says you need help paying them off."

"That was very thoughtful of her." Her hand tightened around the delicate handle of the teacup, ready to crack it.

"It is indeed," Sir Warren agreed as he slapped his knee. "Now *there* is a woman of fine breeding. Nothing beats an English woman and her heartfelt concern for others."

Vivian brought her teacup to her mouth as fast as she could. She didn't want to say what she actually thought about her sister-in-law.

"I'll get down to the brass tacks of it all, little cousin. You need money to pay off your debts. I am getting older in years and would like to be certain that everything I have worked for in my life is passed on into the correct hands if you get my meaning."

"I'm afraid I don't, Sir Warren." Vivian said, a pernicious smile tugging at the corners of her mouth.

Sir Warren squirmed in his seat a bit. After some sputtering and muttering, he finally blurted out, "I want an heir."

"You are in need of some hair?" Vivian found that she was enjoying playing ignorant a great deal.

"Confounded Irish girl. No, I want a son. A little boy to call my own. I want to give him my wealth and title after I pass on. Do you understand that?"

"I believe I do," Vivian let the ignorant act fall only slightly. She knew what Sir Warren was trying to ask and she didn't want to make it easy on him. "You are hoping that I will find you a boy to adopt."

"No!" Sir Warren's face was red from frustration. "I'm asking you to marry me, girl."

"Marry you? Well, why didn't you say that?"

He sighed, rubbing a hand over his sagging face. "So, you will then?"

"I don't see what marrying has to do with debts and sons." Yes, she enjoyed playing ignorant a great deal.

Sir Warren sighed. "If you marry me, little cousin, I will give you five thousand pounds to pay off your debts. And after you provide me with a son, I will give you another five thousand to do with as you wish."

Only ten thousand pounds? That was a large sum, but it wouldn't pay off all of George's debts to Mr. Fletcher. Vivian knew from their brief encounter that Mr. Fletcher would continue to come forward asking for more until every last penny of the debt was paid off, including whatever additional interest had incurred. By the time Vivian had managed to pay Mr. Fletcher all the money, the interest alone could have grown until the debt was near twenty thousand pounds.

"Sir Warren, the debt exceeds ten thousand pounds."

He glared at her. "I'm not giving you another cent. It's kind enough of me to offer you as much help as I am."

She wanted to scream. She wanted to run from the room. She wanted to laugh in his shriveled face at the notion of their marriage. But she didn't. This was an opportunity to get a great deal of George's debt paid off and she wasn't as stupid as she pretended to be. She knew that this was likely the best option for everyone.

"What you offer is most generous, Sir Warren. I would wish to think it over if that is agreeable to you. I am sure that my sister and brother would be able to help me make a clear decision in no time. You know how efficient you English are." She smiled at him, feeling wrong about elevating the invasive country but knowing that flattery worked best on this man.

"I think that sounds agreeable," Sir Warren said after a brief pause. He rose to leave her. "You let me know your answer soon, little cousin."

Once alone again, Vivian collapsed into her chair. She couldn't imagine spending the rest of her life with such a man. But what choice did she have? The more that Vivian thought about it, the more hopeless she felt until her once-elated heart sank. Hot tears of resentment stung her eyes, but she refused to cry. Sir Warren wasn't worth her tears.

"Oh, there you are," Kathleen exclaimed, coming into the room with an air of life about her. "I was at an aid society meeting today. Be grateful you didn't come. It only consisted of talk about slavery. They insisted that we all avoid the purchase of sugar since that comes from the plantations in Jamaica."

As Kathleen talked, she settled into a chair, pulling her embroidery out and beginning to work. Vivian watched Kathleen as she stitched. The brightly colored thread moving deliberately through the fabric on Kathleen's loom. As she pulled, Kathleen's thread snapped.

"How bothersome." Kathleen exclaimed as she began pulling some of the thread out to knot it.

Vivian wondered if her life would ever be peaceful enough that a broken thread would be her biggest worry in a day.

"I almost forgot to tell you," Kathleen went on as she worked. "Sean is doing much better. He's been asking to see you all day. Where were you anyway?"

"I went for a walk."

"All day?"

"No," Vivian said. For some reason, she didn't want to tell Kathleen what had happened to her. Earlier she would have told her everything that happened during every second of every day. That seemed like another lifetime ago. It probably was. Forcing herself into a more cheerful attitude Vivian started again. "No, not all day. I went to Nathan's for a while. After I returned Sir Warren called and we had tea together."

Kathleen let out a groan. "How was that?"

"Just as you would expect," Vivian said with a smile. "I now know that he thinks that Claire is of the highest level of breeding."

Kathleen scoffed. "Those wretched English always stick together," she muttered.

The words pained Vivian. She knew they weren't directed at her, but it still hurt, and she didn't know why. She wasn't English, not all the way. But she wasn't completely Irish either.

For the first time, Vivian realized why her parents kept to such a quiet, country lifestyle. It must have been hard for them to hear what was said about one another, or about the other's country. She thought of how her father must have felt whenever he heard how his wife's people were looked down on. Of what her mother must have felt whenever her husbands' people were spoken of with such loathing. Vivian knew her parents had always cared for one another. It was only now that she realized how much they must have loved each other to be able to withstand the constant criticism from family and friends. Vivian knew she never wanted that for her own life, even though it seemed to be inevitable with Sir Warren. If she had her way, Vivian would find somewhere to live where she would be judged solely on her actions, not the actions of a group of people she didn't identified with anymore.

"Vivian?"

She came back into the room at the sound of her name. Kathleen was smiling at her.

"I think you better go see Sean. You obviously haven't been paying any attention to what I've been saying."

"I'm so sorry. My mind was elsewhere."

Kathleen waved her away. "I can imagine where it was. Maybe with a certain gentleman who needs a good nurse."

"I wasn't-"

"Don't bother explaining yourself," Kathleen said with a wink. "Go see him for yourself."

She went back to her work and Vivian knew she had been dismissed. With nothing else to do, she went to check on Sean.

The room was dim when she entered, the setting sun couldn't be seen out his window. Thinking that he must be asleep, Vivian began to back out of the room.

"Wait, angel," his voice called out.

Vivian looked around the room again and saw Sean sitting up in bed. The sight of him with his tousled hair made Vivian smile. Sean held out a hand to her and Vivian flew across the room to take it. She sat on the edge of the bed; his hand nestled between each of her own. For the first time that day she felt peaceful, almost happy even.

"Tell me of your day," Sean said.

"Where to begin?" Vivian wanted to laugh but it came out as a choked sob. Then she looked into his eyes, those blue eyes she enjoyed so much, and stopped short.

A pain pierced through her heart, rendering her breathless. The room felt like it was spinning. The only point that stayed constant were his eyes. Cool, calm, inviting as a still pool on a summer's day. But if she ventured into those depths, even for an instant she would never be able to fulfill the commitment she had just made.

"Vivian?" Sean's gentle voice called to her.

"I have to go," she muttered.

"Vivian, wait."

"I have to go." In a daze she left. Somehow, she made it into her own room where the pain in her heart grew.

She felt empty inside. Aching for the one thing that could fill the void only to know that it would never be. She put a hand to her heart as if trying to press the empty ache deep inside where it had lain dormant for years. All she felt was the rush of her own pulse, her heart beating rapidly against her ribs. The pain became intense. Gasping for air, she clung to the bedpost until her gasps became sobs. No matter how hard she tried to stop them, the tears fell.

A hand, warm and gentle, turned her around. Arms enveloped her. Vivian sobbed as Sean held her tightly. He spoke no words of meaningless comfort and didn't try to hush her. Sean only held her in his strong arms, letting her tears of regret fall. When her knees threatened to buckle, he didn't force her to remain standing and be strong. Instead he helped her kneel on the ground and cradled her head.

He carried her to bed, letting out a groan as her weight pulled on his injured shoulder. Still, she clung to him as tears continued to fall. He lay beside her, holding her close to his heart. She could hear its rhythmic *thump, thump, thump*. The beat of it pressed into the hollow pain in her own chest, letting her find understanding for what it meant.

XXII.

Vivian woke in the morning to find herself alone. She was tucked under her blankets, still in her dress. She must have cried herself to sleep. The realization made her feel ridiculous. Then the thought of Sean, his soothing gentleness made her want to cry again. Determined to be strong, she got out of bed and rang for the maid.

"I need tea and a bath," she informed the girl the second she appeared.

Vivian set about brushing out her hair. It was a tangled mess from the day before and she attacked it with a fervor. Eventually, the auburn curls were smooth and glossy once again. When the bath water was ready Vivian sank into its depths, letting the heat take away the tension that had been building in her back.

She cleaned away her sorrow along with any dirt from the day before. Taking deep breaths of the steaming water. Leaving the bath, Vivian dressed in her best. A brilliant white muslin day dress edged with navy blue ribbons. She wrapped matching blue ribbons in her hair. Finally, she threw a blue and gold shawl around her shoulders. The look was simple yet striking.

Leaving a note for Kathleen was all that she would allow herself. She didn't trust her emotions today. She worried the instant she saw her friend everything would come bubbling to the surface, leaving her a crying mess again. She couldn't risk that.

The second the carriage pulled into the drive Vivian bounded out of the house. Inside she pulled the curtains closed, hoping to shut out any sight that might make her question her decision. The carriage swayed as the driver climbed onto the box. Vivian settled back into her seat and closed her eyes. She would be in control of her own self once again soon.

As the wheels of the carriage began to move, the door farthest from the house was opened and a man climbed in before Vivian could utter a protest.

"I see you prefer the dark," came the oily tones of Mr. Fletcher.

"I prefer solitude if you don't mind." Vivian curtly replied.

Even in the dark his sly smile was evident. "Mrs. Reed, I thought that you and I had become friends."

Vivian barked out a laugh. "You are not the type of person I would care to associate with."

"Whatever your opinion of me, Mrs. Reed, I would like to remind you that I was not the one who put you in this situation. It was both of your brothers. First George and then Mr. Warren." His tone was cheerful, almost carefree, but Vivian could feel the undercurrent of malice.

Taking a deep breath, Vivian reminded herself to remain calm. This was not a man to be laughed at. He could be dangerous. Vivian didn't want to find out how dangerous.

Being as sweet as possible Vivian tried again. "What might I do for you, Mr. Fletcher?"

"Better," he murmured as he settled back into the carriage seat. "I have a proposition for you, Mrs. Reed. One that should make all your financial troubles go away."

"Oh?" Vivian tried to sound nonchalant, but she wanted to leap at the chance to get out of debt.

Slipping into the seat beside her, Mr. Fletcher leaned in closer and whispered in her ear. "It would be between the two of us. No one else needs to know. But then your debt would disappear." He made the word sound alluring as he twirled one of Vivian's curls around his greasy fingers.

Vivian felt icy fear trickle down her spine. Her voice came out wobbly with nerves "Mr. Fletcher. I don't think I fully understand."

"Don't play daft with me, Mrs. Reed," Mr. Fletcher threatened as he moved even closer. Vivian pressed herself into the corner of the carriage to get away from him, but he came closer still.

"I'm a lonely man," he whispered in her ear. "You are an attractive woman." His hands trailed down her arms, clasping her wrists in his vice-like grip.

"Let me go!" Vivian started to call for help but Mr. Fletcher only laughed.

"Do you really think that they will come to your rescue after I paid them handsomely to leave us in peace?"

So that was how he got here, Vivian realized. Then she would have to get him out by herself.

With all her might, Vivian kicked one of her heavy boots up into Mr. Fletcher's groin. The man yelped in pain, collapsing to his knees. Vivian shoved both feet against his chest as hard as she could, sending the crumpled man to the far side of the carriage.

"Stop the coach!" she screamed as she opened the door and began to climb out.

The horses neighed in protest as they came to an abrupt stop.

"Get him out of there," Vivian yelled at the coachman and groom who were riding on the carriage. "And never, EVER, let some man pay you to ride in a carriage alone with a woman again! You're both lucky that I'm not going to Mrs. Eldon this second to have you dismissed from your posts."

The two men looked utterly ashamed of themselves and apologized profusely as they pulled Mr. Fletcher from the carriage.

"You'll pay for this," Mr. Fletcher seethed at Vivian.

As she began to mount the carriage again Vivian turned to Mr. Fletcher. "I will see that you receive an installment of the debt by the end of the month."

His black eyes flashed with rage. "I will see all of the debt paid by the end of the month or you and your whole family will go to debtor's prison!"

"Then it shall be paid in full by then," Vivian yelled at him. She slammed the carriage door shut behind her and ordered the carriage to move on.

It was only later that she realized the end of the month was two weeks away.

In no time Vivian was standing in the musty drawing room for Sir Warren's castle. It smelled of wet dogs, tobacco, and feet. This was a place that hadn't seen a woman's touch in decades, and Vivian had no desire to touch anything now.

Sir Warren entered followed by a pack of yapping hunting dogs. They ran into the room and jumped on everything, including Vivian. Sir Warren called them off with a gruff command, and while the dogs stopped bothering Vivian they continued to howl and climb on the furniture.

After the chaos of the dogs finally died down Sir Warren turned his attention to Vivian.

"And what can I do for you this morning, little cousin?"

"I have come with my reply to your proposal, sir," Vivian answered as sweetly as possible. Her nerves were still on edge after her episode with Mr. Fletcher, but Vivian was determined to go on with her life.

Sir Warren took her in for a moment. "I see. What is your answer?"

Smiling and batting her eyelashes, she said, "I accept your proposal. I would be honored to be your wife, Sir Warren."

"Naturally," he said.

Vivian stopped smiling and stared straight at him. "Sir?"

"I knew you would say yes. Even if the Irish idiocy that runs through your blood made you think otherwise, I knew your good English relations would talk you into it."

Vivian whipped her fan out of her reticule, frantically trying to cool her cheeks that burned with indignation.

Sir Warren rang a bell, and an aged footman entered the room. "Get the engagement gift," he barked.

"You have a gift ready? But I only gave my answer!"

"As I said before, I knew that you would say yes."

The man's arrogance was beginning to wear on Vivian, and they hadn't been in the same room for more than five minutes. Vivian wondered how she was going to manage a life with this man. Then she reminded herself of the alternative and decided that dealing with Sir Warren, as insolent as he was, was a far better option than debtors' prison.

When the footman returned, he carried a slender leather box, wrapped in a black silk ribbon. He offered it to Sir Warren who thrust it at Vivian with a dismissive, "Here."

Vivian forced on a smile and pulled the ribbon free. Resting on a black velvet cushion was the most dazzling emerald necklace Vivian had ever seen. Each square cut stone was of the brightest green and encased by gold. The largest stone in the center of the necklace was surrounded by a row of sparkling diamonds. It was an older style of necklace, meant to sit high on a woman's throat, but beautiful all the same.

"This was my mother's," Sir Warren said. "She brought it with her from England when she married my father."

"It's beautiful," Vivian admitted.

Sir Warren held out his hand for the box which Vivian obediently handed over. He removed the necklace and placed it around her throat. Being taller than him, Vivian had to bend her knees so that he could see the clasp as he struggled to latch it.

Vivian stood up, letting him see the necklace as it hung around her neck. The cold weight of it rested on her skin, reminding Vivian that she was now his. The thought made her stomach churn. As much as she wanted to rip it off her neck and throw it at him, Vivian remained in control of herself. She curtsied perfectly, thanking Sir Warren for his thoughtful gift.

"I must show my family this wonderful treasure at once," Vivian said as she tried to make her escape.

He caught her arm. "One moment, little cousin," he said in a leering voice.

He pulled her down so that he could give her a kiss. Vivian turned her head in time, so his dry lips only touched the corner of her mouth. The sensation made her skin crawl.

It's better than debtor's prison, she repeated in her head over and over as she rode in the carriage to Nathan's home. All the while the necklace felt heavier and heavier on her neck, reminding her that even jewels could be their own type of shackles.

During the carriage ride into Waterford, Vivian removed the necklace and placed it into her reticule. The idea of ripping the necklace off and shoving it firmly into the bag had crossed her mind but she wasn't one for dramatic actions, so she was careful with Sir Warren's family heirloom. Looking at the jewels as they sat in the bottom of her bag made her think of how much each one was worth. If she were to pawn one emerald would anyone notice? Quickly she pulled the strings of her bags closed to avoid the temptation.

Her spirits were low, even with the good news that she would tell her family. She barely marked where she was until she was sitting on the footstool before her father's accustomed chair. He was sleeping peacefully before a small fire in the drawing-room. With the daylight pouring in through the window Vivian could see how small and frail he was.

"Father," she gently called to him.

The old man opened his grey eyes, joy making them light up.

"I have some wonderful news, Father," She said, nearly choking on the words. They weren't wonderful, they were forced. But what did it matter so long as it got what everyone wanted from her? "I have found a way to get us out of debt with Mr. Fletcher."

"And how is that" Claire asked from the doorway.

Gracefully, Vivian rose to face her sister-in-law. She forced a polite smile on her lips and curtsied. "I have some wonderful news to share with the whole family, Claire. Would you be so kind as to bring Nathan in here?"

Vivian's gentle tone only aggravated Claire further but she went for Nathan without saying anything. When everyone was in the room, Nathan closed the door behind him.

"Sir Warren has proposed, and I have accepted," Vivian said without ceremony.

Claire clapped her hands. "How splendid! I told you it would all work out this way. Didn't I say that Nathan?"

"Yes, you did, dear," he smiled down on his wife.

"I am so happy for you," Claire cheered as she rushed across the room to embrace, Vivian.

Vivian allowed herself to be hugged by Claire but felt nothing close to affection. It was all a show.

Taking a deep breath Vivian continued. "He will give me five thousand pounds now as a type of dowry, and another five after I give him a son."

Nathan scoffed. "But that is only a third of what we need. Where will you get the other five thousand?"

Vivian sighed, rubbing her temples. "I had hoped that you could help with that portion of the money. Claire informed me that you already had two thousand put aside."

"Us?" Nathan nearly laughed at the notion. "Where in the world do you expect us to find such money? This is ridiculous."

"What's more," Vivian continued, talking over him, "we need to get all the money to Mr. Fletcher by the end of the month."

Nathan gasped. "How are we to do that?"

"I have a few ideas. But Mr. Fletcher came to me this morning and informed me that we have to pay him in full or he will have us all sent to the poor house." Vivian left out all the details of the encounter. The thought sickened her.

"What are your ideas?" Nathan asked, a nervous edge in his voice.

Vivian took a deep breath. "We need to sell off anything we can. Jewels, art, fine fabrics, livestock. Sell them for as much as we can and as quickly as we can."

Claire gave a small gasp of alarm, but Vivian paid her no heed.

"To come to this," cried Old Dr. Warren. "Forgive me, my children."

"There's nothing to forgive, Father," Vivian said.

"If I had taken more time to teach George. If I hadn't put all our money into that Argentina scheme. If I hadn't signed away the deed to our home." The old man burst into tears.

"You signed away the deed?" Vivian asked. That would explain why Mr. Kelly was being paid by the bank.

Nathan put his hand on Vivian's shoulder. "Let's get father to bed. He needs rest."

Together they got their father into his room. It took considerable effort to get the old man to rest. Vivian remembered the laudanum Dr. Eldon had left. She prepared a glass for him now.

"It's all right father," Nathan was saying. "You did your best. No one blames you." He continued his soothing words while Dr. Warren took his laudanum. Eventually the elderly man slipped off into a dreamless slumber.

"I feel so guilty," Vivian said as they descended the stairs. "Drugging him like that."

"Don't," Nathan said. "He used to give us laudanum when we were teething."

"Really?" Vivian couldn't imagine her father giving that to a child.

Nathan nodded. "He would give us that and he would rub brandy on our gums to numb the pain."

Nathan called for Claire and the three of them went into Nathan's study at the back of the house.

"So, we are now to come up with ten thousand pounds in just a few weeks' time." He sounded casual as he said the words. He went to a small cupboard and pulled a bottle of whiskey from inside it. Pouring himself a generous glass, he toasted the ladies.

"Nathan!" Claire said reproachfully.

"Well, why not? This is a fine pickle of a mess we're in. There's no clear way out of it this time. Not even marrying Vivian off again is going to save us. No, we really are in a mess with it all." He sunk into his chair and downed his drink in one large gulp.

Vivian and Claire sat in the leather chairs by the fireplace.

Claire said, "What if we could get a loan for part of the expanse?"

Nathan scoffed. "Who would give a loan for such a sum?"

Claire sulked for a few minutes, staring into the fire. After a long silence, she said, "I need to plan the engagement dinner."

"What?" Nathan fumed. "After all this, you want to spend *more* money?"

Claire waved him away. "It doesn't need to be anything elaborate. But we must acknowledge Vivian's engagement to Sir Warren. Once it is publicly announced we can get the bands published. Then Sir Warren will have to give Vivian the five thousand he promised her."

"He may not give that money to her until after the wedding," Nathan said. He had a way of pulling grey clouds over the brightest silver lining.

"Then the sooner the bans are published, the sooner they can be married." Claire left the room in a huff.

When Vivian got up to leave Nathan stopped her.

"Vivian?" Nathan called her back. She turned, looking at her one-time idol as he sat nursing his second drink. "I'm sorry things haven't turned out the way you were hoping. The way any of us were hoping, really."

Vivian smiled at him. Deep inside his prim exterior, he was still her older brother who loved her. "I'm sorry too."

As the day wore on Vivian and Nathan scoured the house for things to sell. They had decided on several paintings in ornate gold frames. There were some vases Nathan felt could be easily parted with. They were going through the books in the study when Claire came bustling in.

"I have all the invitations ready for tomorrow night."

"What's tomorrow night, dear?" Nathan asked without looking up from the books he was sorting.

"Vivian's engagement dinner. We are going to have a small number of guests. No more than twenty, but it should still be a splendid evening."

"Twenty? Claire, don't you think that's too many people?" Vivian asked.

"Not at all," Claire soothed her. "I think it's the perfect amount." Then she bustled from the room again.

"Let her have her way," Nathan said. "Claire is always happiest when she is planning some event or other. Besides, this might be the last one for some time, depending on how many of our possessions we have to sell off."

"You know I'm planning on helping in any way that I can," Vivian said.

"I know. You would sell the shirt off your own back if it would help Father. But let me help you for a change," he said with a smile at her. "It's nice to know that you can't do everything all on your own."

XXIII.

Vivian was curled up on the window seat in the Eldon's library. Wrapped in an old tweed shawl, she watched the rain as it spattered on the window. A sigh escaped her at the sight of it. She didn't remember it raining so much when she was a child. Now, there seemed no end to the light spattering's that happened every few hours. It made everything continuously damp and cold.

Vivian shivered. She despised being cold. She pulled her tattered shawl around her more tightly. She missed the warmth of the Bahamas. Most of the English living on the island's found the heat to be suffocating but she had found it liberating. To be so filled with warmth was one thing she missed. Especially on a dismal day such as this one.

With her finger, she followed a raindrop as it slowly trailed down the windowpane. It collected in a small pool at the base of the window.

"Lovely sight, isn't it?" The voice startled Vivian from her thoughts. She turned to see Sean leaning against the door frame. He had a mischievous glint in his eyes as he looked at her.

"You enjoy the rain?" she asked.

"Among other things that are lovely to look at," he said, his eyes not leaving her. Vivian blushed and looked down at the book that rested beside her, not that she saw it.

Sean sauntered across the room to sit opposite her on the window seat. "What book have you there?"

"Nothing of too much consequence." She held the book out for him to take.

"Lectures on Medical Advances by Dr. Adam Colesmith," He read aloud with a bit of a surprise. "I was honestly expecting a book on poetry or a gothic novel."

"It would have been more likely, I suppose. But I find that the best sort of reading should edify us in some way." She watched as he turned the book in his hands.

"So, what brought you here, angel. Today, of all days? I thought you were staying with your father again?"

Vivian leaned her head against the wall behind her. "I needed to get away from it all."

Sean looked at her expectantly. "Because?" he asked, trying to get her to open up.

Vivian smiled at him. Even when she felt miserable, he was still willing to listen to her. Before she could answer, an involuntary shiver overtook her. Sean reached out and pulled her shawl higher onto her shoulders. He looked at it for a moment.

"Where's your cashmere shawl?"

Vivian sighed and lowered her gaze. "I sold it," she said quietly.

"Why?"

Vivian looked at him from under her lashes. His face showed his concern. "To gather money to pay off Mr. Fletcher. I've sold everything I could. Even my shawls."

"Oh, Vivian." The sympathy in Sean's voice was enough to bring all her emotions to the surface. A tear trickled down her cheek. She brushed it away with the flat of her hand.

"I feel so ridiculous admitting this but I'm mourning the loss of my things," she said between tears. "I mean, I had so few possessions to my name and after I sold them I have even less. I didn't even get very good prices for them. But then, what was I expecting for a few used shawls and that thin fox fur." Vivian pulled out her handkerchief and dabbed at her eyes. "This must sound extremely vain, crying about things. It's keeping us out of the poor house and that matters more." She gave a small laugh as she wiped the tears away. "I feel selfish about it all."

Sean reached out with his warm hand. He cupped her cheek, wiping a tear away with his thumb. "Selfish is the last thing I would ever call you."

Vivian nearly cried again from his kindness. She leaned into his hand, letting his touch soothe her.

"Vivian, have you ever puddle jumped?"

"What?" She sat up abruptly.

"Puddle jumped. You know, jump into the puddles while it's raining," he explained.

Vivian was taken aback. "Not since I was very small," she admitted. "I got in a great deal of trouble for it then, so I never did again."

"Don't you miss it? Don't you miss the things you were able to do as a child?" Before she could answer, Sean grabbed her hand and pulled her toward the French doors that led to the garden. He flung them open wide and said "Let's be free for a moment, Vivian. What do you say?" Vivian nodded in reply.

Sean gave her a wide grin. He threw off his coat, vest, and cravat. He kicked off his shoes and stockings and ran out into the pouring rain with a whoop. Vivian took off her slippers and stockings and followed Sean into the rain with a squeal.

It was a warmer rain than she had expected. Sean grabbed her hand and together they ran down the garden path toward the rising hill beyond. Vivian felt an exhilaration for life fill her that she had almost forgotten.

Sean pulled her off the garden path so they could run up the hill together. The wet grass tickled at her ankles. Vivian couldn't remember the last time she had felt wet grass under her feet. For too long she had been governed by the proper rules of decorum that dictated her society. And what had it brought her? Nothing but disappointment.

With their fingers intertwined, Vivian relished the feel of Sean's strong hand. As they ascended the hill together, he looked over his shoulder with his ever-charming smile. Vivian laughed as she smiled back. She must have looked a sight, soaking from head to toe with her once perfectly arranged curls now long, wet strands of mess. Still, Sean continued to give her his warm smiles and she didn't care how she looked.

At the top of the hill Sean threw out his arms and spun around, tilting his face to the falling sky. Vivian laughed as she watched him, so carefree and wild. He shook his head of wet curls. Water droplets flew from his hair, spraying her even more.

"Here we are free, Vivian," he said as he pulled her into his arms. Together they spun around faster and faster. "There are no debts to be paid. No, I-owe-you's are hanging over anyone's heads. This is our moment of liberation!"

Vivian felt so dizzy from all the spinning that she had to throw her arms around Sean to keep from falling. She held him close, resting her head on his shoulder. He stopped spinning and carefully lowered her to the ground, shielding her face from the falling rain with his own body. She rested on one of his arms as she lay there, looking up into his stormy eyes.

"Vivian," he whispered, his voice unsure. He didn't look at her eyes but at a lock of her wet hair he was twirling around in his free hand. "Vivian, do you think you could forgive me for my past?"

She knew he wanted her to forgive him of his thefts. It was surprising to her, but she hadn't given them another thought after he had confessed everything. She pushed a wet strand of hair from his brow as she thought. "I already have."

Relief filled his eyes. He caught her hand and kissed it. She sat up as he did so, her heart nearly ready to jump from her chest filling her with girlish delight and anticipation

"Do you think…if it were possibly…could you ever see yourself, that is…"

Vivian had never seen him at such a loss for words. She longed to hear what he was struggling to say but feared it as well. Finally, he took a deep breath and offered her one of his winning smiles.

"Vivian, I love-"

She pushed her hand to his lips to keep him from saying the rest. Surprise clouded his eyes.

"Don't," she begged. "Don't say things we are not at liberty to act upon."

He pulled her hand away. "But we are free. Here in this moment-"

"And then what!" Vivian yelled. She pushed him away as she stood up. Sean stood as she started pacing, attempting to salvage the ruined moment.

"Don't you feel the same?" He stopped her and, with both hands on her shoulders, made her look at him. In a voice of pleading desperation, he said "Tell me you feel the same, Vivian. Tell me!"

"What good would it do? We are not free, you and me. We both have obligations on us that prevent us from choosing our own lives." It cut her to the core to admit the truth, especially as she saw the pain in his eyes. Those stormy blue eyes she loved to look into.

"But we could change all of that." Hope filled his voice. A hope for something that could never be.

"How?" she demanded as she slapped his hands away. "By abandoning our families. By stealing from more people. As long as you are under the thumb of that man, and as long as my family is still in debt, we are not free. And we may never be free, Sean. So please, don't make me say something that will only cause us pain."

"How could us loving each other ever cause us pain?" There was a hint of bitterness in his voice as one more piece of a normal life was stolen from him.

"It may not at first. But after a time of knowing how we feel and never being in a position to do anything about it, those tender confessions of love may turn bitter in our memory. I won't have it."

The rain had stopped without Vivian noticing. The sun began to shine as it pressed its way through the clouds. Vivian knew their moment of freedom was over. She left the hill and ran back to the library for her things. Beginning the walk back to Nathan's, she refused to look back at what she was willingly leaving behind.

XXIV.

The next evening came too quickly. Vivian had been preparing all day for the dinner, but she still felt flustered. As she finished dressing, she placed Sir Warren's engagement gift on and realized what the matter was.

Tonight, she would have to face Sean. She had moved back into Nathan's after she accepted Sir Warren. Somehow, staying with her happily married friends and the man she admired didn't sit well with her. She had only given Kathleen the excuse of missing her father when she left. Vivian hadn't even bid Sean farewell. Now she would have to face him.

The necklace sparkled against her throat. She descended the stairs to the foyer, and it gleamed in the candlelight, letting everyone see it.

Let them see my new chains, Vivian thought. That was what the cold metal felt like against her skin.

The instant that she entered the drawing room her eyes met Sean's. He rushed to her side. Taking her hand in his, he bowed deeply, bringing her fingers to his lips. Vivian nearly crumpled at the tenderness of the gesture, but she reminded herself that she still was part English. Even a small part, but English, nonetheless. Giving in to personal emotions was not what brought glory to crown and country.

"It is good to see you, Mr. Kade," she said calmly. "You are looking much recovered."

"Vivian, is all well? You ran off yesterday. I thought of following but you seemed so upset. I've been worried about you." He reached a handout to stroke her arm, but Vivian side stepped his attempt. It wouldn't do to have anyone see such an intimate gesture.

"Everything is fine. I found that I had been away from my father too long." Her reply was cool, her eyes averted, but her heart was screaming inside her chest.

"You could have told me that, my angel." Sean's voice was low, like distant thunder.

The sound of it made Vivian want to throw off Sir Warren's necklace and scream out that she wouldn't marry him. It made her want to curse Mr. Fletcher to the bottom of Poseidon's ocean. Instead, she answered with a calm voice. "Thank you for your concern, Mr. Kade."

"Vivian, I don't understand. Have I done something to upset you? Why are you being so evasive tonight?" Pain flickered across Sean's face. Vivian resisted the urge to run into his arms and hold him until it went away.

"You have done nothing wrong," she answered without meeting his eyes. She looked at anything in the room except him. "I have to help my sister with her guests. If you'll excuse me," and she left him without waiting for a reply.

Dinner went smoothly enough. The Eldon's were present, with their usual cheerful dispositions. Sir Warren seemed more engaged than usual. Even old Dr. Warren was the model of good health for once. If it weren't for the feeling of impending doom that kept slithering up Vivian's spine, she would have called the evening pleasant.

As the ladies left the men, Kathleen pulled Vivian aside.

"We must speak now," Kathleen whispered as she dragged Vivian into Nathan's empty study.

"About what?" Vivian tried not to knock over a stack of books that rested on the floor.

"What is going on between you and Sean?" Kathleen demanded.

Vivian tried to keep her emotions in check. "Nothing at all," she answered lightly.

"Something has been. For days now you have been his sole nurse and I have never seen him happier. Then, as dinner was about to start, you acted as if you hardly knew him. Now, you will tell me the truth Vivian Warren Reed, or I will go in there and tell every member of this dinner party who really stole the money from the poor box all those years ago!"

Vivian remembered clearly how she had been small enough at age eight to slip her slender arm into the opening at the top of the box and retrieve a few coins. She had used the money for candy but had felt so awful after eating it that she spent the entire day sick with guilt in Kathleen's room. No one had ever found out what she had done.

"You wouldn't dare."

"Watch me." Kathleen reached for the door, but Vivian caught her arm.

"Fine. You win." Vivian rubbed her hands over her face. "Sir Warren has agreed to give me five thousand pounds in exchange for my hand in marriage."

"But that's not all of the debt."

"No, it's not," Vivian cut her off. "Nathan and I are doing everything we can to get the rest. Do you understand now?" Vivian asked. "I care for your cousin, but I have to do what I can for my family. Even if that means marrying the likes of Sir Warren."

"My poor friend." Kathleen wrapped her arms around Vivian pulling her close. "I am so sorry for not understanding sooner. What can I do to help?"

A smile spread across Vivian's lips. "Stand by me when I need you."

"I will always do that."

The two women walked arm and arm together into the drawing room. The gentlemen were joining the ladies.

Sir Warren came shuffling up to Vivian. "Should we make the announcement, little cousin?"

Vivian nodded and Claire had the footmen pass out flutes of champagne to all the guests.

Sir Warren called for everyone's attention. "I am most pleased to see so many faces of friends and family. I have a joyous announcement to make. I have proposed and was accepted by Vivian here to be my wife."

The room erupted into joyful congratulations. Everyone embraced and kissed Vivian on the cheeks. There was talk of the upcoming nuptials and questions about who was most excited. Vivian left most of the talking to Claire and Sir Warren. She did her best to slip into the edges of the room away from the crowd.

The only congratulations that seemed as forced as the smile Vivian wore, were the ones from Sean.

"I'm pleased to see you got the old wig after all."

"Sean, you can't mean that."

"Oh, but I do," he said, a disgusted look on his face. "Now if you'll excuse me," and he turned away.

As the evening came to a close, Sean was the first to leave. He nearly bolted through the door to escape. Vivian went to where he had been sitting and discovered that he had left his cigar box behind. Using it as an excuse she rushed out the door after him.

"Sean!" She called after him once she spotted him walking down the street. She could hear the echo of his boots on the cobblestones as he continued to stomp away. She called his name again as she ran after him.

Finally, he stopped. He held his fists at his sides. Even in the dim light from the streetlamps, Vivian could tell his knuckles were white.

"You forgot this," she said lamely, holding out the cigar box to him.

He snatched it from her. "You could have sent it with Kathleen and Eldon."

"I wanted to see you before you left."

"Why?" He demanded. His eyes bore into her with a wave of intense anger that frightened her so much she stepped back. "So, I could wish you well before you go into another loveless marriage? So, I can congratulate you for bagging a rich, old wig so your family can use his money to their own ends? Well then," he offered her a grand bow full of mock courtesy, "I congratulate you, Mrs. Reed, on a most successful outcome to all your scheming."

Vivian was beyond shocked at his rude behavior. She may have made mistakes but at least she tried to be civil to him. "Sean, I had hoped we could part ways as friends."

"I would ask you to refrain from the use of my Christian name, madame," he said, savagely.

"After all we have been through-"

"After all we have been through, I thought we had an understanding."

"Sean, you know my family's situation. I never tried to hide that from you. I have now been given a chance to free my family from Mr. Fletcher and I must take it. You, of all people, should understand wanting to be free from that man."

Sean stepped towards her. "You speak of us not being free, but how much of that is by our own doing." His blue eyes were a storm of emotions. "I love you, Vivian. I have since the first moment I met you. And I would do anything to hear you say the same to me."

Taking another step towards her, Sean reached out his arms, wrapped them around Vivian and pulled her close. He bent her head back across his arms and kissed her, gently at first, then more desperately, as if he were a dying man finding water. She melted in his arms, clinging to him as if he were the only stable thing in all the torrent world.

When they finally broke apart, Vivian was desperate for more, but he held her at arm's length.

"Goodbye, Mrs. Reed." Then, turning on his heels, Sean walked away into the night.

She tried to stifle a sob, but it came anyway. Unable to see through her tears she somehow made it into her room. The moment the door shut she crumpled onto the floor. Tears streamed down her cheeks but she hardly cared. She knew she was losing the only man she had ever loved.

XXV.

The ship creaked as waves tossed it across the sea. The air was thick with humidity, almost as if a blanket of damp heat was laid over everything. Not even the spray of the sea could relive that heat.

Alone on deck, Vivian still felt she was being watched. At sea she felt vulnerable and bare. Wrapping her arms around her middle did little to ward off the feeling of exposure.

The figure emerged from the darkness behind her. She could feel it there even without seeing it. She did her best to run, her steps weighted and slow. As the wind whipped the saturated hem of her dress around her ankles, she was certain she would fall onto the slippery deck. Doubt threatened to consume her. Then the niggling sensation that always remained in the back of her mind wormed its way to the forefront.

She knew this nightmare. She had experienced it many times. But never had that feeling been in it. Thinking there was nothing to lose, she gave in to it. The worm grew inside her, strengthening her. It pushed her to feel something she had never given voice to before. Vivian was angry.

The anger swelled inside of her until it was near rage. She resisted the urge to suppress it, as she had done at every other moment in her life. She gave it room and let it flood her.

Taking control of the nightmare for the first time she turned on the hooded figure as it glided toward her. Refusing to be frightened, she walked toward it.

"I won't fear you!" She screamed over the wind.

The figure slowed its approach. Its arms reached forward, but she refused to be afraid. Instead, she slapped the arms away. The power of that simple action was enough to instill the first ripple of confidence she had ever had.

"I refuse to fear you ever again!"

The hood melted away, revealing a smiling face. Not sinister, not threatening. Loving, caring, smiling Sean.

Wide eyed, Vivian stared at him. Why was he there?

Reaching into the blackness that wrapped around him like a cloak, Sean pulled the Admiral's spyglass out. He offered it to her, clearly pleased with what he was doing. She didn't understand how he had it, but she took it.

The instant her fingers touched the brass it cracked. Splintering apart before her, she watched as gold coins began to pour from the spyglass. The gold came in wave after wave, pooling on the deck at her feet. All the while Sean smiled at her.

Vivian sat upright in bed. The dream swirled around her thoughts, still so real. As she rubbed the sleep from her eyes an idea formed in her mind. There was a possibility she knew what the dream meant.

***

Waiting until the proper hour to call was more than she could stand. She tried to read the newspaper to her father, but her mind was miles away. Or not far away enough. Thoughts of blue eyes swirled in her head. When at last she could stand it no longer, she grabbed her shawl and made for the door.

"Where are you going?" her father asked.

"To make a call."

"But it's only 9 o'clock in the morning. No one is even awake at this hour, except us."

But Vivian didn't hear him. She was running down the street toward the country. This time when the Kathleen's butler answered the door, he promptly led her into the parlor.

Too excited to sit, she paced the room as she waited. She picked up objects only to set the down again without looking at them. The minutes ticked by agonizingly slow. If she had been less certain she would have forgotten all about making this call. But the surety that rested in her felt more real in the light of day. And there was only one person she trusted enough to help her.

"Why are you here, madame?" The contempt that laced Sean's usually gentle voice was painful. Vivian turned to face him and nearly gasped. He looked as if he hadn't slept in days. His hair was disheveled, and it was obvious he was unshaven. What's more, he wore no coat, only an unbuttoned vest over his shirt. Vivian noted his missing cravat that allowed his shirt to hang open to reveal a soft patch of hair on his chest.

"Are you well?" she asked dismayed.

He scoffed. "As if you'd care." He made his way to a sideboard, taking a bottle of brandy from off the table and pouring himself a generous glass.

"Well I do care, so I'd thought I'd ask." She felt a fool. How was she going to ask for his assistance after she had caused him such pain? He must feel used by her, and here she was wanting to use him again.

He threw the brandy down his throat in one swift gulp. Reaching for the decanter, he filled another glass. "If you are only here to inquire after my health then I assure you madame I am well. Never better, in fact," he said as he gave her a smile that left her feeling cold inside. "I am currently making plans." He raised his glass as if in toast and threw it down his throat as well.

"Plans? What kind of plans?" Her fingers flew to her amulet, rubbing in slow circles.

"The kind that don't involve you," he said, his voice calm and icy. Vivian would rather that he yell at her. Then she would be able to be angry with him and allow her blood to boil. His quiet distain sent an unsettling shiver down her spine.

Taking a deep breath, she squared her shoulders and faced him. "I need your help, Sean."

He scoffed, then gave her a mocking bow. "I'm sure you do, but as you can see, I am very busy. I have a great many things to do before I make my journey to America."

"America?" She wasn't sure she had heard him right.

"Yes, America," he said without feeling.

Vivian felt panic rise within her. "But that's so far away."

He glowered at her; his features dark. "That's the point."

Involuntarily she took a step back. She felt her eyes well with tears, but she refused to give in to them. Turning away from him she pulled out her handkerchief to dab at her tears. Her throat felt tight, making it difficult to breathe. She needed to calm down, to control herself, but the deep breath she forced into her lungs made her shoulders shudder.

A hand on her arm, strong and warm, made her turn around.

"I didn't mean…" Sean stammered. "It's not what I wanted."

"No," she said as she forced a smile onto her anguished face. "No, Mr. Kade. You must live your life as you see fit." Then a thought occurred to her. "But will Mr. Fletcher let you alone if you leave?"

Sean sighed, his entire body seeming to deflate with the use of that name. "I've no idea. But I have to try."

"Then I wish you the best," and she meant it. She started for the door, ready to be away from him and the pain that filled her.

"Vivian," his voice came to her, the low murmur that would have excited her had she not been so dejected. Turning back, she met his eyes full of concern. "You wished to speak with me. What about?" After a moment's hesitation he added, "Is there anything you wanted? Anything at all?"

Looking at her trembling hands, she nodded. Now was not the time to be timid. As much as she hated the words that were about to come from her, she didn't know how else to proceed. "I wanted you to steal something for me."

Sean's brows shot up. "Oh?"

"Before the Admiral died, he gave me a spy glass. It's old and tarnished. I've never been able to see anything through it so it must be broken as well. Still, I held on to it for some sentimental reason I couldn't begin to fathom. Then Mr. Fletcher asked for a small trinket as a sign of good faith on my intention to pay him back. The spyglass was all I had so I handed it over. But now I think it might be important."

He narrowed his eyes at her. "Important how?"

"I think the Admiral may have put something inside of it. Something that would help me now. I need to get it back from Fletcher, but I know asking nicely won't work."

Sean chuckled. "No, it most definitely won't."

"Do you think you could get it for me?" Her heart pounded against her ribs as she waited. Without him, she would have no way of retrieving the spyglass. Her only hope was with his help. Silently, she prayed he would help her.

Sean rubbed at his stubbled chin as he thought. Finally, he said, "Aye."

***

The engagement of Sir Walter Warren to Mrs. Reed, wife of the late Admiral Reed of the Royal Navy, was announced in the local papers the next morning. People were lining up to call on her. Everyone had questions and suggestions for her, along with the usual congratulations. All the fuss was giving Vivian a headache.

Amid everything, Vivian and Nathan took piles of their possessions to various merchants. Furniture, art, even Vivian's pearls were sold off. Because of Nathan's standing in the community they had received fair pay. In all, they had gotten three thousand pounds for their sold possessions, a goodly amount, but not enough.

"We're so close," Nathan said that night. "We only need another five thousand and we will be set."

"But how will we get it?' Claire asked. "We sold off everything we could, or at least have it promised to be sold. The last thing of any value we have is the Waterford crystal chandelier, but it won't gather the full five thousand."

The three were sitting in Nathan's study. Vivian looked at the empty shelves. Without the books and artifacts to decorate them, they were a pathetic sight. Even the leather arm chairs that had comfortably faced the fireplace had been replaced with stiff wooden chairs from the attic.

As she shifted on the uncomfortable chair an idea struck her. She shoved it away, fearing it to be as dishonest as burning loan documents or running away. Still the idea pressed at her mind. It was incessant, refusing to be ignored. With nothing to lose but the respect of her brother and wife, Vivian determined to share the idea. If they said it was terrible, criminal even, then she would let it go. It was, after all, just an idea.

"There is the emerald necklace," she said slowly.

"What emerald necklace," Nathan asked, skepticism in his voice.

"The one Sir Warren gave me as an engagement gift."

Claire was on her feet, hands on her hips. "You mean you had something valuable this whole time and you haven't shared it?" Her voice full of ridicule.

"I didn't feel it was mine to share," Vivian defended herself.

"If he gifted it to you then it's yours," Nathan said.

Vivian thought about that. "But it is a family heirloom of his. He will expect to see it on me from time to time. Could we sell it to someone who would let me borrow it on occasion?"

Nathan scoffed. "Don't sell the thing as a whole. Take the emeralds out of the casing and sell them individually. You can always replace them with glass."

"But if Sir Warren notices," she began.

"He won't," Claire said. "He's nearly blind. He'll never know the difference. Besides," she said as she rubbed her hands. "If you are able to get the five thousand from the necklace then when you give Sir Warren and heir you can repay us for our investment."

Indignation rose within her. "Repay?" Vivian asked. She wasn't sure if she was more shocked by the words or offended.

"Certainly," Claire said as she sat down again, a self-satisfied air about her. "You don't expect that we were helping you for nothing. This isn't our financial problem, after all."

XXVI.

"So, do you think you know of a reputable jewel merchant?" Vivian asked Sean.

They walked together along a country lane that saw little use.

She had shared everything with Sean, including the encouragement she received from Nathan and Claire to sell off some of Sir Warrens emeralds. She still didn't feel that that necklace was hers to do with as she chose, so she sought his advice.

He shook his head slowly. "There is one part of this plan that your brother has forgotten."

"What would that be?"

Sean let out a long breath. "Your conscience."

"I don't think that has much of a place here," Vivian said with a laugh, idly kicking a pebble.

"I *know* it does." Sean stopped walking and faced her. He took her hands in his own. Even on this warm afternoon, Vivian reveled in the heat that came from him. "Vivian, you told me once that you would never steal. This is exactly what stealing is."

"But Nathan suggested it and he is a clergyman. Surely that makes it alright." Vivian hoped it did. She needed to be free of this financial burden and she had no idea how to do that. Not on her own anyway.

"Your brother may need to re-read the sacred texts if he thinks this is allowed," Sean said. He held out his hand for the necklace and Vivian handed it to him. He studied it for a long time. He twisted it in the light, making the gems shimmer. From his vest pocket he pulled a thick quizzing glass.

"What is that?" she asked, incredulously.

Sean gave a short laugh. "You're darling when your confused." He held the quizzing glass out for Vivian to see. "This is a loupe. A type of magnifier for jewelers."

He took the loupe from her and held it to his eye. Staring at the emeralds through it, Sean examined them with a seriousness that made Vivian hold her breath.

"Are they valuable," Vivian asked when he finally set the necklace down.

He nodded. "They are. But they aren't for you to use."

"Sean, I-"

"No, listen." Sean said as he held up a hand to silence her. "Sell a jewel or two. Pay off your debts. Then what? You can replace the gems with glass and call the business done. But you would have taken something from an unsuspecting person without their permission. That is the very definition of stealing. Say you do marry Sir Warren, making this necklace yours for the remainder of your life. Do you really think you can hide what you have done forever? Especially with Claire knowing it. She will tell others that there are a few fakes in this necklace. Sir Warren isn't the most forgiving man and will hold you accountable for tarnishing his reputation. Or say that you just 'borrow' a few gems then return the necklace to Sir Warren without marrying him. Knowing what you have done, as much as it helped you, will wear on your conscience, your very soul. Day after day you will think about what you have done but there will be no way to make it right again."

Vivian nodded, feeling her cheeks heat with shame. What had she been thinking? Had she really become so desperate that she would have resorted to theft to get what she needed?

Sean's arm slipped around her shoulders. He pulled her close, and she melted into him.

"It was a good idea," Sean said. "It's just not the right thing for you. You deserve better than this."

"I don't know what else to do," Vivian said, her voice cracking with emotion. "I can't think of any way to fix George's mess and I can't marry Sir Warren. I'd be miserable the rest of my life if I did."

Sean held her close, his other arm wrapping around her. His fingers trailed up and down her arm. Up and down. "We'll think of something," he whispered into her hair.

****

Toward the end of the week, the Eldon's came to call on her. Vivian hadn't seen them since her engagement was announced. Sean was with them, hiding in the shadows with a perfect air of contempt. While Vivian tried to carry on a conversation with Kathleen and Dr. Eldon, she kept being distracted by Sean's sour mood. He sulked in the corner, occasionally scoffing at the news she was relaying. When the visit was over Vivian felt a flood of relief when Sean moved to the door. She didn't feel she could endure his contempt a moment longer.

Before he could leave, Kathleen called him back. "Don't you have anything to say to Mrs. Reed?" By her tone it was a command not a question.

Sean walked up to Vivian, roughly took her hand in his and bowed over it. "My congratulations, madame," he said with mock sincerity.

She felt him press something into her palm, a piece of paper, and Vivian had to hide a smile. He was playing the part of the jilted lover for her benefit, and doing a marvelous job of it, but he wasn't going to abandon her. Sean would always be there for her.

When there was finally time for her to escape to her room, Vivian unfolded the note from Sean. Her fingers trembled as she opened the little slip of paper. In a pristine hand it read:

Meet me at Reginald's Tower tonight at eleven.

Anticipation made the rest of the day unbearably long. In the afternoon, Vivian began to fret about how she would be able to get to Reginald's Tower alone in the middle of the night. A lone female walking around in broad daylight was one thing but to go unescorted so near the docks was another. It was dangerous for a woman to be down there after dusk.

Eventually, she lit upon a plan that should help her move about without detection. As the family gathered for dinner that night, she slipped into her father's room. Helping herself to everything she needed from his armoire she quickly stored the items in her room.

Excitement made it difficult for her to eat, not that anyone noticed. Through the whole meal Claire prattled on and on about wedding plans, and Nathan seemed oblivious to anything that was happening around him. Time slowed, as it always does when one is forced to wait. Every tick of the clock made her heart beat twice. When it was finally time to retire, Vivian felt a wave of relief sweep over her. She bid the family goodnight and tried not to look suspicious as she rushed off.

Making certain her door was bolted, Vivian changed into an old suit of her fathers'. The clothes were from a time when he was a more substantial man and hung on her smaller frame. Still, an ill-fitting suit would be safer for her to go out in than a gown.

Tucking her hair up into her father's old tricorn hat did little to hide her soft features. She hoped that with the darkness would be difficult to tell she was a woman. Taking a last look at herself in her washstand mirror, Vivian wished she was braver than she felt.

Patty mist is an interesting thing to walk through. It is a cloud, thick with unfallen rain, that has decided to rest on the earth instead of float in the sky. So, it was on this night as Vivian made her way to Reginald's Tower. The mist was thick as it hung in the air, like a curtain of water droplets with nowhere to go. It seemed that if she put her hand out, she could pull the curtain aside and pass through.

As impossible as that truly was, the idea made the corners of Vivian's mouth twitch upward. Pulling up the collar of her father's coat and hugging it tighter around herself, Vivian tried to ward off the chill that came with the damp air. Her clothes soon became saturated from the mist and the cold bit clear to her bones.

Reaching the tower, she leaned against it for support to keep herself from shivering. She pulled her hat low to keep any passersby from noticing her features but there was no one about. Not on a night like this.

As the minutes slowly ticked by Vivian let the absurdity of what she was doing sink in. What had she been thinking? To come all the way to the docks in the middle of the night just to rob a man. Her mother would have been shocked and disappointed in her.

She was about to give up the whole endeavor when a familiar voice called to her.

"Reed? That you?"

"Sean!" Vivian felt flooded with relief as she moved through the mist to him.

Sean pulled her to him, giving her a quick but loving embrace. "My angel, you're shivering! Let's get inside."

Sean pulled her along as they moved through the mist. Vivian could see the hazy glow of tavern lanterns. The rowdy sounds that flowed from these establishments let Vivian know these were not proper houses suitable for a lady. She adjusted her disguise in a nervous attempt to keep from being recognized.

Sean pulled her closer and whispered in her ear. "When we get inside the tavern go straight upstairs. Wait for me at the end of the hallway."

Vivian wanted to ask him which tavern, but the building rose out of the mist before them. The tavern was commonplace for this part of town. Not even the faded sign would have stood out if anyone was looking for it. A perfectly inconspicuous den for thieves. Without a word, Sean opened the sagging wooden door and disappeared into the crowd inside. Not wanting to be left alone, Vivian scurried into the tavern.

The scene before her assaulted all her senses. The large room was crowded with all manner of people, each one pressed against the other. It seemed every person who usually found their lives on the docks was inside on this moist night. A thick haze of smoke from too many pipes made it difficult to see more than a few feet in front of her, not that she could even see that far with so many bodies in her way. All this time, she had been worried about being recognized. Now she thought that she should have been more worried about being trampled to death in the throng of people. A shrill laugh from another part of the room reminded her that there was a job to do.

Using her elbows, she pushed her way to the stairs near the center of the room. No one really noticed or cared, since they were doing the exact same thing. Once she was upstairs and hidden in the shadows at the end of the hall, Vivian could breathe easier. She had made it this far. Now all she needed was that spyglass and she could make her way home.

Time seemed to stretch on and on as Vivian waited at the end of the hall for Sean. Every second that passed pulled her nerves taut. She wondered if she had the correct hallway. Had there been another set of stairs she'd missed? Should she go look for Sean? The idea of going to the main room didn't seem a wise one. She had been lucky the first time to get through the crowd unnoticed, she doubted she would be that lucky again. No, sitting and waiting for Sean was all that she could do.

At the sound of unsteady steps on the stairs, Vivian pressed herself back into the shadows. A male form staggered through the flickering candlelight. His shadow wobbled along the narrow hallway. Vivian had never seen anyone drunk before and the sight of Sean inebriated made her uncomfortable.

She was just stepping out of the shadows to give him a well-deserved tongue lashing when the head of another man appeared at the top of the stairs. Sean whipped around, standing in the middle of the narrow hallway. He blocked the man completely from Vivian's view, and possibly she from his.

"Oy, Kade!" The head bellowed. "Whatcha doin'?"

"I's be gettin' more money," he slurred. "And what about you? Ya look like a floatin' head like that."

"Too lazy to climb the last few steps," the man laughed as if his own laziness was the greatest joke in the world.

Sean laughed with him. "So, you be layin' on them steps? Your daft, man."

"Daft and too dry. Be getting some more ale. Get back to the game quick," the man advised. Then he disappeared down the stairs again.

Sean let out a sigh of relief, shaking his head as he heard the man's footsteps on the stairs disappear. "That was close Vivian. Very close," he softly said over his shoulder.

"I thought you were drunk,' Vivian said, surprised by the sudden soberness.

"Not only am I a master thief, I am also a master actor," Sean said with a wink.

Sean turned his attention to the door beside him. Pulling several thin metal instruments from his pocket, Sean began to place them into the keyhole of the locked door. Vivian watched as he fiddled with the lock. It took him a few heartbeats, but the door opened to a dim room beyond.

"We haven't much time," Sean said as they entered the room. "Let's both look for the spyglass but try not to make a mess. We don't want to make it obvious that we were here."

Vivian and Sean moved through the room quickly. They looked in every drawer, under every piece of furniture they could find. Aside from a few items of men's clothing they found nothing.

"Are you sure that this is Mr. Fletcher's room?" Vivian felt anxious as time wore on.

"I know it is," Sean said as he wheeled around again.

She was ready to say they should give up and get out before they got caught when the candle sputtered, throwing shadows around the room. One shadow moved and looked like a large block sitting on a rafter. Or a large box!

Vivian grabbed the candle and held it aloft. Above their heads, resting in the corner of the room on two rafters, was a large leather box. Carefully she and Sean pulled it down, doing their best not to upset what was hidden inside. There was no lock, only leather straps keeping the box closed. Unfastening these filled Vivian with such excitement that her fingers trembled.

When the lid fell back it revealed an assortment of papers. Sean held the candle aloft for more light and Vivian was able to see that the papers were filled with names and numbers. For a moment, Vivian was disappointed, thinking that all this effort was for nothing more than laundry lists. Reading on, she realized that it was filled with names. One name with an amount of money next to it.

"These are his lists of debtors," Sean informed her.

"How many are there?" Vivian asked, her voice filled with wonder and disgust. She picked up list after list. Some pieces of parchment were nearly as long as her forearm covered with Mr. Fletcher's intricate writing.

Sean shook his head. "Hard to say. He has dozens on this list here," he said, indicating the paper in his hand. "Probably more back at his home."

"And each owes him money," Vivian concluded.

"Plus, interest," Sean added. "The man is a leech. He will drain each one of these people and their families dry of all funds."

Vivian was disgusted as she looked at all the paper in her hands, each one covered with names of unsuspecting debtors. Putting them down she looked in the leather box again, finding what she had been searching for. The small wooden box that contained the Admiral's spyglass was sitting in the bottom. She pulled it out as fast as she could, a small piece of scrap paper coming with it. Vivian was about to throw the scrap paper back into the box when the words on it caught her attention.

George Warren was written on the scrap paper, over and over again in a variety of hands. Vivian stared at the paper for a long while.

"What is it?" Sean asked.

She held up paper to him. "I think Mr. Fletcher copied George's signature." she said, questioning the words even as they came out.

Sean knelt by her. He sighed and hung his head. "I was worried about that."

"What?" Her voice a harsh whisper.

He rubbed his hand over his face before he looked at her. "Fletcher's done this before. If getting paid from a family was fairly easy the first time, then he often tries again a few years later."

Vivian felt sick. "So, there's no debt from George?"

Sean thought for a moment. "If Fletcher is practicing signatures then most likely not."

Vivian looked at Sean, anger rising in her. Her family was being swindled by a thief. She was going through hell for nothing.

She stood up, putting the box with the spyglass and the scrap of paper into her pocket. She headed for the door.

"Where are you going?" Sean asked.

"Away," was all she said. She couldn't stand the sight of him.

"Wait. I'll go with you."

"No." The words came out as strongly as she felt. "You can stay here."

"Angel," Sean began.

"Don't," Vivian hissed. She didn't dare yell for fear of being caught in Mr. Fletcher's room, but she wished she could. "You don't come near me. You work with that man. You steal for him, lie for him, and you think that I… that we…" She struggled with words in her anger. "I don't want you to come anywhere near me."

"Vivian."

"Just stay away from me!"

She felt naive. How could she have been so stupid as to trust a thief? She should turn them both in for what they had done, Sean and Fletcher. As she pushed her way out of the tavern, she fought off the urge to find Fletcher. It wouldn't do any good. It was her word against his and men always believed other men.

She left the tavern as unobserved as she had entered it. For the first time in her life she blessed the patty mist. Never had it helped her in anyway before. Tonight, it hid her from prying eyes. Her feet carried her swiftly away from the docks.

XXVII.

In her fury she didn't care about where she went, so she was surprised when she found herself on the steps of her childhood home. The familiar sight looming out of the mist filled Vivian with a sense of peace.

Behind the planks that covered it, the kitchen door was unlocked. There was a gap at the bottom of the planks just large enough for Vivian to squeeze through. The kitchen was barren compared to what it had been in her youth. There was only the large center table left over. A few odds and ends were scattered about. Vivian wandered around for a few minutes, taking in the state of the house. It made her heart ache. The once beloved rooms were now neglected. Curtains hung in dusty disarray. Cobwebs crowded the corners. Any furniture that remained was worn and broken.

Of all the rooms, Dr. Warren's office was the least affected by the family's departure. His large desk still stood in one corner, and his wooden chairs laid on their side's in the other. Vivian righted the chairs and pulled them toward the fireplace. There were still a few pieces of peat moss in the tinder box. Vivian put them into the fireplace and soon had a small fire to dispel the damp chill the patty mist created.

Throwing her coat and hat over the back on one chair, Vivian stretched out on the other. She played with the spyglass, rolling it between her fingers. She had been so sure that it held something important for her, but now all she felt was the cold metal it had always been. Holding it to her eyes she tried to see through it. As usual, she wasn't able to. It was as if something was inside, blocking her view.

A small inkling of an idea formed in the back of her mind.

Vivian jumped up from her chair. She frantically looked through the office and then the rest of the house for something to use to pry the spyglass open. After a fruitless search, she took the glass in her hands, trying to twist and pull it apart. Nothing worked.

With no other ideas coming to her mind Vivian knelt before the hearth. She held the spyglass aloft.

"Forgive me, Admiral," she whispered. Then with all her might she brought the spyglass down onto the hearthstones.

Thwack!

She tried again.

Thwack!

Then a third time.

A deafening sound of shattering glass filled the air. Tiny crystal pebbles scattered across the floor, casting glittering rainbows of light around the room.

Vivian's heart pounded in her ears as she turned the spyglass over. Sitting inside the cylinder was a folded piece of paper. Her fingers moved in slow motion as she reached them into the opening and drew the paper out.

Opening the paper, she laid in before her on the hearth. By the light of the small fire she read it, then read it again, barely believing the words that filled the page.

The final will and testament of Admiral Richard Reed,

> *I, Admiral Richard Reed, being in sound mind and body, do make my will in the view of my witness, Mr. John Clay, my banker and friend. In the event of my death I name my devoted wife, Vivian Warren Reed, sole beneficiary to all my earthly possessions. These possessions include the sum of twenty thousand pounds left in the care of Mr. Clay, as well as her own family home in Waterford which I purchased from her father. She will also be the recipient of a yearly annuity from the Admiralty of one thousand pounds for the remainder of her life. All these things will be given to her upon her showing Mr. Clay the proof of her inheritance, this very will. With this document he is instructed to make arrangements for all my lands and money to be transferred into her name. May these things provide her with the comfort and stability I was never able to give her during my earthly sojourn.*

It was signed by the Admiral with Mr. Clay as the witness. Vivian let the words sink into her. He had provided for her. The Admiral had provided for her! Her home was hers again. It seemed that everything she had ever wanted was in her hands.

Vivian cried tears of joy. She regretted her anger toward so many men who, apparently, hadn't done anything wrong. The evidence of their care and provision for her future were in her hands now. Relief flooded her soul. She collapsed onto the chair, hugging the Admiral's will to her heart.

XXVIII.

In way of apology for the soggy night before, the morning sunlight was exceptionally golden. With head held high, Vivian walked into Mr. Clay's office. She didn't look as regal as she had the first time she visited him. Lack of sleep made her eyes puffy, and her furs and finery were sold. But the determined look on her face made everyone accept her requests without question. Which is how she ended up in his office, unannounced and uninvited.

With a flourish she laid Admiral Reed's will on the desk. "Mr. Clay, the document you requested."

She sat in one of the uncomfortable chairs as Mr. Clay perused the document. After what felt like an eternity, Mr. Clay looked up and smiled at Vivian.

"My congratulations, Mrs. Reed. You are now an heiress."

As it happened, the money the Admiral claimed to own was indeed in Mr. Clay's care. He was only too happy to transfer it into the name of Mrs. Reed, now that the will had been found. Vivian was still annoyed at him for not doing so before, but she was willing to forgive him now that everything had been righted.

She also had the deed to her family's country estate. A few years ago, Dr. Warren had signed it over to Admiral Reed for a substantial sum. Vivian knew it was the money that had been used for her mother's treatments. While the treatments hadn't worked, knowing he had done all he could to help his beloved had eased the old man's mind. Dr. Warren would have done anything for his ailing wife, even give up his home.

Vivian glanced at the paper, feeling very official as she looked at its gilded letters. Her childhood home was her own. Her husbands' money was hers. She was going to take care of everything for her family, just as she always did.

She was putting the deed into her reticule when she saw a familiar figure across the street. Sean Kade looked anything but happy. Regret pricked at Vivian's conscious. She had treated him poorly and she knew it. Her fingers went instinctively to her amulet. She rubbed it a moment to summon her courage, then marched across the street.

His back was to her. Placing her hand lightly on his arm, she called his name. She wasn't sure what she had expected him to do, but the look of complete disgust he gave her had never crossed her mind. Without a word he turned and walked swiftly away.

"Sean, wait. Please." She raced after him.

"We have nothing further to say to each other, madame," he said without breaking his long stride.

"I have something to say to you, if you would stop and listen."

He stopped at a crossroads, waiting for the carriages to clear a space for him to cross. Vivian grabbed the opportunity. She jumped in front of him, looking right into his angry face.

"Sean, I'm so sorry. You did everything you could to help me and I turned on you. You did nothing to deserve that. I was wrong and I beg your forgiveness."

"Why did you blame me?" Sean asked, his eyes blazing. "You know I've never supported that man. I may know of his methods but that doesn't mean I condone them. You knew that I was disgusted with Fletcher, with myself for working for him, disgusted with the whole thing. And yet you blamed me? Why?"

"I don't know," she admitted. "I saw the evidence of Fletcher's lies. Then you confirmed he was swindling us. I was so angry at him, at Nathan, at Claire, at Sir Warren, at everyone really. It all just came bubbling to the surface and I took it out on the first person I saw. You."

Sean sighed. "I would hate to see what you would do to someone you were really angry at."

She gave a short laugh. "At this moment, nothing. I couldn't be happier than I am right now. I have you to thank for that." She watched him a minute as he stared out over the street. "Oh Sean! I know I've made a mess of things. I am so sorry. Please say that you'll forgive me?"

"And if I did? Then what?"

"What do you mean?" Vivian looked at him, watching the emotions swirl through his eyes.

"Say I do forgive you. Will you still marry that oaf?" Sean's voice rose with each word. "Are you going to lead me on again only to cast me aside the moment something better comes along?"

"I never meant to," Vivian said, her own anger starting to rise.

"But you did. Will you do it again?" Sean looked at her, the intensity in his eyes making her nervous.

"No," she said. Vivian squared her shoulders and looked Sean in the eyes. "I may have acted badly in a moment of shock, but I can assure you, Mr. Kade, that I have no intention of letting my anger get the better of me. Now, I have apologized for my poor conduct. I would hope that as a gentleman you would forgive me."

He scoffed. "I'm no gentleman. Never have been and never will be." His look was hard. "Are you going to marry him?"

"Sir Warren?" Bile rose in the back of her throat at the thought of the upcoming wedding. "Do you really think I would want such a life?"

"It's a simple question," he snarled. "Yes or no, are you marrying him?"

If she were wearing a sturdy pair of boots, she would have kicked him. Unfortunately, she gave in to the fashion of delicate slippers. "Saying you forgive someone is a simple question as well."

"I asked mine first."

"You're intolerable!"

"And you're a prude!"

Vivian gasped. "You take that back."

"Not until you answer my question!"

She fumed. Gritting her teeth, she said. "I will not ever marry him, Mr. Kade."

"There. Was that so hard?" He asked, the fire in his eyes ebbing away a tad.

"I think I might die now," she sarcastically said.

He smiled then, and his once stormy eyes brightened. "We should get off the street," he said with a wink. "I think we're causing a scene."

She let him lead her away, even though she was still furious at him. She told him all the details about the will as they went, even how she had to smash the spyglass open to retrieve it. He was immensely pleased for her. He gave her his congratulations again and again. As they walked, her annoyance with him faded, until she was able to forgive his impertinence earlier. Vivian's happiness began to know no bounds, which was why she was so startled when he stopped walking.

"What's the matter, Sean?" She looked at his serious expression. The storm clouds returning to his eyes.

"You're going to be free of Fletcher," he said slowly.

"Yes," she said slowly.

"You're free but I'm not." His voice was flat as the words fell. The dampening of Vivian's good mood was instantaneous.

"Oh," she said softly.

"Neither are the others."

"What others?"

"The other people who were on that list. On all the lists," Sean said emphatically, referring to the lists they found alongside the spyglass. "Just think about it. Every name on those lists is one person who owes Fletcher money. Just one person! But each of those people have families which Fletcher will have no scruples about manipulating. He will use their mothers and fathers to get as much money as possible. He will use their sisters," Sean looked at Vivian. "It's up to us to stop him."

"How?" Vivian felt overwhelmed by the very idea of it all.

"I have a stash of jewels-"

"What?" Vivian nearly screamed.

Sean led her off the main road and toward a garden. It was surrounded by hedgerows, hiding them from any passersby. Together they sat on a bench. Sean took Vivian's hands in his own, rubbing his thumbs on the back of her knuckles. He looked solemn as he stared into her eyes.

"I have a number of valuables from the area. I was going to wait to sell them, but I think giving them to Mr. Fletcher will be much better. Making sure the local magistrate is present, of course."

"You're going to use stolen jewels to frame a man," Vivian asked in a harsh whisper. She feared that someone might overhear their conversation. Even talking about stealing could get them both into a great deal of trouble.

Sean looked ashamed, but he nodded. "Yes. That's my basic plan."

Vivian was appalled. "Not only is that against the law, Sean, but it's also against the commandments. We are told not to bear false witness."

Rage flashed across his face. "We're also told to love our fellow man. To help those in need. To do unto others as we would have them do to us. Do you really think that Miles Fletcher is the type of man who cares what the Bible says? I have been under this man's thumb for years, Vivian. Years that I can never get back. All I want is a chance to have a normal life and he keeps taking that from me. Not only me but all those other people who find themselves on his lists. Think about how they must all be feeling when a man like Fletcher comes into their lives and destroys it?"

Sean sounded desperate as he spoke. Vivian's heart went out to him. So many people were finding themselves in the same situation as her family. She wished to help them just as she wished to help her father and brother. But to lie?

"I'm going to do this," Sean continued, "even if you aren't willing to help me. But it would mean the world to me to have your blessing."

"To frame a man?"

"Not a man," Sean broke in. "A liar and a thief. He uses the innocent for his own ends. He takes from them until they have nothing left to give and then he moves on to their loved ones. His greed knows no end."

Vivian wanted to say no. But the image of Mr. Fletcher in her carriage, his leering eyes, his wandering hands filled her mind. Had he done that to other women? Had they been unable to refuse? The thought made her sick to her stomach.

"What if we get caught?" She couldn't keep the fear from her voice.

"Then I will take the fall," Sean assured her. "I'll tell the authorities that I forced you into it. You know they would believe me."

Vivian almost smiled. "Everyone always believes you. But what if things go horribly wrong, Sean? What if you get hurt again?"

"I have to try, Vivian. If I don't act now, then the opportunity to get rid of Fletcher will be gone and other innocent people will get hurt." Sean paused. He looked at their joined hands for a moment. "Please tell me that you will support me in this?"

She wanted to say no. Anything to keep Sean from doing something rash. She could just pay off Fletcher and move into her family's estate with her father. But then Mr. Fletcher would simply move on to another family and ruin their lives with his greed. For them, the unknowing next victims, Vivian said yes.

Sean smiled, a forced expression that did nothing to dispel the ice that formed in Vivian's gut. "Everything will be fine, you'll see."

XXIX.

"I can't do this Kathleen," Vivian said as she paced her friend's parlor. It was the day before the wedding, and Vivian still hadn't paid Miles Fletcher off. "What if I actually have to get married tomorrow?"

Vivian felt her stomach churn. She had felt sick all week, often relieving the contents of her stomach into a chamber pot. Never in all her life had she felt this nervous.

"Please sit down," Kathleen pleaded with her. Offering her a cup of tea, she said, "you are wasting away, Vivian. I fear for you. We all do."

"And yet no one has offered to cancel this ridiculous marriage."

"Because no one but you can. If you are so set against it then call it off. Only you have that power."

Sighing, Vivian set the tea down and rubbed at her sleep deprived eyes. "Sean told me to keep up the illusion of an engagement. How would it look if I called it off?"

"And if Sean told you to jump from the cliffs of Moher, would you?" Kathleen asked, her voice dripping with sarcasm.

"Will he be at the bottom to catch me?"

"He'd not catching you now." Kathleen said. "Vivian, you haven't slept, you barely eat. You look weak and I'm worried you will become ill if you don't take care of yourself soon."

"Sean said-"

"Oh, pooh on Sean! Take care of yourself, girl. Don't wait for some man to come along and smooth the road before you."

"That's easy for you to say. You were left an inheritance from you father."

Kathleen sighed, finally defeated. "All I'm saying is that if this engagement is causing you so much grief a marriage to Sir Warren might kill you."

Vivian nodded. The movement shook loose her fortitude, and tears began to trickle down her hollow cheeks.

"Oh, my darling friend," Kathleen said as she sat beside Vivian. Wrapping an arm around her, Kathleen held her close and rocked her as the tears fell. "It will be alright. If Sean said he'd help, then he will. Don't give up yet."

"It's tomorrow. The wedding is tomorrow!" Vivian bemoaned. "How am I to get out of it by tomorrow.

"You don't." The masculine voice at the door made both women jump.

Vivian looked up, hoping it was Sean, but only Dr. Eldon stood in the doorway. His plump frame filled the doorway, his hands tucked behind his back. He walked into the room; his face solemn as he took in Vivian. Without a word, he pulled a box from behind his back, offering it to Vivian.

It was about the size of box a lady would expect for a new pair of slippers. Covered in a light blue satin, it reflected the sunlight coming through the windows. Vivian took it, and nearly dropped it. Its weight belied its size.

"Good heaven's Eldon," she said as she hefted the box onto her lap. "Did you fill it with rocks?"

"Not I. But Sean might have," he said as he shut the parlor door.

With shaking hands, Vivian opened the lid of the box. She wasn't sure what she expected to find, but it wasn't a letter in a neat hand.

Mrs. Reed,

On the eve of your wedding I present you with the token of my esteem, and these instructions.

Send a note to Mr. Fletcher, asking him to meet you at the church minutes prior to your wedding. Give him the contents of this box, with promises that he will receive the remainder of his money from Sir Warren after the service. Leave the rest to me.

Forever your humble servant,

S.K.

Removing a layer of tissue paper revealed Sean's gift. Gems of every shape and size lay in the bottom of the box. They glistened in the sunlight, sending a rainbow across the ceiling.

"It looks like he *did* give you rocks," Dr. Eldon said.

"Hush," hissed his wife. She looked at the contents over Vivian's shoulder. "That must be everything he ever kept aside for himself. He didn't let you down, my friend."

"No, he didn't." Vivian said. With a relieved sigh, she closed the box. "Now all I have to do is summon Mr. Fletcher."

The thought of that man sent a chill down her spine. She shivered as it went.

"Is all well?" Kathleen asked.

"I'm frightened."

Dr. Eldon huffed. "You'd be a fool not to be scared. But have no fear. Mrs. Eldon and I will be right there with you every step down the aisle."

Vivian nodded. The weight that had hung on her shoulders all week now felt like it was sitting in a blue satin box in her hands.

That night, Vivian sat next to her father. She kept a tight hold on his hand, wishing to feel anything but the fear that filled her.

"And to think," Claire prattled, "that tomorrow you will be a married woman. Lady Warren. Are you excited?"

"I feel rather ill," Vivian confessed.

Nathan huffed. "Prewedding nerves. All brides have them. You'll be fine."

Dr. Warren patted his daughters' hand. "Your mother spoke to you before your last wedding. What did she say?"

"She said I was saving my family," Vivian said. The memory barely brought a smile to her face. An image of her mother's face, desperate and pleading, came to her mind. The memory was bittersweet. It was the last time she had seen her mother alive. The last time they had spoken in person. Her mother's words from that day came back to her.

"Please, Vivian, we are desperate. You are the only person who can help us."

But now they had someone else who was helping them. Someone else who was doing all he could to assist in their struggle. Vivian sighed as her fingers reached for her pendant. If only Sean were here now.

XXX.

Vivian paced in the tiny room. It was little more than a cloak room, but a mirror had been wedged into one corner, and a small side table and stool had been placed in the other. She was dressed for her wedding in her best muslin gown with her green velvet spencer over it, the same outfit she had worn to the bank, minus the fur. She hoped it brought her more luck than it had the other day. Her hands shook with nerves. She reached for where her mother's pendant always rested against her skin, but it wasn't there today.

Instead, she stroked the handles of a leather bag that sat on the small table. It was a respectable looking black bag with black painted handles. It had been one of Mr. Eldon's but had been retired.

A knock came to the door.

"Yes," she squeaked. She took a deep breath and tried again. "Yes, come in."

Mr. Fletcher came in. "Ah Mrs. Reed. You look stunning," he said as a fake compliment. His eyes looked her up and down in his appraising leer that was supposed to make her feel small.

She forced a smile on her face and did just as she had practiced earlier. She motioned for Mr. Fletcher to sit down.

"As you know, sir, my brother owed you a great deal of money for many years now. The interest of which has become excessive. I wish to pay off this debt with the money that has been left to me by my deceased husband, Admiral Reed."

"You found the will of Admiral Reed?" Mr. Fletcher nearly fell off his chair.

"Yes, sir. He was most generous. He left me nearly the sum that you now require in precious jewels. Most of which he acquired during his travels. I can pay you these jewels, plus an amount that Sir Warren has offered to provide once I am his wife. The total of these two amounts comes to the same amount that my brother owed you. Interest included. If I pay you with these," she said as she motioned to the bag, "will you consider my brother's debt paid in full?"

Mr. Fletcher sat rubbing his chin. He wanted the jewels; Vivian could see that. She waited, breathless for his answer.

"Agreed. So long as I do receive my money from Sir Warren."

"Wonderful," Vivian tried not to reveal her excitement. "If you will provide the contract that contains my brother's loan then I will give you the jewels." She motioned to the bag. Mr. Fletcher's eyes took on a hungry kind of look.

"You mentioned two sums, Mrs. Reed. How much do they equal? I would like to make sure I get all my money back."

Vivian nodded. "Of course. The jewels equal ten thousand pounds. I had them appraised to confirm that amount. Sir Warren will give you a note for five thousand pounds once the vows are spoken. With all my calculations that is the exact amount we owe you. Not a penny more."

Mr. Fletcher chuckled. It was an unpleasant sound. "Very good Mrs. Reed," he said. "Very good indeed." He retrieved an envelope from his jacket pocket and handed it to her. "I trust that you will find all in order," he sneered. "There is no need to insult me with checking the letter in my presence."

Vivian snatched the letter from his hand, opening it. "You will forgive my impoliteness, but I would rather be thorough in this matter." She scanned the letter, looking very hard at the signature at the bottom. It matched one of the signatures she had on the scrap of paper. The evidence of Mr. Fletcher's lie made her know she was doing the right thing. "Mr. Fletcher, I would like to invite you to stay for my wedding. Once it is finished, Sir Warren will pay you the last of the money I owe you." She folded the letter and placed it in her reticule for safe keeping.

Mr. Fletcher merely nodded. His attention was on the black handbag. The moment it was in his grasp he opened it, becoming completely engrossed in the contents.

A knock at the door meant that everyone was ready to begin. Vivian walked Mr. Fletcher to the chapel and showed him a seat near her father. The older man looked stricken with fear at the sight of his lender. There was little for him to do except squirm since he had difficulty moving about freely.

"What are you doing out here?" Claire was at Vivian's elbow faster than a fox to a hare.

"I was showing a guest to a seat," Vivian said. She was growing weary of Claire.

"The groom has spotted you," said the older woman as she grabbed the bride's elbow. Claire all but shoved Vivian to the entryway of the church. "Do you want bad luck on your wedding day?" She raised her eyebrows at Vivian, giving her a pointed look.

Vivian openly rolled her eyes. "So long as you get out of debt, what do you care about my wedding?" She shoved past her speechless sister-in-law toward the entryway.

Dr. Eldon was waiting for her there, ready to walk her down the aisle since none of the men in her family were able. Vivian looked at the altar of the church to see Nathan was fumbling with his bible, as he tried to find the correct verses for marriage. Sir Warren stood by him, standing as straight as he was able with the help of his cane. Vivian sent a silent prayer to heaven that Sean would make it in time. If he failed, her life would be miserable.

Kathleen came over to them. "I wanted to wish you luck. I hope that you are very happy in your new life." She was trying to be kind though it was easy to tell she was sad.

Vivian embraced her. Even if all didn't go as planned, at least she would always have the support of her friends.

"It's time," Dr. Eldon said when he noticed a signal from Nathan. The few assembled guests rose for the bride to pass, even Mr. Fletcher.

Dr. Eldon walked Vivian slowly down the aisle. So slowly, it was almost painful to endure.

"Why so sluggish, Dr. Eldon?" Vivian whispered behind a handful of flowers she was holding.

"To give Sean enough time to get here," Dr. Eldon whispered from the side of his mouth.

"He won't make it in time?" Vivian froze in fright from the thought.

"Of course, he will," Dr. Eldon reassured, moving her along again. "I'm just giving him all the time I can."

The two had reached the front of the chapel to the visible relief of the guests. They both looked back at the door then at each other. Dr. Eldon gave Vivian what should have been an encouraging smile, but it was weak. Vivian ascended a few steps to where Sir Warren was waiting. She stood beside him as Nathan began the ceremony but could only look at the flowers in her hands. She squeezed her bouquet in an attempt to stop her hands from trembling.

Where is Sean, where is Sean. She found she could only repeat the question to herself.

As Vivian was beginning to repeat the wedding vows, the door of the small chapel burst open. Sean stormed in, followed by the local magistrate and his men. At the sight of them, Vivian's knees nearly went weak with relief.

Sean marched up the aisle and pointed at Mr. Fletcher. "That is the man who stole his lordship's jewels. Seize him!"

Before Mr. Fletcher could do more than jump up in alarm, he was grabbed by several of the magistrate's men. All looked ready to fight him if need be. Mr. Fletcher struggled and kicked at his captors. He threatened and cursed them, but they held firm.

"What is the meaning of this?" Sir Warren demanded of the men.

"This man is a thief," said the magistrate. "He has stolen jewels from a number of homes in the area."

"That's a lie!" Fletcher was red faced with fury. "I would never have committed such a crime."

"Then how do you explain this?" Sean said as he held up the handbag that had been in Mr. Fletcher's lap moments before. He turned it over, allowing the contents of the bag to pour out onto the church pew. Catching the weak sunlight that filtered through the led windows, a cascade of gems sparkled for everyone to see.

Sir Warren hobbled forward. "My word. I've never seen so many jewels in my life." He was almost giddy with excitement until a particular object caught his attention. He picked it up with shaky fingers. "That is my family's crest on that necklace. This is my great-grandmother's ruby necklace. This scoundrel has been in my home as well. He stole family heirlooms from me. I want to see this man brought to justice!"

"I never touched it!" Mr. Fletcher screamed. He twisted in an attempt to get free, but he was held fast by the magistrates' men.

"My mother's amber pendant. And Sir Warren's engagement necklace." Vivian picked up the emerald necklace, letting the light sparkle off the emeralds. "I couldn't find it this morning and was searching for it everywhere."

This was more than Mr. Fletcher could stand. "You gave me the bag. You must have taken the necklace. You stole everything!" His face was red with rage as he screamed at Vivian.

"What in the devil is he talking about?" Sir Warren asked the magistrate.

"No idea," the magistrate said. "Fear not, Sir Warren. This man was caught in possession of your property. We will make certain he pays for his crimes." The magistrate gathered the jewels into the bag and motioned for his men to take Fletcher away. Fletcher fought them, trying to get free.

Sir Warren looked very sternly at the magistrate. "I don't want to see him pay for his crimes. I want to see him hang for them."

"NO!" Fletcher screamed, continuing to struggle. "I never stole anything! It was Reed. She set me up. Mrs. Reed is your thief!"

"How dare you accuse a lady of such villainy, sir," Sean said.

"Lady? Bah!" Fletcher continued to yell as he was drug toward the door. "I will see her pay for this. You think you can best me? You think you are done with me? I will make you pay for this. You hear me Reed? You will pay for this for the rest of your life! You will never be free of me!"

With that, Mr. Fletcher broke free of his captors. He ran down the aisle, burning with anger directed at Vivian. She stepped back, a scream in her throat, but before she uttered a sound Sean jumped in front of her. With one well timed blow, he landed his fist squarely in Mr.

Fletcher's face, sending the disgusting man sailing backwards. Mr. Fletcher landed onto the stone floor with a resounding *thwack*. He groaned as he laid there, barely conscious.

The magistrate offered Sean a grateful look. Mr. Fletcher was quickly carried away by the magistrate's men and thrown into a barred wagon.

"What will happen to him?" Vivian asked the magistrate.

"Having found him holding a bag of valuables that clearly belong to upstanding citizens, and with Sir Warren's own accusations, this man will hang by the end of the day. Now, if you will excuse me," he said with a bow. The magistrate followed his men out of the church.

The small group of spectators moved to the door. The view of their oppressor being carried away to his demised sent every person into a flurry of emotions. Claire burst into tears, falling into Nathan's arms as she sobbed onto his arm. Dr. Warren, overcome with relief, collapsed onto the stone steps. If it had not been for the vigilant Mr. Kade, the old man may have come to injure himself. As it was, he was caught and carefully moved into a waiting carriage. Vivian followed close behind, eager to care for her father.

Her own emotions were less obvious to the party than that of her father's or sister-in-law's. She had expected to feel guilt over her actions. After all, any normal human being would feel guilty over sending a person to jail. Vivian instead felt immense relief filled her heart and with that relief, a lightening of her spirits. This was truly the happiest day of her life.

XXXI.

"I shall paint you a fickle and false!" Sir Warren bellowed at Vivian a week later.

Sitting calmly in her own home, Vivian didn't care how she was painted by such a man. No one that she respected listened the old lord anyway.

"Then let it be so," she said. She followed him as he stomped toward the front door of the manor house. "I bid you a pleasant day, Sir Warren."

He huffed and stomped off toward his carriage.

"What be that all abou'," Mr. Kelly asked as she came up the gravel drive.

Vivian smiled at him. In the past week he had been more help than he could have imagined. Under his direction, the manor house had been restored to its original glory. Craftsmen had worked nearly round the clock the make the home ready for Dr. Warren and his girl Vi. While the home still lacked many of the grander extravagances such as hall rugs, paintings, and many pieces of furniture, it was sound, warm, and a perfect place for Dr. Warren to rest in his old age.

"He's just upset that I called off our engagement."

"Bout time, ye did," Mr. Kelly said with a wink. "He'd be no good for ye. What abou' that young buck that's been seen sulkin' round the countryside. He might do."

"He has yet to call," Vivian said. The tinkling of the bell called her attention back into the house. "That would be father."

"See bout getting' him a maid. You don't need to always be at his beck and call."

"The maids start tomorrow. Are you sure your niece doesn't mind coming all this way from town?"

Mr. Kelly laughed. "That little thing? She's just happy to be away from Mrs. Warren. Ye've a steadier nature. My niece will be as happy as a basket of kittens."

Reassured, Vivian smiled and left Mr. Kelly. Her father was situated in his study, one of the few rooms to have been furnished with the recent move. His desk had been polished and restored, a fine leather chair had been purchased, and the tinder box was once again full of peat moss.

"What did you need, father," Vivian asked as she came into the room. She stoked the fire and tucked the tweed blanket around her father's lap.

"Only to see how my cousin was fairing." Dr. Warren settled farther into his chair. He had missed his study. Vivian smiled to herself. She hadn't told her father, but she felt as if this room had missed him as well.

"Sir Warren wasn't overly pleased with my decision, but I'm sure in time he will see that it is for the best."

"And until he does, you have Mr. Kade to talk to," Dr. Warren said.

A momentary melancholy overcame Vivian. "I'm not sure if Mr. Kade wishes to speak with me. He hasn't said-"

"He wants to talk to you, girl. Don't be daft. No man risks all he has to help a woman if he doesn't wish to speak with her again."

"How do you know that?"

"I may be old, but I'm still a man. Trust me on this. Find him, tell him how you feel."

"I'm not sure I have the courage," Vivian said as she sat in the chair opposite her father.

He took her small hand in both of his. "My girl, you have sailed oceans, seen places many will only ever dream of. You stood up to a thief and a bully and protected your family. You have enough courage to tell one gentleman how you feel about him."

Vivian thought that over. Maybe she would be able to share her heart. Before she could ponder it more, the sound of a carriage pulling into the drive drew her attention to the window.

"Whoever could that be," she said to no one in particular. She didn't expect an answer from her father.

Moving to the window, Vivian could clearly make out the occupants of an open carriage. "It's the Eldon's, father. I see they even brought their children. You don't mind, do you?"

"No, no. I believe Mr. Kelly promised the wee one's a look at the new puppies."

Vivian made her way to the front door to great her guests.

"Kathleen! I didn't know you were coming today."

"After the morning we had we all needed to see a smiling face," Kathleen replied as her husband helped her step from the carriage. Dr. Eldon went into the house to check on his patient, while Kathleen and the children started toward the garden.

"What happened this morning?" Vivian asked as she walked with the children toward the garden shed. The yelps of new puppies could be heard from inside.

Kathleen sighed and hung her head. "It's Sean, I'm afraid."

"Is he alright?" Vivian's heart leapt into her throat.

"He's fine," Kathleen reassured her. "Only he's leaving."

"Back to Dublin?" Vivian tried to sound casual but inside she was frazzled. How could he leave without telling her?

"Nowhere so close," Kathleen said, trying to hide her tears. "He's going to America."

"What?" Her shriek of disbelief startled the puppies into yelping more.

"He leaves on the ship today. He said his goodbyes this morning and walked out the door. The children and I are distraught."

"He's still going. After everything?"

"You knew of this plan?"

"He mentioned it once, but I had thought that his plans would have changed." Vivian felt her spirits' plummet. He must have changed his mind about wanting her. That was the only explanation. If he wanted her, he would have come for her.

"He left this for you," Kathleen said, holding out a small velvet pouch to Vivian. "he asked me to give it to you as soon as possible."

Vivian took it, hardly knowing what to think. She emptied the contents of the pouch into her palm. Out fell her amber amulet from her mother. Vivian stared at it, her heart beating in her ears. Attached to the chain with the amulet was a simple gold ring.

"What is this?" Vivian asked Kathleen, but her friend only shrugged. Vivian checked the velvet pouch again and found a note written in Sean's clear handwriting.

My Angel,

I return to you the treasure from your mother. I am glad that you have found the freedom you worked so hard for. My congratulations on this, and hope you find every happiness in your new life. I, too, will begin a new life, even though my heart will forever remain behind. The ring you find belonged to my mother. She told me to give it to the woman I loved. You are my first thought in the morning and my last though every night. You are the reason my soul finds peace. I love you more than my own life. So, I leave both the ring and my heart in your keeping.

Yours forevermore,

S. Kade

Vivian hadn't realized she had been holding her breath until her body screamed for air.

"What did he give you?" Kathleen asked.

Vivian showed her the note and jewelry. Kathleen stared at them wide eyed.

"Oh, Vivian. I'm so sorry."

"Sorry? Why? He loves me. That's all I needed to know." She ran toward the front of the house, the gravel crunching under her slippers.

"Where are you going?" Kathleen asked as she raced after her. The children were right on their heels, wondering why the ladies were all a flutter.

"I have to stop him," Vivian said.

"How? The harbor is nearly five miles away." Kathleen scooped up her son who had fallen on the gravel drive. She kissed his sore knee as she chased after Vivian.

"I have to try." Vivian saw the carriage. "Driver. We must hurry."

The driver, bewildered, came around from the front of the carriage where he had been tending to the horses. He looked at his mistress for permission to heed Vivian.

"Eldon!" Kathleen shouted toward the manor. She took a few steps toward it, before she turned back to Vivian. Changing her mind, she turned toward the house again. "Eldon, hurry!"

Vivian climbed into the carriage, ready to take the reins if need be. Dr. Eldon appeared at the door, looking between his wife and coachman for clarification as to the commotion.

Hopping up and down, and pointing furiously, Kathleen shrieked, "She's going after him!"

That was all the information that Dr. Eldon needed. He sprang toward the carriage, mounted, and ordered the drive to get to the docks as quickly as possible. The carriage lurched as it sped off. Looking over her shoulder, Vivian waved at Kathleen and the children before the carriage turned a corner and was lost from view.

"Thank you for coming," she said to Dr. Eldon.

He patted her trembling hands. "Of course. If you are going to do this, you will need a friend by your side. No telling what we will find when we get there."

Vivian didn't want to admit it, but she was worried they would arrive too late. She could picture Sean's ship sailing down the Barrow River, never to return, as she watched from the dock. The image made her eyes burn with tears.

To comfort herself, she reached for her amulet, expecting to find it in its accustomed place. How surprised she was to then find in in her hand, the delicate chain hanging between her fingers.

"What have you there?" Dr. Eldon asked.

"A good luck charm, I hope."

Putting the necklace on, Vivian rubbed at the amber stone, praying the horses would run fast enough to catch the ship. As her fingers brushed the smooth gold of the ring Sean had placed on the chain, Vivian calmed. Make it to the docks or not, she would find Sean again.

When, at long last, they arrived at the docks of Waterford, Dr. Eldon inquired after the ship that was to set sail for the America's.

"It's over there," a surly dock worker said. "The Kensington."

Vivian ran to the ship to find Mrs. Seymour, the captain's wife, promenading on deck.

"Mrs. Seymour," she called. "have you seen Mr. Kade?"

"Who?" the startled woman asked. Then she recognized Vivian. "Why Mrs. Reed, what a pleasure. You know I was just saying to the captain 'I wonder what became of that young widow?' And would you believe it, he said it was unlikely you were still a widow. I told him that-"

Vivian grabbed the woman by her shoulders and looked at her sternly. "Mrs. Seymour, I'm looking for Mr. Kade. You remember, the man who rescued me when I fell overboard. Is he on this ship?"

"He is," Sean said from behind her.

She hadn't thought what she would do when she saw him. Getting to him had been the premiere thought in her mind. The notion that Sean Kade wouldn't want her once she did reach him hadn't even entered her thinking. He gave her no time to think now.

As she turned to face him, his arms slipped around her waist, gathering her against him. Wrapping her arms round his neck, Vivian buried her face into his collar, inhaling deeply. He still smelt of earth and fresh linen. What's more, his heartbeat as furiously against his ribs as hers did.

"Where were you going?" Vivian whispered to him.

He drew back to look at her, but Vivian kept her hands on his shoulders. She wasn't letting go of him again.

"I wanted to become worthy of you," he said. The words ripped at Vivian's heart.

"You are worthy. You stood by me, helped me, fought with me when everyone else would have simply dismissed me."

The smile that touched the edges of Sean's mouth was full of sorrow. "But you deserve someone who has something to offer you. Someone who can shower you with all the beautiful things of this world. I have nothing to give you. I don't even have the good name of a gentleman."

"Sean, I have no need for a gentleman or his name. I need you."

He reached up and stroked her cheek with his thumb. "Even with all the problems I've caused?"

"Especially then. Because you also solved all of mine. You gave me everything you had. Sean you are the most generous, selfless man I know. There is no one better than you on the whole of this earth." Vivian paused, watching his blue eyes as they swam with emotion.

"You could do so much better."

Vivian put her finger to Sean's lips, silencing his arguments. "But I choose you, Sean Kade."

His hand slipped into hers, pulling her hand away. A devilishly charming smile spread across his lips. "Well now. I can't argue with a woman who has her mind made up."

Sean leaned closer to her, tilting her chin towards his. He brought his lips to hers, tenderly, gently pressing their mouths together. It wasn't as passionate as their last kiss, but far purer. As Vivian surrendered to the warmth that was Sean, she knew their kiss held a promise of a future. A future where she had finally found the home she had been looking for.

Made in the USA
Middletown, DE
20 November 2021